# *What* the critics are saying...

༈

## ~Lion Eyes~

"An amazing story that kept me guessing first over the identity of the attacker, then over how Liddy became a shape shifter herself, and finally over what would happen with her mother who is so opposed to anything that'd be considered different in her community. A wonderful story with a beautiful ending!" ~ *Euro-Reviews*

"A suspenseful, fast-pace story that will keep you glued to your seat trying to solve the mystery of this tale. Ms. Copeland did a magnificent job of "who did it" and kept me guessing until the very end. ...the love making between Liddy and Kevin is scorching hot and leave nothing to the imagination!" ~ *Romance Junkies*"

A suspenseful novella whose characters all have tremendous secrets they are hiding. Lion Eyes is a nice opener for Lions and Tigers and Bears with a dramatic love story between two complex yet interesting characters with secrets to hide." ~ *Cupid Reviews*

## ~Tiger Eye~

"Dr Zinsa Senghor, who might be one of the boldest heroines ever, makes Tunstall's Tiger Eye a great read. There is a civil war and, for safety reasons, Zinsa's practice is moved to a clinic run by Dr. Grant Hayden, a vet who improbably resists Zinsa's sexy temptation. This story starts with a vicious attack that changes Grant's life forever. Then, a couple of decades later, Zinsa shakes up his life again." *4 Stars* ~ *Leigh Rowling.*

## ~*Hidden Heart*~

"Kate Steele weaves a fantastic story of a shape shifter and his desire to be normal, with a sexual romp that is hot and steamy. A great read!" ~ *Coffee Time Romance*

"Hidden Heart is a fantastic short story filled with humor, wonderful characters and emotion. Ms. Steele captures Rafe's multitude of emotions throughout this story realistically and with great depth. His feelings and heart are an added dimension I just fell in love with. Lindy, likewise, is a character with great heart and compassion. Because of Ms. Steele's ability to make these characters so believable, their love story from the start is one that touches the heart. The attraction between the two sizzles and when they are intimate, it's an inferno." ~ *Cupid's Library Reviews, Cupid Plot Factor: 5, Cupid Pleasure Factor: 5*

## ~*Lions and Tigers and Bears*~

"Three heart-touching tales of shape shifters that each take the shape of a specified animal. The stories contained in this anthology are each vastly different and endearing to the reader. Definitely a keeper!" ~ *Euro-Reviews*

"This is a definite read for paranormal romantic erotica fans –particularly those who enjoy shape shifter plotlines." ~ *Elizabeth, Fallen Angels Reviews (5 out of 5)*

"This anthology is a must-have for all those who love shape shifters, hot sex, and romance. All in all fabulous read. A definite keeper." ~ *Coffee Time Romance (5 out of 5)*

# Lions and Tigers and Bears

## KIT TUNSTALL
## KATE STEELE
## JODI LYNN COPELAND

ELLORA'S CAVE
ROMANTICA PUBLISHING

An Ellora's Cave Romantica Publication

www.ellorascave.com

Lions and Tigers and Bears

ISBN # 1419953109
ALL RIGHTS RESERVED.
Lion Eyes Copyright © 2005 Jodi Lynn Copland
Tiger Eye Copyright © 2005 Kit Tunstall
Hidden Heart Copyright © 2005 Kate Steele
Edited by Briana St. James, Raelene Gorlinsky, Heather Osborn
Cover art by Syneca

Electronic book Publication June 2005
Trade paperback Publication January 2006

# Warning:

The following material contains graphic sexual content meant for mature readers. *Lions and Tigers and Bears* has been rated *E-rotic* by a minimum of three independent reviewers.

Ellora's Cave Publishing offers three levels of Romantica™ reading entertainment: S (S-ensuous), E (E-rotic), and X (X-treme).

S-*ensuous* love scenes are explicit and leave nothing to the imagination.

E-*rotic* love scenes are explicit, leave nothing to the imagination, and are high in volume per the overall word count. In addition, some E-rated titles might contain fantasy material that some readers find objectionable, such as bondage, submission, same sex encounters, forced seductions, etc. E-rated titles are the most graphic titles we carry; it is common, for instance, for an author to use words such as "fucking", "cock", "pussy", etc., within their work of literature.

X-*treme* titles differ from E-rated titles only in plot premise and storyline execution. Unlike E-rated titles, stories designated with the letter X tend to contain controversial subject matter not for the faint of heart.

# ~ Contents ~

**ɞ**

## Lion Eyes
Jodi Lynn Copeland
~11~

## Tiger Eye
Kit Tunstall
~103~

## Hidden Heart
Kate Steele
~183~

# Lion Eyes

*Jodi Lynn Copeland*

ℰℬ

# *Trademarks Acknowledgement*

# Chapter One

$\wp$

Unease prickled over Liddy Freeman's skin as the black and white police cruiser pulled up outside her office window. She'd heard about the latest attack on the news this morning, and had known it was only a matter of time before the cops returned to the animal sanctuary for another round of the question and answer game. The answers would be the same this time as they had the previous three—no there were no lions missing from the sanctuary, no she hadn't let any out for a late night stroll last night and no she wasn't lying to protect anyone.

If the cops would open their eyes, they would see it wasn't one of the eight lions that called the Hanover Wild Animal Sanctuary home responsible for the attacks. Given the wintry weather outside and the odds of a lion surviving in it for long, the more likely conclusion was that the attacker wasn't a normal lion at all, but a shifter. The residents of Hanover were as liable to entertain that possibility as the cops were.

That shapeshifters existed among the human population in various forms—tigers, bears and, oh my, even lions—wasn't a point of question but fact. According to Annette Freeman, Liddy's mama and the mayor of Hanover, it also wasn't a point of question if any of those shifters resided in Hanover. According to Annette not a single one had ever ventured within five miles of the city limits and not a single one ever would, because Hanover was a normal city, and normal cities didn't cater to genetic freaks.

Liddy snorted at the thought. If only her mama knew...

A knock sounded on the office door, and the sanctuary receptionist popped her blonde head into the room. "Detective Riggs is here to see you."

*Big surprise.*

Liddy forced a smile. "Thanks, Ann. Go ahead and tell him to come on back."

Less than a minute later, Tanner Riggs stepped into her office. He was the cop who'd been out to question her on all of the other attacks, and was typically what she would have thought of as a good looking guy between his dark blue eyes, brown hair and chiseled facial structure. With Tanner she couldn't get past the odd aura he gave off long enough to appreciate his looks. He made her uncomfortable in a way not even her mama could accomplish, and that was saying something.

Tanner pulled off his cap. He glanced at the chair in front of her desk, but then remained standing. "Good morning, Miss Freeman."

No, it didn't appear that it was a good morning. Not when it started off with the cop standing in her office. She hadn't even finished her first cup of coffee yet, damn it.

Struggling to keep her smile in place, Liddy inclined her head in greeting. "Detective Riggs. What can I help you with today?"

He gave her a look that said she already knew, but then offered, "Been another attack. Same markings as the other times. I'm having the body run for prints or anything else that might turn up, though it's pretty clear what's to blame."

The automatic reaction to protect her animals shot through her. She opened her mouth to remind him that the lions in the sanctuary were retained by high wattage fencing and that most of them were as docile as kittens. Then Tanner's words caught up with her, and the unease she'd felt on first sighting his cruiser returned times ten.

"Body? She died?" The victim had been a woman, like those attacked before her, and Liddy had believed she was recovering in the hospital.

Grim determination settled on his face. "She bled out on the way to the hospital. The way her wounds look she didn't stand much of a chance. This thing's getting worse with every attack, Miss Freeman. If you know something now's the time to come forward. We find out you have something to do with this on our own, you won't be liking the consequences of your silence."

Tanner glanced around the office. His gaze landed on the twin white lioness portraits that always brought Liddy a sense of comfort, then moved out the window to the acres of rolling snow-laden fields and woods and the large heat moderated buildings that kept the animals warm during the winter months. "This place is nice, big. You strike me as someone who values that." He looked back at her, gaze narrowed. "Where you'll go if we catch you lying won't be nice or big."

She'd been prepared for his accusations, and still they had her temper spiking. She stood and rounded the desk. "I told you before that I don't know a damned thing about the attacks. I wish I did. I wish I could tell you who or what is responsible, so I could get you off my back." Reaching the door, Liddy jerked it open. "But I can't. So unless you have any *real* questions for me, I need to get on with my day."

Tanner eyed her a few seconds, assessing her in a way that made her skin itch, then pulled his cap back on and crossed to the door. "You have my card, Miss Freeman," he said none too friendly, "don't be afraid to use it."

She might just do that. To start a fire in her fireplace tonight.

Liddy walked the detective to the door. Grabbing her coat from the rack, she shrugged it on over her green knit sweatshirt and followed him out. He took his time getting into the cruiser, started the engine just as slowly, and kept his attention fixed on her as he backed out of the parking lot and turned down the drive. Finally the car disappeared beyond the trees that lined either side of the drive as far as eye could see.

Inhaling breaths of icy cold air in the hopes of flushing out her frustration, Liddy made her way across the shoveled walk to the first heated viewing building. The winter months were slow for visitors, but a handful came by daily. One was a regular.

And breaking from routine today, she noted the moment she opened the door to the building and heat rushed out to greet her. Kevin Montcalm had been coming by on his lunch hour for the last six months without fail. In many ways, his blue eyes, dark hair and chiseled facial structure was similar to the cop's, but on Kevin impossible to ignore.

He stood in front of the fencing that housed two of the lions, his hands pushed into the pockets of his dress slacks with his back to her. He might as well be looking at her, his intense blue eyes sweeping over with open invitation, for the way her body responded to his presence. Her pulse picked up while her nipples tightened in a way the cold could never accomplish.

Chastising herself for her reaction to a man she knew was wrong for her, at least in her mama's eyes and most the people of Hanover, Liddy swept off her coat and hung it by the door. She'd taken two steps toward Kevin when he turned around. His smile came slowly, and when it was finished took up much of the lower half of his clean-shaven face. His teeth were white, straight, even. His lips full, firm, sensual.

Despite the facts so many thought they were wrong for each other and that Liddy had spent the last months convincing herself they were better off as friends, she'd imagined those lips on her more than once. And more than just in her daydreams. It was often Kevin's face that filled her mind as she curled up at night with her favorite vibrator. Kevin who stroked her bare, open body. Kevin's mouth that moved between her legs, his tongue that slid between her folds and sucked at her pussy. She'd come with his name on her lips more times than she even wanted to acknowledge.

And this was definitely the wrong train of thought to be having so early in the morning and on half a cup of coffee no less.

Ignoring the wetness that had gathered between her thighs with her thoughts, Liddy crossed to Kevin and focused on the lions lazing on the other side of the fencing. "Lose your watch?" she asked after a few seconds. "You're early."

"I couldn't concentrate on work, so I figured I might as well stop in for a few minutes. I saw the cop car out front. They giving you more trouble about the attacks?"

She chanced a look at him, and found him watching her. Twenty feet away, the potency of his eyes could make her hot on sight. One foot away, it stopped the breath in her throat. He was successful businessman, one who was respected in the community and had the wealth to prove it. He wasn't, however, more successful, respected or wealthy than some of the other men Liddy had dated.

So what it was about him that drew her in?

She had no idea of the answer, and she wasn't going to question it any longer. She was going to do what was necessary to keep peace in her family and, as she'd been doing for the last six months, pretend her heart didn't stutter and her panties grow wet whenever Kevin walked into a room.

With a shrug, she turned back to the lions. "Same old thing. They're convinced one of my cats is responsible. You know my theory on that."

"That it's a shifter? Did you say anything to them about that yet?"

"Right. And have them laugh in my face? If my own mama won't believe me, why should anyone else?"

"You're mother's the last person who will accept this city isn't so normal. You say so yourself all the time."

Liddy's mother would also be the last person to accept him asking Liddy out on a date, Kevin knew. Annette Freeman was about as anti-liberal as one could get. That the bulk of Hanover was the same way was how Annette had come by the position of mayor. That the bulk of Hanover was the same way was also the reason that Kevin could never ask Liddy out, no matter how hot the chemistry between them grew.

More than her African American roots and his Caucasian ones separated them—if it were only that and how their dating would be perceived by others, Kevin would say to hell with everyone else's opinion and ask her out here and now. But his identity was the real problem. He was the one thing this city feared and, though Liddy loved her animals, he sometimes wondered if she might not fear him too, if the truth of his being a shifter came out. It couldn't come out—he'd worked too hard to make a name for himself to be shunned by all those who now respected him.

It wouldn't come out. Not so long as he kept his distance from Liddy.

Between her killer curves and eyes so dark brown and soulful he found himself wanting to sink into them, into her, on a daily basis, he knew if he acted on the attraction between them he'd never be able to stop from letting himself go completely. He'd be trapped by his hunger for her, the lust that had been building for months now, the insatiable want that no amount of fucking other women, or even other lion shifters, had managed to lessen.

"The woman who was attacked last night died," Liddy said quietly.

Kevin pulled his attention from below his belt where his cock stirred to rock-hard life. He should stop tormenting himself by coming here, but he valued his time with the lions. And, hell, he valued his time with Liddy even more.

He looked back at her. She'd wrapped her arms around her body, and the stiffness of her posture was a dead giveaway to her anxiety. He considered offering her a comforting hug, then realized how bad of an idea that was. Not only would his erection be obvious, but if her mouth got that close to his, he'd never be able to stop himself from doing something about it.

"I hadn't heard," he said simply.

"Detective Riggs just told me."

"You'd think with things getting worse they'd want to consider every possibility, including that the attacker might not be an animal."

That the attacker, now murderer, could well be one of his own kind, had Kevin's thoughts moving away from Liddy and the attraction between them.

As leader of the local pride—a responsibility passed down to him three years ago when his father died—it was his job to see that all lions followed a strict set of rules. Breaking those rules meant expulsion from the pride and area as a whole. Breaking those rules by committing murder could well mean death. It wasn't a circumstance Kevin had encountered before, and one he hoped to not have to face now.

One thing was for certain. It was time for another gathering. "I need to get going. I have a ten o'clock appointment."

Liddy looked over at him. "Will you be back for lunch?"

He didn't want to acknowledge the tinge of hopefulness in her eyes, and knew that any normal man wouldn't even notice it. But he wasn't quite normal and he also couldn't ignore it. She wanted to see him again today, and he wanted to see her again just as badly. "Do you want me to be?"

She blinked, but then said nonchalantly, "That's your call. I was thinking about picking up some Chinese, and they always give me enough for two."

He laughed, recalling the struggles she'd had the last time they'd shared Chinese. "You going to try to eat with chopsticks again?"

Her full lower lip pushed out in a pout, while her eyes gleamed with amusement. "I was thinking about it."

"Then consider it a date. There's nothing quite as entertaining as watching you try to get those things in your mouth with the food intact." Nothing short of trying to get something else in her mouth, that is. His tongue seemed as good as option as any, he thought when her lower lip pulled back in.

Though he knew how bad an idea it was to stand here and ogle her mouth, Kevin couldn't pull his attention away. Her lips shimmered as if she wore lip gloss, and he wondered if it were the flavored variety.

What would she taste like? Feel like beneath him? What sounds would she make when he slipped into her body and filled his hands with her generous breasts?

Liddy's tongue came out, a slip of pink dampening her lips, and his breathing heightened. With that slight lick, he knew she would taste better than any woman or female he'd ever kissed. She would taste like he would never be able to get enough.

It was the biggest reason he shouldn't reach out to her, shouldn't bend his head, but he found himself doing both, found himself watching her pupils dilate until her eyes were almost completely black. He found himself savoring the moment, and then he found himself cursing it when Liddy stepped back, away from his touch.

She took another step back and looked at the lions. "Yeah, um, so I'll see you at noon then, right?"

If he had any sense, he would say no, that he just remembered another meeting. Something about her obliterated his logic, though.

"Count on it," Kevin said, already anticipating the next time he would see her, when she'd be fighting to get the chopsticks in her mouth, and he'd been fighting himself to stop from imagining those sticks were something else entirely.

\* \* \* \* \*

Most would think that a pride gathering was instigated by sound, an instinctive growl or cry. And maybe some gatherings were brought about that way. Kevin preferred email. Judging by the number in attendance tonight, most in their lion form, some in a state of semi-transformation and others still in their human form, his method worked well.

In his lion form, he stood in the center of the pride. The blackness of night and the thick canopy of woods and new fallen snow shrouded the group from uninvited company. He addressed them in thought — whether they chose to listen and to let him hear their thoughts in return was up to each individual cat.

*There's been another attack. This time the woman died. I've asked before if any of you are responsible or if you know who might be. No one came forward. If you come forward, I'll do all that I can to help you. Until you do, it puts us all at risk. You know how our kind is hated by this city, by most beyond this city. We need to avoid having our identities revealed at all costs.*

"They don't hate us, they fear us," a half-transformed male said off to Kevin's right. Tufts of tawny fur stuck out from beneath the cuffs of his ski jacket and a mane of long, thick hair covered his chin to disappear beneath a navy stocking cap. "They're scared of the unknown and that prig they've elected to mayor doesn't help."

*You're right. It is fear. And the mayor condones it. That doesn't change what's happened. Doesn't make it right. The rules of this pride are firm. We don't need to live off of humans, and when one of us takes it upon themselves to do so, it affects us all.*

An unfamiliar lion with splotched yellow-gold fur stepped forward. His mouth was pulled back into a snarl and the anger in his eyes clear. *A real leader wouldn't hide what he is. A real leader would take pride in it, glory. He would have us do the same.*

*Identify yourself,* Kevin demanded. Uprising in the group was rare, but when it happened had to be dealt with immediately.

*I'm the first of many. One among the masses who will soon see what it is our kind was put on Earth for. Not to cower in the dark and take our pleasure in the same way, but to be the rulers we were born to be. We should be the ones controlling this city. The others can hide what they are. They already fear us, taking over this city will be no effort at all.*

Kevin skulked forward, circled the other lion, then came to a stop in front of him. Sniffing his scent, he attempted to read the cat's thoughts but came up empty. *There will be no taking over the city. And we won't hide what we are forever. We strive for equality, but it has to come slowly, in measured ways. Anyone who can't understand the reason for that shouldn't be a part of this pride. They will not be welcome in this city.* He pulled his teeth back, growled. *Do I make myself clear?*

*You waste your breath. You can't change what is. What will be soon?* The unfamiliar lion turned, addressing the group. *All of you have listened to him for years. Where has it gotten you? Hiding what you are? Fucking behind closed doors and in the dark of night. That's not what I want for my life. That's not what my life will be. I intend to start a new pride, one that is proud of what we are, one that sees we earn our rightful place. Any of you who wish to join, follow me now. Follow me and I will take you farther in a month than this lion has in years.*

The lion looked back at Kevin, bared his teeth in a snarl and then darted off. Silence descended over the pride. Kevin waited, expecting at least one among them to take what the other lion had said to heart and follow. But not even one moved, and he realized all eyes were trained on him, waiting for his lead.

He should speak more about the attacks, about the consequences they could face if the shifter responsible failed to come forward. But after what had happened with the other lion, he knew giving them what they wanted, the one thing many had come here tonight for, would get him that much farther in the long run, at least in maintaining their faith in him.

Tossing his head back, he roared into the night. A thunder of cries responded and then all died into snarls of pleasure and growls of relief as lions paired off.

This was the real reason they responded to his emails and came to these gatherings. Not to listen to him, though he liked to think at last some of them did, but because it was the one time they could give into their natural urges surrounded by others of their kind. It was the one time they could truly allow their feral side to come through without fear of being caught.

The sight of so many around him in various states of transformation, most down on four legs and thrusting aroused cocks into their mates' pussies and asses had Kevin's own cock thick and solid, his blood pulsing with the urge to join in. Rarely did he give in. Most nights he would watch, inhale the lusty scent of sex and take delight in the roars of ecstasy filling the night. Tonight he thought would be no different—he would watch, enjoy playing the part of voyeur and then go home and find pleasure at his own hand—then he saw her, practically camouflaged against the snow.

She was the only white lioness he'd ever seen in the area, had ever seen period, and she came to these gatherings far too seldom. Kevin had figured out some time ago her attendance depended on if he flagged his emails as being of high importance. She always responded to those. Always said she would be here.

In the past, she'd done the same as him, watched the fucking taking place around them, occasionally meeting his eyes with lust burning hotly in hers, and then left without finding fulfillment. Tonight her gaze was trained on him, and now that he'd connected with it, he couldn't take his own away.

Only one other female—make that woman—had ever captured his attention so completely. Kevin thought of that woman now. His body told him he must go to the lioness and use the pull she had over him to erase his desire for Liddy. His mind feared it wouldn't matter if he had the lioness tonight. Come tomorrow, when he saw Liddy at lunchtime, the desire that rocked him to the core would still be there.

Aware he had to forget his want for Liddy and more aware of the anxious way his cock twitched at the thought of taking the stunning lioness, he moved through the pride. He stole glances around him as he went, his hunger becoming that much more acute with each thrusting pair he viewed. A trio in their human forms stripped of most of their clothing caught his attention.

Without their fur, the winter air should have felt icy. Instead, as the blond man kneaded the woman's full, pale breasts and pumped into her ass and the dark-haired one pushed his cock into her pussy, they appeared hot, sweaty. The look on the woman's face as she tipped back her head and wailed skyward, was that of pure ecstasy.

It was the look he wanted to see on his lioness's face.

Kevin turned his attention back on the female, intrigued by the way he'd taken possession of her. Maybe he'd been wrong. Maybe she could make him forget about his desire for Liddy.

He attempted to penetrate her thoughts as he continued toward her. She wouldn't let him in. It was a rare trait for a female, but so much about her was rare. Her eyes for example. The darkest brown. A startling contrast to her snow-white fur. And familiar, in a way he knew went beyond these gatherings. Or perhaps it was a premonition that made him believe that. Some of the great kings had been known to have the sight. Until now, Kevin had never even considered he might be amongst them.

Among true lions, many things were different. Prides were dominated by females and cubs and the females were often the dominant ones when it came to sex. Among shifters, there was an equal ratio of males and females and control was shared. Females were taught young to cast their gaze downward when the king looked upon them, however. The lioness appeared to have missed that lesson, as she didn't look down when he reached her, but continued to look at him with those dark, hungry eyes.

Her tongue came out, long, wet and silky, to swipe along her mouth. Kevin's cock jerked. He would like to feel that raspy tongue on his length, only tonight he wasn't patient enough. Tonight he wanted to assert dominance, take hold of her neck and push into her slick pussy from behind. As ruler, he could do so without question, without thought to her wishes. He didn't do so, because she wasn't a typical female. She was special and she deserved to be treated differently.

Lying down at her paws, he rolled onto his side, exposing his belly and offering himself to her. He'd never behaved so subserviently among the pride, and he hoped she understood the message in his doing so now.

The lioness studied him a silent moment, then asked, *Why me?*

Because he wanted her in a way he'd only ever wanted Liddy.

Liddy's face filled his mind, her full lips curved into a teasing smile. Her eyes inviting him into her office, onto her desk, where she would sit back while he undressed her one layer at a time. He would savor every inch of her beautiful body, her smooth dark skin. He would love her with his tongue before he did so with his body, have her writhing beneath him, screaming his name as she came.

He would, if he was a normal man.

Kevin focused on the lioness, on her engaging eyes. Yes, he could sink into them. He could lose himself in this one.

He reached a paw up, cupped her face. *I could ask the same.*

She preened against his paw, purred low in her throat. *Any female would be foolish to say no to you.*

*Any male would be the same. You are beautiful, rare. Tell me your name.*

*Sierra,* she said after a moment.

The hesitation told him the name was not her human one, but her feline. For fear of it harming him professionally, he chose not to use his human name among the pride, either, so he could not fault her. As far as he could tell there was no fault with this cat, only perfection. Exquisite beauty that made rubbing her cheek not nearly enough. He had to be inside her, now.

*Sierra, would you like me to fuck you?*

Another moment of hesitation, then, *Yes please.*

Eagerness coursed through his veins. His cock thrummed. Fervent cries and rapturous roars of those around them filled the still night air. He bounded to his feet and brushed his face against hers, flicked his tongue across her mouth. She licked him back, her laps urgent, needy. Her taste was warm, explosive on his tongue. The scent of her arousal filled his nostrils. She was wet for him. Hot. Ready.

He flicked his tongue to her ear and then down along her nape. With a low growl, he bit her neck. She reared back and he came over her, brushed his cock against her ass. She reared a second time and he thrust hard into her slick sheath.

Kevin growled against her neck, while his heart slammed against his ribs.

Sierra fit him in a way no other female had, no other woman. Her pussy loved him tight, hard as he pulled out and thrust again. She mewled with each push, then those mewls grew to throaty cries and finally, as her muscles clenched his shaft, a low roar that resounded through his ears and pitched all the blood in his body directly to his cock.

He could no more hold back his climax than he could stop from biting her harder, marking her as his. Soul blistering release sliced through him as he poured his cum into her hot, wet body and, while he rarely spoke in his lion form, his teeth let up from her neck and a name growled from his lips.

"Liddy!"

# Chapter Two

### ஐ

"Late night?"

From where she stood at a low counter in the first of the large heated buildings, doling out vitamins into small plastic containers, Liddy looked over at Samantha Redding. The young woman was doing an internship with the sanctuary and came by three mornings a week to help with the animals' weekly nutritional plan and to log their behavior.

Liddy reflected on her own time spent interning while attaining her veterinarian degree—that summer had shaped who she was, literally. While she'd never regretted what had happened to her—outside of the strain keeping it secret from her family sometimes caused—she hoped Sam's internship was uneventful.

As for being tired… She'd stayed up way too late. Used muscles she hadn't used in far too long. Last night had been gratifying to the fullest extent…and she felt guilty as hell about it. Not for what she'd done—she was entitled to sex at least once a year—but because of who she'd done it with. Or rather who she hadn't done it with.

God, she was in so deep with Kevin that she thought her lover had called…

No. She was not going to drive herself crazy by thinking about last night and what she did or did not hear.

Liddy stood and stretched. Arching her back, she let out a long yawn. "I met up with some friends and stayed out a bit late. But I'll get my bearings soon."

"Lack of sleep causes wrinkles, baby. You're too pretty and too single for that."

Arms still over her head in stretch mode, Liddy spun around. Annette Freeman stood just inside the building doorway, wearing the fur coat that always made Liddy's belly ache when she thought of the foxes slain to make it. Killing for sustenance she understood well, but never for luxury's sake.

"Mama. What are you doing here?"

Keeping her coat on, Annette came over to Liddy. She glanced at the lions behind the fencing thirty feet from where they stood and attempted to cover a shiver. Liddy saw it, sensed her mama's alarm, and fought off a frown. How anyone could fear such beautiful creatures she would never know.

"I heard the police were out to see you again," her mama said.

Frustration coiled in Liddy's belly with the reminder of the annoying Tanner Riggs. He was the reason she shouldn't feel regret over selecting a near stranger to have sex with. The cop's accusations had had her wound up tight and in need of stress relief. Admittedly, so had the idea that Kevin had wanted to kiss her yesterday before she'd stepped away from him. But she was not to going to think about that.

"Detective Riggs was by yesterday. I told him again I know nothing about the attacks, that there's no way any of my animals could get out and then back in without my knowledge, and all of them are accounted for."

"Well, you let me know if he doesn't leave you alone. He hasn't lived in Hanover long enough to know much about us, but that won't stop me from using a connection or two to get him off your back." Annette pursed her lips, and her face took on the look Liddy had termed her "I'm about to give advice you don't want to hear" one, years ago. "Now, about this single status of yours. Baby, you're not getting any younger. Another few days and you'll be thirty and from there it's all downhill."

More like a year and ten days until she turned thirty, and last thing she knew the downhill birthday was the fortieth one. Considering her mama was in her early fifties and, with her smooth mocha skin and shoulder-length black hair, still as fit and lively as she'd been when Liddy was a girl, she had no plans to worry about the aging process. She also had no plans to have this conversation yet again.

"Yes Mama." Liddy returned her attention to sorting out vitamins, hoping her desire to change the subject was clear.

Apparently it wasn't. "There are plenty of fine looking men in this city, Liddy love. All you need to do—"

"Sorry for interrupting, but I need a moment with Ms. Freeman."

Liddy's antipathy over discussing her love life with her mama faded to irritation with Detective Riggs' deep voice. She glanced over to find him making his way toward her, then looked around the building out of instinct. It was too early for visitors, and Sam had moved into the small computer room, closing the door behind her.

As much as they had their differences at times, Liddy loved her mama and trusted her with anything the detective might say. "We can talk here."

The cop's gaze went to Annette, staying there for several long seconds before he looked back at her and nodded. "If that's how you want it."

"It is."

"They were able to pull DNA off the body."

Liddy paused midway to dropping two large pills into a small plastic cup. Unease stiffened her spine. If the cop had come here to tell her that, it could only mean one thing… "Oh," she managed to get out calmly.

Tanner's gaze honed in on her face, as if assessing her to see how calm she really was. The impulse to bar him from her thoughts was automatic and absurd. The cop couldn't read her thoughts. Only between the way his lips twitched at the corners and the hint of amusement that rallied through his eyes, it almost seemed that he could.

"It's not a lion," he finally said.

She breathed an audible sigh while her heart pounded madly against her ribs. Thank God. Outwardly, she allowed smug satisfaction. "Told you it couldn't be. At least, not one of mine. I keep them under—"

"It also isn't a human," Tanner continued, all trace of humor gone.

Liddy's satisfaction burst. "What?"

"Just what are you saying, Officer?" Annette asked in a tone just this side of snippy. The way she managed to look down her nose at the cop who was a good six inches taller than her wasn't much better.

Tanner bristled. "It's detective, Mayor Freeman, and I'm saying we've got ourselves a shifter in Hanover."

Annette's face paled. The color quickly returned to her skin and she shook her head at the cop. "That's impossible. Hanover has no shifters. Everyone knows that."

"Looks like it is possible," the detective returned, his voice steely, "and since it seems no one's gonna come forward and say they're the shifter responsible, we're gonna have to think of some other way to catch this thing."

"*Thing*?" Temper shot through Liddy in an instant, coiling rage in her belly. She glared at the cop. "Shapeshifters are not things, Detective. They have the same rights as humans."

Annette sniffed. "That amendment should never have been voted in."

With an inward growl, Liddy turned her glare on her mama. "A lot of people would probably say the same thing about people of color being allowed to vote, or carry a governmental position, for that matter."

"Don't be illogical, Liddy," Annette chastised. "That's a totally different issue."

"Why," she snapped, "because you happen to be someone who benefited from it?" She looked back at Tanner. "Whoever— not whatever—is responsible for these attacks, once you track them down, deserves a fair trial, not a lynching."

The twitch was back at the corners of the cop's mouth. Amusement more than clear in his aura. To think she'd entertained the thought yesterday morning that he shared similar looks with Kevin. Kevin was gorgeous. Tanner was disgusting.

"We'll see to it that we do what we can, Ms. Freeman," he said.

Liddy managed to hold in her snort, but not her sarcasm. "Yeah. I bet."

"Liddy Marie!" Annette warned. "That's no way to talk to the officer."

"Detective," Tanner corrected again brusquely.

Minutes ago her mama had been ready to use her influence to get the cop off Liddy's back and now she was acting like she was on his side. Of course, the stakes had changed the moment Tanner had mentioned a shifter was involved.

Liddy put her hand out, palm forward. She would no sooner disrespect the mayor in front of one of her citizens than bring about a family war over this. "Please don't start, Mama. I know how you feel about it, and I'm sorry."

Annette looked mollified. "Well, that's better, and I forgive you, baby. It's hard to accept one of those freaks could have found their way into our city. Detective, you will be keeping this speculation under wraps, I assume?"

Okay, so maybe she would disrespect the mayor and start that war after all.

Liddy had grown up listening to her mama persecute others for being different. She should have been prepared to hear her call shifters freaks. It wasn't even the first time. She wasn't prepared, and it riled her temper to the breaking point.

"I wasn't apologizing to you," she bit through her teeth. "I was saying I'm sorry that the bulk of this city is so damned narrow-minded." She started toward the large coolers that held ground meat and small animal carcasses. "Thanks for stopping by, Detective, Mama," she said without turning back. "Now I need to work. Of course, you're welcome to stay and help me feed the lions."

The idea of feeding the detective to them held too much appeal to not smile over. As for Mama...well, she was family. Maybe she'd just let the cats nibble on her a bit.

* * * * *

Liddy stood up for him.

Not for him alone, Kevin acknowledged as Annette Freeman swept out of the first heated building followed by the cop who'd been giving Liddy trouble the past few months, but for shifters as a whole. Did that mean they could have a chance?

Hell, he shouldn't even be considering it after last night.

He'd wanted Sierra to know how beautiful she was, how special, how she appealed to him on a level no other female did. He'd been doing a good job of it, up until the moment he'd come into her while growling Liddy's name.

The lioness had taken off nearly the moment he'd pulled out of her. She'd claimed it was late and she had to work early, but he'd known the truth of the matter. He'd hurt her. He felt guilty over it and yet not nearly as guilty as he should.

Not half as guilty as what he felt when he stepped into the building and spotted Liddy stalking to one of the lions' enclosures, a container of meat in her hands. Even as culpability weighed on his shoulders his body responded to her, his cock hardening and his blood thundering between his ears. Having Sierra last night did nothing to curb his hunger for Liddy, if anything it made it that much more acute.

Damn it.

"Morning," Kevin said.

She stopped filling the lions' feed bin and swiveled around. Loathing flashed over her features and then was quickly replaced by another emotion, one just short of happiness. As a matter of trust, he never ventured into Liddy's thoughts. But now he was tempted. He had heard much of her conversation with the cop and her mother, but not enough to understand the extent of her fury.

"I take it the detective wasn't just making a social call?" he asked.

She finished filling the bin, then stepped out of the enclosure and ensured the electricity that ran through the fencing was turned back on before responding. "He just confirmed what I'd already guessed. I shouldn't be so upset over it."

"But?"

She sighed loudly. "Mama."

She looked beyond upset, moving into severely hurt terrain. He crossed to her, but knew better than to reach out and offer his shoulder. Instead, he gave her a reassuring smile. Annoyance aimed at her mother knotted his gut when she didn't return the smile. What had Annette said to her that he'd missed?

Kevin broke his own rule and searched Liddy's mind for the answer. Only Liddy's mind wasn't open to him.

He frowned. It wasn't unheard of for a human to be able to block their thoughts from a shifter, but it was rare. That Liddy was strong enough to do so built his appreciation of her all that much more. "I'm sorry. As you know my father died several years ago and I rarely see my own mother, so I can't imagine how you must feel."

Her smile came now, weak and still able to snag the breath in his throat, while making his fingers itch to touch her. Hell, not just touch. To take her into his arms and make her his. "Thank you," she said softly.

"For what?"

"Not trying to pretend you know what it feels like. You're a wonderful friend."

The claim was like a physical blow. His gut knotted further. Hatred for his own desires swamped him. It was no wonder Liddy had backed away from his kiss yesterday. She wanted nothing from him but friendship. The chemistry he always sensed between them had to be one-sided.

Kevin could handle that. Was glad for it in fact, at least logically—they were too different for a lasting relationship that went beyond friendship. Then there was the fact not opening himself up to Liddy meant not risking his identity being discovered by anyone else in Hanover. Yes, keeping their relationship on a friendly level was a good thing.

He pushed an easy grin into place, even as his body rebelled at the thought. "Also a great listener, I've been told. Care to talk about it?"

She looked uncertain for a moment, then glanced around them. She looked back and nodded. "Just let me finish feeding the animals."

Ten minutes later, Liddy settled onto a stool on one side of the low counter that held her medicinal supplies. He took a seat opposite her.

She sorted pills as she spoke. "It turns out a shifter is behind the attacks, the way I've always believed."

The calm that had come over Kevin as he watched her work was replaced by dread. He nearly snapped out the need to know more before he could gather his senses. He had to look like he was merely curious, not that the safety of his pride might hinge on her response. "What makes them think that?"

"They were able to get DNA off the last victim."

Shit. "Were they able to match it to anyone?"

"Not by the sound of things." Liddy secured another handful of pills. "Detective Riggs said since no one's coming forward, they'd have to find another way to catch this thing." Her hand shook as she upended it over a small plastic cup.

She looked up at him. Her eyes had always been soulful in the past, now they held rage. Gathering the cup in her hand, she squeezed until her brown knuckles shone with whiteness. "That's what he said," she snarled. "Thing. Like a shifter is a fucking object or something. And my mama, she's worse. She called them freaks. Shifters are not freaks!"

It wasn't just her hand shaking now, but her entire body. Her lips were pressed tight and she looked capable of vibrating off the stool with her anger.

No longer fearing what might happen if he touched her, Kevin reached across the counter and covered her fisted hand with his. Heat radiated from her skin, shot up his arm and fired his blood with awareness.

The hardness of his body had retreated since learning she wasn't attracted to him. The way the temper in her eyes sizzled to passion, the way she blinked at him, the way her tongue slipped out of her mouth to swipe along her lips... It all suggested she wasn't immune to his touch. It suggested she wanted him as badly as he wanted her. And it had his cock stirring back to life and right into painful hardness.

"You know one?" he asked, wary of the roughness of his voice.

Liddy didn't break eye contact or attempt to pull her hand back. "I've met them before, and they're just like anyone else with a few extra abilities. They have feelings, hopes. Desires," she added in a sultry voice. Her lips curved into the inviting smile he adored, and for a moment they sat in silence, staring at each other. Then she continued, "Most of them have jobs and even families. And I hate to be the one to break it to Mama, but they do live in Hanover."

Kevin nearly let go of her hand with the shock of her words. She knew his kind lived among the residents of this city. How? "I know," he ventured.

She looked as stunned as he felt. "You do?"

"Yes. I've met them before, as well. I know several who live in the city."

"Why didn't you say something before?"

"I wasn't sure how you would respond," he admitted, still uncertain of how she would respond if she learned he not only knew shifters, but was one himself.

Would she fear him, or would she embrace the truth?

His heart squeezed with hope for the latter. Maybe it was a foolish thought to even entertain, but if there was a chance… "I could ask the same of you."

"I guess I kept quiet for the same reason." Liddy's fist uncurled beneath his. She turned her hand until her palm connected with his. It wasn't soft, but the hand of a woman who wasn't afraid of hard work.

Either that, or one who spent a lot of time on her hands and knees.

Heat splintered through him with the visual that formed in his mind. Liddy naked on the floor before him, her curvy ass in his face, her thighs splayed wide to expose the rear of her pussy and the nest of black curls that covered her mound.

Sliding into her would be a lesson in control. Feeling her wetness, her warmth around him, milking his cock would surely drive him insane. Kevin's shaft gave an impatient twitch, while his balls drew tightly to his body.

Fuck, he wanted to be there now, buried deeply inside her pussy, listening to her full, sweet mouth crying his name. Hearing her growl as she came.

Women didn't growl, females did.

Fine then, she could moan or scream. He could live without her growling if doing so meant having the lovely Liddy in his life, his arms. His bed.

He focused on her face, determined to do something about this heat between them. Now that he knew where she stood on the shifter front, it wouldn't be such a grand wager to ask her out. If she learned the truth about him and couldn't handle it…well, hell, he'd deal with the consequences if and when it happened.

He didn't believe she would turn him down, not after seeing the want that burned in her eyes with a simple touch. Still his heart pounded madly as he said, "If I asked you out, what would you say?"

The smile fell from Liddy's lips. She blinked at him. Several Times. Fast. The blinking stopped and she looked at their joined hands, then back at him. Emotions swam through her eyes. Emotions that like her thoughts, he couldn't read.

Seconds passed. Nearly a full minute. His heart felt ready to beat from his chest.

Her mouth parted, her tongue slipped out. Licked over her lips, slowly. Sweetly. God, he wanted that tongue on his body. Wanted it up against his own.

Kevin rarely exerted his dominance, on women or lionesses. This time he couldn't stop himself. This time it seemed action was exactly what was needed. He rose to his feet and tugged Liddy to hers. Watched the emotions play through her eyes as he leaned across the counter. Worry. Anticipation. Fear. Relief.

He could read them all now. And every one of them tuned his body into hers all that much more. He could scent her arousal. See her desire. And then taste her want, as their lips met. Hers were wet from her tongue and soft as a dream. They tasted not of the lip gloss he'd imagined, but rather…familiar. Maybe nothing more than the sensation of coming home. Or maybe, as he'd thought of Sierra's eyes last night, it was a taste of his future.

Both Liddy and Sierra could not be his future.

Anger surged through him with the thought. He ceased the brushing of his mouth and stabbed his tongue deep. The throaty moan against his mouth wasn't one of fear, but of urgency. Her tongue moved against his, wet and rough and needful. Her fingers untwined from his, her hands moving to his chest. Pushing his own into her long dark hair, he gripped the thick curly length. Her hands slid beneath the open sides of his jacket, her nails pressing through his dress shirt. He'd never noticed if they were long, but he felt them now, long and sharp and biting into his flesh, bringing pleasure just this side of pain.

She was wild, wanton. His need for her was fierce. He had to have her now.

"I hate to admit it, but it looks like I'm gonna need a jump."

Liddy broke from his arms with a gasp at the sound of the detective's voice. Cursing under his breath, Kevin stepped back and stood on the side of the counter opposite her. Passion darkened her eyes to near black, flushed her stunning face, and had the breath leaving her lips in hot little pants. They were sexy as hell and he wanted to swallow them with his mouth. Instead, he turned to the cop.

"I have jumper cables in the back of my truck." He started toward the door, then glanced back at Liddy and grinned. "I'll be back in a few minutes to finish the conversation."

\* \* \* \* \*

Kevin returned inside ten minutes later. Liddy's heart was still racing, her panties wet, her nipples aching points and the need to feel him inside her wild in her blood.

She'd gone without sex for months at a time. Considering she'd just had it last night with someone far more ideal for her than Kevin, her pussy shouldn't be tingling with the need for it now. But it was, and she wanted him so badly it bordered on pain.

She should say no to his date offer. There were too many consequences that could come from it, not the least of which was a family feud with Mama. Only she wanted to say yes. No, she wanted to scream yes, preferably when she was fucking his gorgeous body.

Oh boy. How had things reached this point so quickly after months of denying herself the urge to so much as touch him?

The question was forgotten the moment Liddy noticed the streak of red on the side of Kevin's hand. Her senses attuned to the blood and his possible pain in turn.

Concentrating on the latter, she rushed to him. "Are you hurt?"

"Nothing a Band-Aid or two won't cure." He held his hand out for her inspection. A jagged scratch ran the length of his palm. Not deep, just bleeding a good deal. "The detective dropped the hood before I was ready. Luckily I pulled my hand out in time and only managed to cut it on the latch."

"Luckily," Liddy returned, disdain for the detective making her irritable. She'd only been joking about feeding him to the lions, but the idea held some real appeal.

The rich metallic scent of Kevin's blood took over her thoughts then. Her nostrils flared, her tongue ached. They had to get the wound covered. She took his good hand and warmth shot from their joined fingers directly to her womb. Her pussy pulsed. She was still so wet for him. Wetter with this simple touch.

First things first.

She guided him to the low counter and instructed him to sit down on the stool he'd occupied before kissing her. Memories of that kiss, of how desperate he'd made her feel clouded Liddy's thoughts as she pushed vitamin containers aside. She settled his hand on the empty space. Her tongue swelled with the sight of his blood. Her pulse sped. She was back to desperate, this time in a completely different way.

She hurried to grab the first-aid kit that was mounted in each of the large heated buildings for precaution's sake. With shaking hands, she pulled out antiseptic and a large, square Band-Aid. Kevin's hand needed to be bathed before she could apply the antiseptic. There was a sink less than four feet away. But her tongue was so close and his blood smelled so good, warm. Enticing.

Unable to take her eyes from the oozing red liquid, she lifted his hand to her mouth. Just a kiss. The kind Mama had given her boo-boos when she'd been a little girl. She brushed her mouth across his palm, telling herself she'd leave it at that. Kevin's grunt wouldn't allow it. The guttural sound reached deep down inside her, stoked her hunger, her natural need. The side of her she denied to all but a few.

The first taste of his blood was exquisite, like nothing she'd ever experienced, like nothing she could ever have imagined. With the second lap, raw energy soared through her body, deep into her veins. Her breasts felt heavy, her nipples hard peaks. She licked fervently, urgently, stunned by the way it affected her. It was more than a hunger, it was a want, a lust. Her pussy felt aflame, wetter with each lap.

Was it possible to come from licking someone's blood? There was so much about herself she didn't know. So much no one had ever told her. So much she thought she could live without. Only now it seemed she had been wrong.

"Liddy?"

Kevin spoke her name roughly, and when she lifted her eyes to his, she saw his want for her clear. She also saw his confusion.

She was confused herself, but knew better than to let it show. Lowering his hand, she applied the antiseptic and Band-Aid, explaining in a voice that only trembled slightly, "I, uh, thought it might help. Mama used to kiss my hurts."

He should have asked more. She would have. Instead, he said, "It did," and reached to her face with his good hand, stroked her cheek. "Your saying yes about going out with me would help even more."

His touch was so good, so lulling Liddy could simply purr over it. "Mama will never let me hear the end of it. I mean, not because she doesn't like you but because…well, I'm me and you're you. We don't exactly match."

Amusement lit Kevin's blue eyes, turned them dark as night. He chuckled deeply, then quickly sobered. "If it bothers you that much, tell me no. I'll understand."

"No."

Disappointment flashed through his eyes and he pulled his hand back. Liddy mourned the loss even as she realized how he'd taken her answer. "I meant no," she clarified, "that I don't want to say no to you. I want to go out with you. Mama's mama. Very set in her ways. The important thing is that she loves me and respects my decisions. One date isn't going to change that."

At least, nothing more than consuming his blood like a feral animal had.

# Chapter Three

**ഇ**

One date, Liddy had said, but Kevin had every intention to see this first date led to many more. Especially after today. After the way she'd licked his wound.

His cock hardened with the memory of her hot, wet tongue on his hand and the sultry look in her eyes as she lapped at his blood. Hell, he'd been ready to pounce across the counter and claim her as his with the first lick.

He was still ready to claim her as his, lioness or no.

Kevin didn't want to speculate on Liddy's behavior meaning she was one of his kind. But cleansing his wound with her mouth wasn't something a normal woman would do. The ability to keep her thoughts from him was potentially something a normal woman could do, but the odds were slim.

As were the odds he was right about her being a shapeshifter. He wanted it to be true for his own selfish reasons. But he had to consider the other possibility, namely that she had an incredibly soft spot for animals. Her behavior could have been something she'd picked up from spending so much of her life around them.

Wrong or right, Kevin had every intention of finding out tonight. There were ways of drawing out a lioness and he'd yet to meet a female immune to them.

Before he could pick Liddy up, however, he had a few things to deal with. The most important of which was setting up another pride gathering. Now that the police were pointing fingers in the direction of a shifter, discovering who was behind the string of attacks was critical. If the wrong lion was brought in, he could spill every one of the pride's secrets, including the identity of all those who struggled to keep their lion side private.

The unfamiliar cat from last night topped that list of wrong lions. Kevin had no idea who the male was, but given his open disrespect for the way Kevin ran the pride, it was clear he would do anything to see him usurped.

He had to have answers, and he had to have them immediately. As much as he wanted to end this night with Liddy in his bed and slipping away from her unnoticed would be unlikely, the gathering needed to be tonight.

Of course, maybe he wouldn't need to slip away from Liddy. Maybe she'd be attending the gathering with him. Maybe she'd been attending them all along.

\* \* \* \* \*

"You look hot!"

Shrugging into her long winter coat, Liddy cast her sister Chenille, who sat cross-legged on the living room couch, a "knock it off" look. She was incredibly nervous about going out with Kevin. Knowing her sister would be home when he arrived made her all that much more so.

As younger sisters went, Chenille was great but had a big mouth. Liddy knew the moment she walked out the door on Kevin's arm, her sister would be on the phone to Mama. Unless she could think of something to blackmail her with first, that is.

Fortunately thinking of ways to blackmail her sister wasn't so hard. At twenty-five, Chenille had a penchant for late nights spent partying with her guy of the week. It was the reason Liddy has been shocked to hear she was staying in tonight. It was also the reason she could smile now.

At least until she met her sister's eyes, then she was careful to keep her expression bland. "Did you ever tell Mama you were the one who ran over the mailbox last summer?"

Chenille's eyes went wide. Her relaxed position grew tense. "What? No. Why?"

"Just wondering." Liddy turned to the mirror that hung on the closet door, pretending to inspect her appearance. "I know how much she loved it. Daddy gave it to her for their twentieth anniversary. She always said how much the windmill design reminded her of their honeymoon."

"Yeah, I know." Concern was apparent in Chenille's voice. "But why bring it up now?"

Liddy spun back to look at her sister meaningfully. She believed what she'd told Kevin. Mama did respect her decisions. Annette would pitch a fit over Liddy's dating a white man, possibly not even talk to her for a while, but eventually she would have to see how happy Kevin made her and get used to the idea, or at least learn to live with it.

Of course, just in case this date didn't go so well, prolonging the moment when her mama found out about it wouldn't hurt anything. "I was thinking how heartbroken she was about the mailbox and how mad she'd be with the person responsible. Probably wouldn't make them carrot cake for at least a dozen Sundays or so."

Whether it was the mention of the cake that happened to be her sister's favorite and the dessert Mama made every Sunday for their weekly family luncheon, Chenille's gaze narrowed. She came to her feet and lifted her chin, attitude clear in her stance. "She's not going to, so don't worry about it."

"I hope not."

A knock sounded on the door before Chenille could respond. Liddy's belly tightened as she crossed the short distance to the front door. With an indrawn breath, she yanked it open, and had to fight to hold in her roar of appreciation.

Between tight fitting dark jeans she could guess would hug his ass like a glove and a black leather jacket over a tan sweater, Kevin looked more than good enough to eat. His mouth tugged into that wide, full grin that showed off his teeth and her panties grew moist. Vaguely she was aware of the cold air rushing in, but it wasn't the reason her nipples felt hard as rocks. No, that would be the way his intense gaze traveled over her body, lingering on the swell of her breasts.

She'd put on her coat, but hadn't bothered with shutting it, and her cleavage suddenly felt ready to escape the bodice of her casual dress. Right into his hands would be the ideal place for her breasts to go.

Kevin's gaze met hers and he whistled. "Wow. You look —"

"Hot," Chenille's voice carried over Liddy's shoulder. I told her…" Her sister's words trailed off, and she knew Chenille had stepped into sight of Kevin. "He's your date?"

Liddy retreated to the couch to grab her purse and give her sister a warning look. "Yes. And we're leaving now. Don't wait up. And don't forget about the mailbox."

Understanding filled Chenille's eyes followed by amusement. With a sigh of relief, Liddy returned to the door. Her sister seemed mostly accepting of her dating a man outside their race — at least, the parts of her race that involved pigmentation — now to see how the rest of the city responded.

* * * * *

"I like mine blood red. How about you?"

Liddy frowned a little, but then responded to Kevin's question. "Same way. It zaps all the flavor out of the steak when it's cooked too much."

He'd been asking her minor questions meant to unravel the mystery of what she really was — a woman or a lioness — for the last half hour. The major questions would come later, when he had her in a position where he wasn't afraid she would bolt.

Given the frowns that had come with his latest questions, he opted to avoid even the minor ones for the time being. A glance across the small candlelit table revealed a topic he wouldn't mind spending several hours talking about, the way Liddy's lush breasts pressed against her black gown and tempted his fingers to reach out and touch.

The candlelight played off her golden brown skin and made the generous curves glisten, as if they were damp, as if he'd had his mouth on them. He hadn't yet, but he would before

43

this night was through. The sensual smile that curved her lips as he lifted his attention from her cleavage ensured she was as anxious to take this relationship up a step. Heat sizzled in her dark eyes as he reached for his wine glass, purposefully brushing the hand she'd settled on the table next to her own glass. The intensity of that heat had him aching to take the next step here and now.

It was dark in the restaurant, the lighting set low to add to the atmosphere. The tablecloth hung well over the edge of the table, far enough to hide most of their legs from view. Far enough that unless someone was pointedly looking at their feet, they wouldn't notice movement under the table.

Kevin could give her casual conversation, but they shared that daily during his visits to the sanctuary. What they hadn't shared during those visits—hadn't even come close to sharing until yesterday—was intimacy.

His cock lengthened, thickened with the idea overtaking his thoughts. Dare he, when it was clear how anxious Liddy was about the two of them being seen on a date?

He lifted his wine glass and took a long drink. The answer to his unspoken question was in the way her gaze went to his mouth. Her pupils darkened, dilated. Her tongue slipped out, swiped at her lush lower lip.

Dare he? Oh yes, he dared.

Kevin set his glass back, and hitched his elbow at the precise angle to send his spoon flying to the floor. Finely arched black eyebrows darted together and he gave her an innocent smile. "Woops. It would seem your date has a clumsy side."

He sent a covert glance around, and noting no watchers, pushed back his chair. Slipping to the floor on his knees, he pulled the chair back in. The spoon had fallen inches from his feet. He grabbed it and crawled the short distance to Liddy's slender feet decked out in strappy black heels. Her pantyhose were sheer black and her legs neatly crossed. He set the spoon against the inner curve of one of her legs, and they came unfolded, still too close together for his liking. He remedied that with his mouth.

Nibbling at the inside of one knee, he set the spoon aside and caught the other knee in his hand, squeezing the soft flesh, then slowly working his way up. Liddy was silent above the table, but her hands moved beneath it, letting him know she wasn't unaffected by his actions. He parted his lips and stroked his tongue along her thigh. Her legs opened wider, while her fingers delved into his hair.

*Yes. Higher. All the way up.*

Her thoughts hit him hard, and made his cock throb. That she was sharing them was a good sign. They were also a silent plea he had no plans to resist.

Kevin placed both hands on her thighs and slid them upward. The air lodged in his throat momentarily when he met with the lace edges of the silky material that covered her legs. Not pantyhose, but stockings. And that meant her pussy was easily accessible.

His blood heated as he lifted the hem of her dress, moved it up her shapely thighs and bunched the material beneath her curvy ass. Her panties were black and miniscule. The scent of her arousal all consuming. Nostrils flaring, he slid his thumbs to the apex of her thighs and beneath the crotch of her panties.

Liddy's hips shot forward with the first swipe of his thumbs over her swollen clit. Then harder a second time, as he pushed one thumb against the tender pearl and used the other to pull her panties aside. It was dark under the tablecloth, and this was one time Kevin praised God for his abilities as a shifter. Thanks to his night vision, he could see the tangle of black curls glistening with her essence as easily as if the sun shone on her sex. He parted her folds with his thumbs and once more Liddy's thoughts came to him.

*Your tongue. Now. Please. Fuck me with it.*

If he'd had any concerns over her not wanting to end this night in his bed, they were wasted. The months they'd spent as friends, carefully avoiding the chemistry between them had her dancing on the edge of need as acutely as he himself was.

Her need he planned to do something about, now.

*So hot*, Kevin thought, pressing his nose to her slit. He inhaled her heady scent and her essence fired his blood to fever pitch. It stole through him in a flourish, making his veins ache with the urge to do so much more than sink his tongue into her wet flesh. His body throbbed, his cells felt afire. This wasn't a normal reaction to a woman. It was a reaction to a female. It was the way he felt before he shifted.

He wouldn't shift here, but that he wanted to do so nearly confirmed what he'd guessed. Liddy was no woman. She was a shifter. The female that he would make his. Later with his body, now with his mouth.

He sniffed her sexy scent one last time, then placed his tongue to her slit and licked the length of her damp folds. Her hold on his hair tightened, her nails nipping into his skull. A soft little mewl left her throat. Kevin grinned against her pussy and sank his tongue deep. His extrasensory hearing might have allowed him to be the only one to hear that mewl. But more than likely there were other shifters in the restaurant. Others who knew exactly what was going on beneath the table.

*Oooh yes! More. Deeper. So close…*

He responded to Liddy's silent pleas with deep thrusts of his tongue into her sex. Warm wetness coated his tongue, growing damper with each push. *So wet.*

Palming her upper thighs, he kneaded the soft, dark flesh while he returned the pad of one thumb to her clit. With each plunge of his tongue into her pussy, he pressed at the swollen pearl. The muscles of her sex shuddered around his tongue. Her hips jerked against his face. He could taste how close she was to climaxing. *So sexy.*

More gentle mewls reached his ears. His answering growl was low but automatic. Her nails nipped harder against his head. Her pelvis jerked toward his face.

*Oh God. Oh God. I'm going to come…*

Her pussy convulsed around him. Cream drenched his tongue. One long, low cry lit the air. His cock thrummed with the animalistic sound. His balls hugged his body. He ached to pull her under the table and fuck her breathless.

Instead, he eased his finger against the inner walls of her sex, bringing her down from the climax. He took one last lap of her heavenly body, then fixed her panties and righted her dress. Mindful to grab the spoon, Kevin returned to his chair. The grin that took over his face as he looked across the table felt ridiculously huge, but he couldn't do anything about it.

Liddy's face was flushed, her eyes glazed and her lips dark and puffy. Her breath came out on fast, excited pants and he could hear her blood traveling at a rush through her body. She looked as though she'd been thoroughly loved. She hadn't yet, not thoroughly, but she would be soon.

She reached for her wineglass as their server approached the table. Guilt flashed over her face as the man set their appetizer down. "Did you, uh, find your spoon?"

Kevin reached across the table when she set the glass back and took her hand in his. He rubbed over the pounding pulse at her wrist. "Yes, but I'm feeling awfully clumsy tonight. I'll probably drop it again before the meal's over."

\* \* \* \* \*

Kevin hadn't dropped his spoon again. Liddy's entire body had been keyed up for the moment when he would do so. Outside of rubbing her wrist before they began eating and flashing hot looks her way throughout dinner, he hadn't even hinted at touching her again. That had to be the reason the silent ride back to her place had her nerves stretched to the snapping point.

Their conversation had been lagging since the moment he'd crawled beneath the tablecloth. It had stopped completely the instant they climbed into his truck.

Maybe he felt awkward about conversation after what he'd done to her. Only that didn't seem like the Kevin she knew. Then again she never would have guessed the Kevin she knew would give her oral sex in a fancy restaurant, either.

Liddy's sex grew wet with fresh moistness at the memory of the way his masterful tongue had licked at her folds and pushed deep into her sheath. He'd had her ready to come from the first lick. She wanted to come again just thinking about it. But, no, this time when she climaxed, she wanted it to be with Kevin's thick cock impaled in her.

When they came together, it would be unforgettable. The way her body reacted to his tongue ensured it. He'd had her blood sizzling and the rest of her aching to give into her baser side. No other man had ever been able to accomplish that.

Something so amazing was too much to do without for even another night. She had another seven blocks to convince Kevin of the same.

Liddy glanced across the cab of the truck and flashed her most temping smile. "You don't have to take me home. I told Chenille not to wait up for me. I meant it."

His left hand moved to the steering wheel while his right one uncurled from the wheel and started slowly toward her. His palm settled on her knee where it peeked out from beneath her coat. A glance in her direction revealed lust burning hotly in her eyes. "I know. That's why I'm not. I live out this way, too."

"Oh. That's good. I'm glad." And she was. She really didn't want to stoop to begging in order to get her hands all over his scrumptious body tonight, but if that's what it took she might well have.

Kevin glanced at her a second time, humor lighting his eyes. "Why is that, Liddy? Why are you so glad to know I'm taking you home with me?"

Well, she'd wanted conversation… This was franker than what they'd ever had before, and yet she found herself eager to respond no-holds barred. "Because I've wanted to go there for months now. Every day when I see you at the sanctuary, it's so hard for me to stay at a friendly distance. What I really want to do is pounce on you and rip those stuffy dress clothes off your gorgeous ass."

The hand on her knee squeezed. His rich chuckle filled the cab and ignited every one of her nerve endings. "I'm glad we've finally gotten past the friendly stage, because that's what I've wanted too. I've imagined the way you would taste for the last six months." He braked the truck and pulled into a long drive surrounded by a cluster of trees. Killing the engine, he looked over at her. "You taste hot, Liddy. Hot and sweet."

Would he reveal his desire for her so completely if he knew she could see his face in the dark? Liddy had only seconds to ponder the question before Kevin was out of the truck. He came around to her side and opened the door. Moonlight spilled down, calling out the sharp angles of his face, as well as the want etched into his features.

Yes, she realized, he would let her see his desire, because he wasn't a man to keep secrets. She could trust him, and she did so now by taking the hand he offered. Silently, he led her up the front steps of a two-story townhouse. He released her hand to unlock the door, then gestured for her to go inside. Silence ensued as he reclaimed her hand and led her to the center of the living room. Hardwood floors filled the room and a vivid rug sporting a collage of animals spread out beneath their feet. An unlit fireplace dominated the wall in front of her and off to her side, large bay windows reflected the moonlight off the snow making it nearly as bright as day. She knew with the aid of the moon he could see her almost as well as she could see him.

"I want to see all of you, Liddy. Undress for me."

Kevin's voice was rough yet soft, not what she'd expected. After the way he'd gone down on her at the restaurant, she'd assumed this night would end with fast, furious sex. She rather liked the slow approach. It stoked the fire kindling in her belly into a restless need. "You too," she responded just as softly. "I want to see all of you."

With a nod, he shrugged off his leather jacket and cast it aside. Liddy followed his move, unable to take her eyes off his body. His sweater came next to reveal a dark T-shirt molded to his torso. She'd never seen him outside of his business attire and until now hadn't realized how toned he was. He was tall, lean and graceful. He had the build of a runner. The kind of build that had always made her salivate.

Long fingers went to the hem of his T-shirt. With held breath, she inched the straps of her dress down, working at lowering the bodice as he raised his shirt. His gaze flickered to her chest. From the way his pupils darkened to the catch of his breath, she knew her dress had moved past her breasts. Her nipples beaded under his gaze, and her breasts grew heavy. Then all that much heavier when he pulled his shirt over his head and his sculpted chest was bared. A vee of dark hair started at his flat nipples and tapered to a fine line that disappeared into his jeans. The vee stood out in stark contrast against his white skin, and in some strange way seemed familiar.

The question of how it might be familiar was knocked from Liddy's mind as Kevin's fingers moved to the waist of his jeans. He unzipped the fly and pushed the jeans down his legs. His briefs moved with them, until both, along with his shoes and socks, were in a pile on the floor. He straightened and grinned, and her heart took off.

Absently freeing her body from her own clothes, she assessed him. He was a big man. And the length and girth of his cock was no exception. Her pussy pulsed as she stared at the head of his penis. Pre-cum wept from the slit and her mouth watered with the desire to lick at the salty sweet substance.

"Go ahead, Liddy. It's all yours."

For an instant, she met his eyes, stunned by the way he'd seemed to have read her thoughts. Then she dismissed the wonder to cast aside the remainder of her clothes and go down on her knees in front of him.

Taking his shaft into her hand, she lapped at the velvety fluid on his cock head. His taste filled her senses, cruised through her body and had her cells tightening.

She tipped back her head to find him watching her. Her heart stuttered at the way his sexy grin had become one of exultation. The way he looked at her now was primal, predatory. He looked at her as no other man ever had. No other male...until last night.

Guilt passed through her with the reminder. If she'd known there would be a chance with Kevin, she would never have given herself to another, no matter how hot the male made her with his gaze alone.

No matter how right it had seemed at the time, last night had been a mistake. Tonight was perfection.

Liddy swirled her tongue over his cock head, dipping into the tiny hole and pleasuring in his answering groan. "You taste so good."

"Just good?"

She teased her tongue over the sensitive head once more, then stroked the length of his hard shaft. The scent of his blood had riled her arousal. The scent of his sex stimulated her to the breaking point. "So much better than good. You taste...like mine."

Something flashed through Kevin's eyes, some unnamable emotion. In the past, she had left his thoughts alone. Now she wanted to look into them, to know if he feared the connection growing between them. Before she could do so, his fingers spilled into her hair and he encouraged her mouth to slide onto his penis.

"I'm yours, Liddy. Yours to do with as you will."

The words captured her heart and filled her soul. The feel of him, the texture and taste of his sex stole over her senses. He was huge in her mouth, hot and hard, and she wanted to suck every inch of him, wanted to show him how effectively he'd become a part of her life.

She'd feared taking their relationship to the next level for a number of reasons. None of those reasons mattered now, nothing did but finally making love with Kevin.

Watching the emotions play across his face, Liddy captured his balls, massaging the sac while her tongue slid over the rigid veins of his cock. She murmured against his hot flesh, delighting in the way his mouth parted, the increased rhythm of his breathing. She could hear his heart beating, loud and fast. Her own pounded in tandem. Her pussy pulsed nearly as fast, as loudly when she milked his cock with her mouth and his hips jerked toward her face.

Kevin's fingers squeezed into fists in her hair, tugging. "You're so hot. So good. And if you keep that up, you're going to have me coming in that sweet mouth of yours. I want to be inside you. I want to feel your orgasm. Let me love you, Liddy."

That she wanted him to fuck her was obvious from the straining points of her nipples to the scent of her arousal thick in the air. That he asked for her approval regardless of her aroused state raised her affection for him all that much more. She had nothing to fear with this man. He was a man she could trust, a man she could love.

Warmth filled her as she took a last suck of his cock, pulling away from the head with a lusty, lingering lick. He lifted his hands from her hair and offered them to her. Liddy thought he would bring her to her feet. Instead, he took her hands and came down on his knees in front of her.

Once more the predatory look gleamed in his eyes. Strength exuded from the lines of his body. Wordlessly, he pulled her flush to him and slanted his mouth over hers. For all that they'd shared tonight, this was only the second time he'd kissed her and the rush of heat and longing that spiked through her nearly brought her to her knees. The brush of his lips was intimate, the lick of his tongue familiar. The urgency that claimed her as he rubbed his tongue over her teeth and then against hers all consuming.

Kevin's fingers untwined from hers. His hands came over her breasts, palming, stroking, circling her aching nipples. The damp head of his cock nudged her opening and her pussy flamed with need.

Tracing the hard contours of his chest and the furl of dark, silky hair that covered it, Liddy's voice came out low, sultry, in a way she'd never before heard it. "I want you now, Kevin. All of you. Take me."

Silence had been a consistent part of the last half hour, now the look in his eyes was deafening. So much more than predatory—it spoke of power, of command. His fingers closed over her nipples, twisting the peaked dark flesh until pleasure just this side of pain arced through her. Her cry was automatic, the rush of wetness in her sex the same. That rush was repeated when he took hold of her arm and turned her around.

One hand still toyed with her nipple, while the other locked around her middle. His cock rubbed against the crack of her ass, her anus puckering in response.

Kevin's breath was hot against her ear, his voice rough. "You have the most beautiful ass, Liddy." His finger replaced his shaft, pushed into it her hole, and the breath snagged in her throat. "Do you want me to fuck it, Liddy? Do you like that?"

The change in his mood should have surprised her. But like the command in his eyes, it only thrilled her. His finger pushed deeper into her hole, thrusting in and out, milking her anus. She couldn't keep from rearing back, whimpering her response, "I've never tried it this way, but yes, I want it."

"This way?"

"As a hum—" No. As much as she trusted him, she couldn't admit so much so soon. Even feelings were safer to discuss than the fact she wasn't quite human. "With someone I care for. Please, Kevin. Fuck me now."

His fingers thrust twice more and then his cock head rimmed her damp crack. He slipped into her pussy with two fingers and stroked her sheath until the pressure building within her was nearly unbearable, and finally he gave her what she craved, pushing into her ass with a solid plunge.

Liddy's ecstatic gasp was met with one of Kevin's own. His hips thrust against hers, pushing his large cock further inside her yet. His thumb settled over her clit, circling and stroking the swollen pearl. Need built hot and heavy in her belly.

"Hell, you're so good, Liddy. So tight. So perfect." His lips touched down on her neck, his tongue licked over her hot flesh, and then his teeth bit down lightly.

She purred with the tender nip. She wanted it much harder, wanted to feel his teeth sinking into her skin, marking her for all to see. When bitten in her female form the marks faded almost instantly. When bitten as a woman they would stay for days. "Bite me."

"Yes."

The rush of his teeth sinking into her skin was blinding. The scent of her blood drove her wild. The slow tempo was no longer enough. She needed fast, needed furious. She needed to make him hers.

Curling her fingers into the rug beneath them, she thrust back hard, tipped her hips and took him to the hilt. The movement of his fingers picked up in turn with their hips, plunging into her wet sheath, strumming over her clit, driving her to the edge in seconds. Climax pounded through her like a tempest, ripping through her body and screeching the air from her lungs. A roar tore from her lips as he shot his cum into her ass. The sound was wild, feral. It wasn't human, but she couldn't stop it, and concentrated instead on riding out the wave of orgasm as it thundered through her.

With the last of the tremors, Kevin slipped from her body and turned her around, until she was on her back on the rug. Placing a hand on either side of her head, he came over her. He lowered to her mouth, nipping a kiss at each corner, before raising concerned eyes to hers. "You okay?"

Liddy allowed the elation filling her to reflect in her smile as she lifted a hand to his cheek and stroked. "So much better than."

"Good, because I need to ask you something and I want a truthful answer."

Something in his voice and the way his concern stayed intact even after her assurance she was okay called forth her anxiety. Her fingers stilled on his cheek.

She could trust him. She wanted him to feel the same way about her. No matter the question, she would answer. "I'd never lie to you, Kevin. What do you want to know?"

"Are you a shifter, Liddy?"

# Chapter Four

ගා

Liddy's hand jerked from Kevin's cheek and her eyes went wide. She attempted to push him off her, but then clearly realized he wasn't going anywhere and gave up the efforts to squeak out, "Why would you think that?"

He smiled at her anxiety while happiness soared through him. If she wasn't a shifter, she wouldn't be acting this way. "The way you licked my wound today. The way you wanted me to bite you. The way you roared when I took you in the ass. And for so many other reasons." He added solemnly, "Liddy, you affect me in a way no normal woman ever has."

"What are you saying?" she asked, her voice tremulous.

He brushed a reassuring kiss across her mouth. "I'm saying it's okay to admit what you are. It won't scare me. I told you I know shifters, many who live in this city. They mean more to me than you could ever guess."

Her lips pulled into a thoughtful pout. Long, silent seconds passed. Finally, she admitted, "No one knows about me. Just a few other shifters I've met through the years. No one else even suspects. If I hadn't licked your hand today, we might not be here now and you wouldn't know either, would you?"

She looked scared, like telling him the truth had cost her dearly. Kevin hated seeing the fear in her eyes—she was too strong of a woman for it, too strong of a lioness. At the same time, he gloried in her unease. Liddy believed he was human and had entrusted him with her secret. It spoke highly of her feelings for him, her faith in him.

He captured her hands in his. Linking their fingers, he brushed her lips a second time, needing to show her that she had nothing to fear. "Eventually I would have figured it out."

"How can you be so sure? You didn't know for the last six months, did you?"

The words were barely a whisper. Kevin pulled back to meet her eyes. The glimmer of tears made her eyes seem as bright as the moonlight and tugged at his heart. This was a good moment, the best he could remember. The only tears in her eyes should be happy ones. Thankfully, he knew how to accomplish that. "I didn't know, but I should have. I never tried to read your thoughts until yesterday. When I couldn't it made me wonder and then, when you cleaned my cut with your tongue, everything began to fall into place. Still I was afraid to hope."

Liddy's fingers went limp against his. Her eyes narrowed. "Afraid to hope. Read my thoughts. What are you saying, Kevin?"

He smiled supremely, relieved beyond measure to have the truth out between them. To think he'd been ready to give up on ever having anything beyond friendship with her. "I'm saying I'm one, too. Like you only other shifters know. And honestly very few of them know who I really am. Making it in this city hasn't come easy. If the people I do business with knew what I really am... I was afraid to tell even you, Liddy. As much as I know you love your animals, I was still worried you would reject me."

Kevin was sure the admission would be followed by Liddy's enchanting smile, her delighted laughter. Instead, her hands stayed limp in his, her eyes narrowed in speculation. "You go to the gatherings?" she asked quietly.

"I lead them."

"You...?" She broke off and shook her hands loose from his, once more attempted to push him away. When it proved unsuccessful, she implored, "Please let me go."

His smile erupted along with his happiness. His gut tightened. He'd been so sure she would be pleased. Damn it, she *would* be pleased. There was so much good between them. She had to see that. He shifted his position over her, applying the weight of his lower half fully to hers. His cock cradled against her pussy. That she was still wet both thrilled and angered him. She couldn't leave him.

"You're not going anywhere, Liddy," he growled, asserting the power he so rarely used. "This is where you belong and I'm not letting you go until you see that. Don't even think about telling me no. I'm your leader, your king. You have to abide."

Unlike his power, Kevin asserted his strength regularly through his business dealings. It was met by anxiety with some and hostility by others. Laughter was a new reaction. But laughter was exactly what came out of Liddy's mouth, throaty and low and sensual in a way that fired his libido anew.

Tears shimmered in her eyes once more, but this time they were those of amusement. "I wasn't going anywhere, you big lug. I just wanted to show you something." She sobered to add, "Now that I know you think I belong here with you, I want to show you more than ever."

He huffed out a breath as the fight left him, and rolled off her. She'd never planned to go anywhere. If he'd been operating on logic and not his fear of rejection, he might have understood that.

Kevin reclined on his side and came up on an elbow. He gestured to the room in front of him. "Show me."

Liddy came to her feet, a lithe move that had her body open to him and her lush breasts thrust high and hard-tipped. Moonlight tangled with the curls at her mound, making them seem so much lighter than their typically black shade. Almost white. Thoughts of sinking his tongue past those tight, wet curls to lick at her delectable pussy pounded through his brain and had his cock solid and aching for her again.

He pushed to his knees, ready to crawl across the floor and skewer his tongue into her pussy. He only made it a few inches when the reality of how white and thick the fur at her sex had become. His focus pulled from her mound and all thoughts of crawling to her were forgotten.

Liddy the woman was gone. Liddy the lioness stood before him, strong and graceful and brilliant white. Soulful dark eyes fixed on his and her mouth pulled back in a familiar smile.

Kevin grinned back as understanding dawned. He should have known. No other woman had ever appealed to him the way Liddy did, just as no other lioness had ever appealed to him the way the white lioness he'd fucked the previous night did. The white lioness looking upon him now. "Sierra."

*Balendin*, she thought his feline name with an incline of her head. *I didn't know who you were. I thought... I felt so guilty about the other night. From the first time I saw you, something about you captivated me in a way no other lion ever had. Now I know why.*

And now he knew why he hadn't been able to resist Sierra.

Kevin shifted into his lion form, wanting to be both physically and emotionally as close to Liddy as possible. He went to her and nuzzled her neck, inhaled her scent. How could have he missed the connection? Regardless of her form, she was the same incredible Liddy. His Liddy.

Joy pressed at his heart as he lapped a kiss at her mouth. *I felt guilty, too. Like you I was drawn in. It was your eyes for me. Dark, soulful. I couldn't place them before, but now I can. I was looking into Sierra's eyes and seeing Liddy. My Liddy.*

She purred against his mouth. *I want to be yours, Kevin. I want you to teach me. To show me everything. There's so much I don't know.*

His joy turned to curiosity as he recalled her saying only a few other shifters knew about her. Most shifters came from a line of the same. That Liddy hadn't, could only mean she had been turned, clearly by a lion who hadn't stuck around long enough to instruct her in their ways. *How did you become this way? When?*

She brushed his mouth a last time and moved to look out the window. He'd purposefully surrounded his home with trees so no passersby could look inside and catch a glimpse of something they would fear.

*Six years ago, when I spent the summer interning with the sanctuary.* Liddy's thoughts came across quietly, as if it pained her to share them. *I was studying the lions' behavioral patterns when one of them went wild. It lunged at me, pinned me down. I was out back, too far for anyone to hear me screaming. Eventually someone came looking for me. They found me asleep. Seemingly untouched. And gave me a lecture about taking naps in the lion preserve.*

Kevin's heart squeezed with hurt for her at the picture she painted. Poor Liddy. He had heard tales of the turning process and it sound painful and often unwanted. Had she wanted it? Did she regret it even now? No, she couldn't. If she did, she wouldn't be asking to learn more. *But you weren't untouched?*

*No. The cat didn't hurt me, just bit me and exchanged enough blood to turn me. At first I was fine, then little by little I started feeling sick. I figured out slowly why that was, what was missing from my diet. I had been a vegetarian up until then.*

Her thoughts had grown stronger as she shared, and he took that as the sign it would be okay to approach her. He moved to the window beside her and glanced over. It was hard to hang on to his sorrow for what she had gone through when he was looking at her, seeing her, his beautiful white lioness in his home. Remembering how amazing she'd felt in his arms, her body joining with his. He wanted that forever.

*You weren't scared?* he asked, fighting back the urge to declare his love here and now. He'd been falling for Liddy since the day they'd met, but as much as he knew how authentic that love was he wasn't certain if she was ready to hear the words.

*I was scared of telling my family or pretty much anyone else, yes, but otherwise, no. I was happy, content in a way I'd never felt before. For the first time, I felt truly comfortable in my own skin. At least, behind closed doors.*

Some of Kevin's happiness faded. No matter how great his feelings for Liddy, there were some things he couldn't accomplish for her or anyone else. *I wish we could feel that way with those doors open, but you know that's going to take years to accomplish. If your mother felt differently about shifters it would help, but obviously she isn't going to change overnight. You would have told her long ago, if you thought there was a chance of that happening.*

*Mama struggles with accepting people from different ethnic backgrounds dating. She'll never accept shapeshifters into her city, let alone her life.*

Her eyes shimmered with tears of unhappiness. He wished he could make them go away, but all he could do was speak his heart. *I'm sorry your mother is so old-fashioned, but I won't hide my feelings for you, Liddy. I already have to hide my identity.*

A smile pulled back her lips and reached into her eyes, banishing the tears. *Oh Kevin, I don't want you to hide anything. Mama loves me and she's going to learn to accept you in my life. And if she doesn't...* She would. Liddy would make her. But if for some reason she couldn't... Fresh tears pricked her eyes. *I hate the idea of her not speaking to me, respecting me, but I won't give you up for her beliefs. I want you. I need you to teach me.*

*Everything I know,* Kevin promised, closing the short distance between them to nuzzle her nose reassuringly. *You can count on that, Liddy.*

*I know I can. I trust you. I care about you so much.*

He ceased his nuzzling to stroke his tongue along her lips. Slipping inside her mouth, her taste ignited his senses and brought his cock to aching awareness. He had once dreamed of the day he would find his mate and make her his. In some ways he had already done that when he'd taken Liddy in her lioness form at the gathering. But he hadn't really known it was Liddy, hadn't known what they were meant to be. This time he knew and he planned to lavish her with every carnal indulgence she deserved.

\* \* \* \* \*

Liddy knew falling asleep each night and waking each morning in Kevin's bed was not the best way to keep it secret from her mama that she was dating a white man. Still, she couldn't make herself leave him after they made love. Not only did that lovemaking lead to more lovemaking, but talk of both the mundane and things about her and what she was capable of as a shifter that she had never known.

Now wasn't a moment for talking though, Liddy acknowledged with a laugh as Kevin returned to the bedroom and rejoined her on the bed. He'd gone to find food. She had believed to eat. The playful gleam in his eyes as he set the plate of fruit next to him on the bed and plucked a grape off the plentiful vine suggested otherwise.

"Hungry?" he asked, raising a dark eyebrow.

For what she could guess he had in mind, definitely. She returned his sensual smile with one of her own. "Always."

"Then open up." He didn't direct that question to her mouth, but her legs. The momentary thought to be embarrassed passed through Liddy's mind, but then was quickly forgotten as she spread her thighs.

Kevin's expression went from playful to carnal as he moved between her legs. He slid the cool grape along the inside of her thigh and upward until it caressed the length of her slit.

She shivered against the hedonistic sensation. "That feels so…"

"Good," he supplied, using one hand to splay her labia wide and the other to dip the grape into her sex.

Her pussy pulsed forth a stream of juices, and her fingers dug into the sheets. "Fucking amazing," she bit out as he rubbed the fruit against her sex.

With a chuckle, he brought the grape to his mouth and popped it inside.

Liddy squirmed with the bliss that stole over his face as he chewed. How could it be possible watching him eat that grape, knowing her juices coated it, was more arousing than watching him fuck her with his mouth?

The answer was forgotten as Kevin returned to the plate of fruit and lifted a peeled banana. She gasped as he skimmed the soft banana along her thigh and toward her dripping pussy. "You aren't serious?"

He looked at her face, dark desire written in the depths of his eyes. "I'm never not serious about making love with you, Liddy. I want to taste your arousal on this banana. I want to lick it from your delicious pussy."

Heat flared in her cheeks while tension tightened her limbs. Liquid warmth coiled in her belly. Her pussy pulsed. Maybe it was strange of her, but she suddenly wanted that banana in her more than her next breath. "Do it."

Kevin moved back between her thighs. Dipping his head, he ran his tongue over her pussy once, just enough to have her spinning with the ache for more, then pulled back and pushed the banana deep.

It felt like nothing she'd ever experienced, soft yet warm, small yet firm. His mouth returned, nibbling at the end of the banana while his hands drew lazy circles along her thighs. The sluggish action didn't suit the mood, and yet managed to send her spinning all that much higher. His teeth brushed her pussy lips and he ate at the banana until the hot press of his tongue mingled with the warm, soft fruit.

With each lick, each nip the difference between tongue and fruit became harder to decipher. The feel of his hands caressing her thighs more difficult to distinguish from that of the rest of his body. Sound was all she was aware of, that of his lapping tongue and the slippery suction of her pussy as he continued to feast. Then even sound slipped away and all Liddy could do was hang on as Kevin consumed her into soul blistering climax.

An arrogant grin she'd come to see more regularly the past few days tugged his mouth wide as he pulled back. "Hungry for more?"

Breathless, floating, Liddy could only nod. And then gasp as he reached for the plate and came back with not a fruit but a vegetable. His grin became wicked as he produced a long, thick cucumber his human teeth could never bite into the way they had the banana. Even as she thought it, his teeth shifted, transforming into fangs that the mere sight of sent a pang of desperate want and urgency racing through her.

Those delectable fangs teased her inner thighs as the head of the cucumber brushed her dripping pussy, and Liddy knew there was no doubt about it. She was in love.

\* \* \* \* \*

"Your mother is here to see you."

Liddy tensed at the sanctuary receptionist's words. The smile that had claimed her lips the moment she thought of Kevin and the incredible night they'd spent together again last night disappeared as she swiveled in her chair to nod at Ann. "Thanks. Give me a minute and then send her back."

She did not want to see her mama. She had been putting if off for the last several days, though she knew doing so was pointless. As she'd already surmised, Hanover was only so big and her spending every night at Kevin's home wouldn't go unnoticed for long. Particularly not when those sleepovers were bound to rile the mayor.

"You don't make your mama wait, Liddy Marie."

Her thoughts burst with her mama's words, and she focused on the heat coming off her mama's aura. Annette didn't look any happier to see Liddy than what Liddy was to see her. Too bad Liddy knew her mama wouldn't go away until she got whatever was on her chest off it. As if she couldn't guess what that something was.

Self-consciously, Liddy tugged at the turtleneck she wore beneath her work sweatshirt. Shifters healed fast from normal wounds, but the bite marks Kevin had left behind their first night together in their human form were still fresh. She would be thrilled to keep them that way forever. Looking at the marks made her happy, like she finally had someone in her life who both cared for her and understood her. The thought of Mama questioning her about the marks, however, didn't make her happy in the least. She already had enough on her hands making Mama see how right she and Kevin were together, regardless of skin color.

Satisfied the marks were covered, Liddy gestured to the seat across the desk from her, struggling to maintain a casual air. "Sorry. I just wanted to straighten up a bit first."

Annette ignored the gesture and pinned her with a disappointed glare. "If there's one thing you've always been, it's neat. I had believed you were sensible, too, but now I wonder. What is this I'm hearing about you being seen with Kevin Montcalm? He's a nice man, baby. Well off and respected in this city, but he's not for you."

Liddy's tension threatened to turn to temper with her mama's expression. She forced her voice to remain even. If she was to convince Mama of anything, she needed to be level-headed. "You don't even know him, Mama. You're basing your opinion on the color of his skin. It's not the twentieth century any longer. People of mixed color date all the time. They even get married and have babies together."

Annette bristled. "Not in this city, they don't."

Oh God! How was she supposed to stay calm, when her mama was tossing out such idiotic remarks? "Because you make it seem like a crime," Liddy managed just a little hotly. "It's a free country, Mama. For everyone, including shifters."

Her nose went up. "This isn't about those...things."

So much for her temper. It was far too combustible to keep in check when she could guess damn well that Mama's next accusation would be about shifters being freaks.

Liddy pounded her fist down on her desk. "They are *not* things and it *should* be about them. You would react the same way if I was dating a shifter or a white man."

"You will not date a shifter! The thought of you letting one of those animals touch you..." Annette shuddered. "Oh Liddy, how can you even say something so awful? You're not in your right mind, baby. All the time you spend around this place has gotten to you. You need a vacation, somewhere you can meet a nice black man."

"I don't want a vacation or a nice black man! I want Kevin!" Liddy winced at the knowledge she was both acting like a child and yelling loudly enough for the entire office and most of the sanctuary to hear. Why couldn't Mama just understand?

"I can't stop you from seeing him, but you won't bring him by my house. So long as you're with that man, you won't come by the house, either. I've worked hard to get where I am, Liddy. I won't jeopardize it over your wild behavior."

The air pushed out of Liddy's lungs in a hard wheeze. She'd known dating Kevin would come to this, her mama not speaking to her until the truth of how right Liddy and Kevin were together finally sank in. Still, Annette's answer to her unspoken question hit her like a physical blow.

The last threads of Liddy's control snapped. She rounded the desk, ready to throw her mama out of the office. "You have no idea about my wild behavior, Mama. If—"

"Sorry to interrupt," Ann cut her off loudly, "but Detective Riggs is here and demanding to see you, Liddy."

Great. Just great. As if this morning needed to get any worse.

"Send him in," Liddy growled to the receptionist.

The cop appeared in the office seconds later, his mouth set in a hard line and his aura giving off enough blackness to tighten Liddy's belly in knots. Ignoring her mama, she forced a smile for Tanner. "What can I help you with this wonderful morning, Detective?"

"We caught the shifter responsible for the attacks."

The knotting sensation turned to painful burning with the accusing way the cop looked at her as he spoke. Before Liddy could question him, Annette said severely, "Not possible. You cannot tell me that you have proof the attacker is a shifter?"

"We have proof, Mayor Freeman." Tanner's eyes never left Liddy's face as he responded to her mama. "We also have reason to believe your daughter's known the attacker's identity for some time and failed to come forward. Abetting a felon is a crime, Ms. Freeman. Depending on exactly how much you know and how much you've taken part in these attacks, a jail cell could be the least of your worries."

A jail cell... "Oh God, I don't know what you're talking about. I know nothing about the attacker. I've told you that a hundred times."

The cop's lips firmed into a smirk. "You know nothing about Kevin Montcalm? Way you two were carrying on when I walked in to ask for a jump the other day, I find that hard to believe."

Shock. Horror. Disbelief. Denial. They all clawed at Liddy's stomach as the detective's words sank in. She gasped, "Kevin?"

Tanner nodded. "He is the shifter responsible."

"Oh Liddy," Annette moaned. "What is wrong with you? It isn't bad enough to be dating a white man, but he has to be a shifter on top of it? I know I raised you smarter than that, baby."

The detective's eyes narrowed and Liddy caught the flicker of amusement as he added, "You forgot the part about him being a killer."

"No." Liddy gave her head a fierce shake. "Kevin is not a killer." He couldn't be. She would know. After all they had shared, she believed in him, trusted him. "Kevin only wants equality for everyone."

"I hate to be the one to break it to you, Ms. Freeman, but DNA doesn't lie. After coming up empty on matching the DNA we pulled off the last victim with anyone on file, we started doing random checks. There was blood left behind on my hood latch from when Mr. Montcalm cut his hand. I noticed it last night and had the lab run it. Results came in this morning, a perfect match."

Liar. He was lying. The truth was in the gleam of his eyes. The sarcastic curve of his lips. Somehow Tanner had learned about Kevin being a shifter and was now trying to blame him for the attacks as a way to expunge him and the entire pride from the area. "Someone set him up. They had to have. Kevin is not a killer. I would know."

"I look forward to hearing how as soon as we get back to the station." With a last smirk, the cop looked down at his hip where a pair of cuffs dangled. "Now you planning to go freely, or do I need to assist?"

\* \* \* \* \*

*I'm not responsible for the attacks. You have to trust me, Liddy.*

Liddy's heart squeezed painfully at the sight of Kevin behind bars. Before he'd always looked so clean cut and put together. Now he looked tired and, if she was to admit the truth, worried, like he thought he might not get off. Or maybe like he was guilty.

Chastising herself for that faithless thought, she started to reach for his hand through the cell bars, then stopped. Touching of any kind would have the guards pulling her out of here before she even had a chance to share anything important with Kevin. *I believe you. It's just that if you didn't do it...who did? And why did your blood match the DNA they found on the dead woman? Detective Riggs —*

*Whatever he's saying is wrong. The DNA had to have been planted there. By who...? Remember that lion who came to the gathering last week? He made it clear he thought shifters should rule humans. He also made it clear he thought I was running the pride wrong, that taking human lives should be okay. My guess would be he has something to do with this.*

Maybe. And if it was that lion responsible, then Liddy had no idea how to do anything about getting him to own up to the truth. She didn't even know where to look for him, or what he looked like in his human form.

Helplessness brought tears to the back of her eyes. She'd felt alone many times since being turned, but she'd never felt this powerless to help someone she cared for. *I don't know how to help you, Kevin. The cops are already trying to lock me up right beside you. They think that I know something, that I covered for you. They don't have anything to hold me with, but if I start snooping around and get caught, they're going to assume that I'm guilty.*

Kevin's eyes went cool blue and he fisted his hands around the bars of the cell door. Quiet command radiated from his body. *I won't have you in here beside me, Liddy. That isn't a request.* His gaze softened along with his thoughts. *They want this case taken care of immediately. They're going to start trying me the day after tomorrow. Maybe I'll get lucky and the jury will have a shifter or two on it. Any one of them who believes in me, would help to see that I get off.*

Liddy smiled weakly. It would be so nice to think that could happen, but she couldn't believe it any more than she could stop thoughts of snooping around despite the potential consequences. Yes, she could get caught and prosecuted. But maybe — no matter how slim the odds — she also could locate the lion who was really responsible for the attacks. If the worst happened, at least she would end up beside Kevin.

*But what if you don't get lucky? What if there isn't a shifter on the jury?* she pressed. *They aren't going to give you a trial, Kevin. They're going to give you a lion lynching.*

"Time's up," one of the guards called from where he stood sentinel at the door which lead into the cell area.

Kevin looked toward the guard, then back at Liddy and smiled reassuringly. *I'll figure something out, Liddy. Just have faith in me.*

*I do. I trust you. I...* Had come in here intending to share her feelings with him, to show him her support in the strongest way she knew how. Knowing she would have to go against his order to help him made sharing her feelings now seem not quite sincere. Still, she had to do it, in case she didn't get another opportunity.

Fresh tears threatened with the thought. She shook them back and chanced brushing her hand against his knuckles. *I love you, Kevin.*

His worry lifted for an instant as happiness filled his eyes. The worry returned as concern with his next thoughts. *I love you,*

*Liddy. Too much to see you hurt. Promise me you won't try to find the real attacker.*

She wanted to promise him that, wanted him to trust her always. Just right now she couldn't. *I promise I won't get caught trying to find the real attacker.* She brushed his knuckles a last time, and as the guard called a second "time's up" headed for the door.

*Liddy, please...*

Liddy's heart ached with the anguish behind Kevin's thoughts, emotions pricked at the backs of her eyes. She refused to turn back, knew it would make her weaker if she saw his concern for her again. Without looking back, she sent a last *I love you* thought to him and disappeared through the door.

# Chapter Five

#### ❧

Liddy should have accepted a ride back to the sanctuary from the police station with her mama. Only she couldn't stomach the thought of seeing the disgust on Mama's face again so soon. She knew Annette's displeasure would have been voiced in further words, as well. Liddy would talk to her mama, make her understand this all somehow , but she couldn't even think about doing so now. She couldn't think period. And it didn't help that she was sitting next to Tanner Riggs.

The detective bothered her enough when they were within five feet of others. Alone in his police cruiser, the mass of negative energy he gave off made her feel physically ill. She'd tried reading his mind to see if it gave some indication as to why he affected her so badly, but she couldn't get a single thought from him.

It made sense, she supposed, for a man in a position of authority to be strong enough to keep his thoughts secret from others. Now if he would just keep his leering glances to himself...

Tanner's gaze moved from the road unwinding before them to give her what had to be the twentieth bodily assessment since they'd gotten into the vehicle. The sanctuary was less than five minutes away and Liddy had promised herself she would endure, but with every one of his looks, her skin itched a little harder and her temper riled a little further. Thank God it was winter and her body was fully covered.

"With Montcalm going away the nights are gonna be a lot longer and cooler."

She should have ignored the words and whatever it was they hinted at, but her natural reaction was to look at him and snap, "What is *that* supposed to mean?"

He pulled his attention from the road once again. A smile curved his mouth, this one apparently more genuine than any he'd given her in the past as it showed off his teeth and took up the better half of his face. It reminded her of Kevin's smile.

Liddy shivered at the comparison and how completely inaccurate it was, as the detective focused back on the road and said, "You're an attractive woman, Ms. Freeman. It also looks like you might be an innocent one. Once this case is over with, I'd like to take you out. I know how the Mayor feels about you dating white men, but I'm sure between the two of us we could get her to come around."

Her shivers grew to all out shakes. To make it seem like her trembling was from the cold and not revulsion, she reached to the heater and turned it up a notch. She might have walked away from the police station today, but Kevin hadn't. She had to at least attempt to be decent to Tanner. "I'm flattered, really, but no thank you."

"I saw the tears in your eyes when you left the cellblock. You know as well as I do that he's not gonna get off. Better to move on now before saying goodbye to him hurts any more than what it already does."

"Kevin will get off, and I am not saying goodbye to him ever." And even if she eventually had to face that horrific outcome, her answer to the detective's date offer would still be a vehement no.

He remained silent in response, and Liddy drew a breath of thanksgiving and then an even longer one when he reached the long, tree-lined driveway that led to the sanctuary office and heated viewing buildings.

Tanner brought the cruiser to a stop next to her car. She reached for the door handle, eager to put this ride behind her.

"You love the freak, don't you?"

The words reached her, thick with abhorrence, and her hand froze in the air, then curled into a fist. For her own sake and Kevin's, she'd wanted to stay on decent terms with the cop. But she couldn't stay on decent terms with any person who called a shifter a freak.

The barb pricked deep and set Liddy's temper to boiling. She turned back to the cop, teeth bared and the urge to use them on the man stronger than any she'd ever experienced. She wasn't a violent person, but now she felt capable of anything. "Kevin is *not* a freak, and how I feel about him is none of your goddamned business."

Smirking, Tanner took her fisted hand in his and gave it a squeeze. "One date. You know deep down how good we'd be together."

The only thing she knew deep down was that if he didn't get his hand off her this instant, he was liable to lose it.

Liddy jerked her hand from his grasp, for once not bothering to hide the fact she was stronger than any normal woman could be. "I would rather be the *real* attacker's next victim, then be seen anywhere with you by choice."

The smirk vanished from his face as cold hardness settled in his eyes. They were no longer the dark blue that she'd once thought of as being similar to Kevin's, but near black and deadly. "Well now, Ms. Freeman, that might just be possible to arrange."

\* \* \* \* \*

Kevin lay back on the lone bed in his cell. Apparently between believing he was a killer and knowing he was a shifter, the cops had been afraid to lock him up with anyone else, or allow him access to a visitation room. He'd been surprised they'd even allowed Liddy in to visit him in the jail cell for the short while they had this morning.

Liddy. If she did something to risk her life to try to save his… He shut his eyes against the many possible outcomes from

Liddy attempting to find the real attacker. All of them ended with her in trouble, too many of them ended with her in pain, dying.

Shit.

He'd been so afraid of the people of Hanover learning his real identity and how the truth would affect him from a business standpoint. Now that his shifter side had been revealed, he couldn't give a damn about what it would mean to him professionally. All that mattered was getting out of this jail cell and getting to Liddy before she did something that couldn't be undone.

While the last day had dragged by as one of the longest of Kevin's life, his watch revealed it was almost nine in the evening. He wouldn't be getting out of this cell tonight. The best he could do was attempt to get a solid sleep that would leave him clear minded and ready to face whatever tomorrow might bring.

* * * * *

Liddy tossed her car keys on the end table in the living room, unsurprised to have found her sister's car missing from the driveway. Friday nights were not meant to be spent at home in Chenille's mind, and since the last thing she wanted to do was talk to another person about Kevin being locked up and accused of murder, Liddy couldn't be happier.

She'd spent the day secured in her office, calling every shifter contact she had and could trust, in the hopes one of them would know something about the unfamiliar lion that had shown up at the pride gathering earlier in the week. For a moment, when she'd been in the police cruiser with Tanner and he had turned uglier than she'd ever seen him, she'd nearly dismissed the lion as having anything to do with the attacks. She'd nearly pointed that finger at the detective.

Then she'd remember the DNA left behind on the last woman's body and the report the first three, still-living victims had given of their attacker. All of them had said it was a lion, not a person. That ruled out Tanner. Obviously he'd only turned ugly because she'd injured his ego by refusing his date offer.

Shrugging out of her winter coat, Liddy laid it on the back of the couch and headed for her bedroom. She didn't want to think about Tanner Riggs another second. Since she'd worked late trying to get information on the unfamiliar lion and had come up empty-handed every time, she also didn't want to think about him. She sure as hell didn't want to think about her rift with her mama. All she wanted to do was sink into a hot bubble bath and doing some closed-eye praying that somehow everything would work out. Kevin would be let off, the real attacker would be found, and Mama would change her narrow-minded ways and do her best to see the rest of the city did the same.

Liddy went to her dresser for clean underwear and noted the blinking red light on the phone base next to her bed. Whoever it was could probably wait, but on the very off chance Kevin had managed to get to call her, she hurried to the base and pressed the message button. The first message was what sounded to be a long-winded speech from her mama, so she quickly skipped it. The second message was a man informing Sierra of an emergency gathering tonight.

Liddy had long ago requested all messages about the pride be directed to Sierra, so if her sister overheard them she would assume that they were a wrong number. Up until now the request had never needed to be followed, as Kevin conducted all pride dealings via email for security's sake. Whoever had organized this meeting using the telephone had clearly done so because of its urgency. The gathering was scheduled for tonight, and in less than a half hour from now. So much for the bubble bath and prayers, but maybe this meeting could accomplish more than prayers ever could.

Holding tightly to that thought, Liddy returned to the living room, gathered up her keys and coat and hustled to her car. The gathering place was less than a mile from the sanctuary.

It was far less risky to park her car there and shift in the safety of the woods.

Ten minutes later, she pulled into the empty sanctuary lot. With a surreptitious glance around, she started for the woods. She kept a small box just inside of the woods to store her clothing in after she transformed. Tonight, she barely noticed the cold air or the icy nip of snow beneath her feet as she stripped and deposited her clothes and boots inside the box. All thoughts were of Kevin and what would need to be done to free him as she quickly shifted and then sprinted through the woods to the gathering place.

There was no moon tonight, but that wouldn't have stopped her from being able to see the pride of lions on the snowy clearing ahead when she crested the ridge directly before it. There wasn't another cat in sight.

The hair on the back of her neck rose as she slowed her pace to make her way into the clearing. The threat of danger danced through her mind. She scented the air, but came back with no smell worthy of fearing. There was no reason to be nervous, she was early is all. The others would be here soon.

Seconds ticked past. Then minutes.

Liddy attuned her ears to the night, waited to hear the near silent brush of paws against snow. She didn't realize how madly her heart was beating until finally the sound of fast falling paws came. Her nose conveyed it was another lion. The anxiety that had filled her from first finding the clearing vacated turned to relief.

And then icy dread as the lion stepped into the clearing. From his splotched yellow-gold fur to the feral gleam in his eyes, Liddy recognized the cat as the unfamiliar one from earlier in the week. Panic slid through her body and into her limbs. She stood her ground, raised her head high and snarled, *What are you doing here?*

The male advanced, his mouth tugging back into a welcoming smile while the gleam in his eyes softened. *I came for the gathering, just as you did.*

*Where is everyone else? They should be here by now.*

The lion came closer, moving in a half circle around her. His gaze roamed over her body, then flicked to her face. *Maybe they don't think their ruler's life is worth their time.*

The tension that cloaked her, head to toe, suggested it would be wise to act nicely around this lion, but she couldn't allow him to think badly about the pride's faith in Kevin. *No! You're wrong. They respect him, revere him. They will be here.*

He moved closer still, circling again, this time all the way around her, as if stalking her. *Maybe we should use the time until they are arrive wisely. You are a beautiful cat, Sierra. I will be king soon and I want you to be my queen.*

Liddy fought off the impulse to turn with him. It might make her seem weak to expose her back, but it would make her seem afraid if she spun back on him now. She was afraid, desperately, and growing more so by the moment, but she couldn't allow him to know that. *How do you know my name?*

*I heard you sharing it with Balendin.*

Balendin, Kevin's feline name. Any cat from his pride would know it, but this male shouldn't know it any more than he should have known hers. *You were already gone by then,* she pointed out, struggling to keep her thoughts even, her paws planted firmly.

The lion rounded to her front side, his face mere inches from hers. Cold amusement glimmered in his eyes. *I came back. I saw you give yourself to him. I heard the way you roared when he was fucking you. You were so hot for him, but you'll be even hotter for me.*

The amusement bled into his mouth as a chilling smile of razor sharp teeth. Liddy's panic arced. She couldn't stop from taking a step back. *There is no gathering, is there?*

*Sure there is, between you and me.*

The male was on her in a high-pitched hiss of laugher and a flurry of yellow-gold fur. He knocked her onto her back and pinned her with his large, powerful body to the snow beneath them.

The automatic urge to pound her fists into him slammed into her. She realized the ridiculousness of that thought immediately. She was a lioness, not a woman. She had no fists to fight with. No knees to bring up against his balls. Not even paws to swipe at him with, as he held her legs captive with his own. She had only her strength of mind and her mouth to defend with.

Struggling to pull herself from beneath his massive weight, she growled, *Get off of me, you bastard!*

He lifted from her, and for an instant, she thought he had given in to her command. Then he rolled her onto her belly and lunged on her again. Hot, stale breath rolled along her ear and the hard length of his cock cradled against her ass, making her stomach quiver. *I don't think so, Liddy. Not until you give me what I want.*

The compulsion to rear away from his appalling touch died as the name he called her sank in. He'd called her Liddy, and that meant he knew who she really was. *Wh-who are you? What do you want with me?*

The male's tongue lolled along her neck and up her cheek. He thrust his hips forward and the head of his cock pushed against her anus. She pressed her lips together to hold in her whimper. She was stronger than this, so much stronger.

*My name is Hidari, and I want you, Liddy. I want you as my queen. I want your help in proving to all the others what a failure Kevin is at leading this pride. He's afraid to show anyone other than his own kind what he is. Afraid to show the people of this city what they have to truly fear in shifters. He was never meant to be ruler, Liddy. I was. Everything of his should have been mine. You should have been mine. I've already started showing the people of Hanover what they have to fear from me, from us. Now I'm ready to take what is mine, starting with you, right now.*

* * * * *

Kevin woke from a nightmare to the sound of Liddy's terrified roar. He jerked to a sitting position and quickly remembered where he was, in prison and the sound of Liddy's roar had to have been part of his nightmare.

*Oh God, Kevin. I'm sorry. So sorry for not listening.*

He shot to his feet with the thought. Liddy's thought.

The roar hadn't been part of his nightmare, it had been real and she was in trouble. She was also almost fully his mate now, that their thoughts could be so perfectly clear to one another while miles apart. *Where are you, Liddy? What's the matter?*

*Gathering place. Hidari – the lion from the other night. You were right. He's the attacker...he's trying to claim –*

Her thoughts were cut short by a keening wail that twisted at Kevin's heart.

Now what the hell to do? He had asked her not to go after the real attacker and she had done it anyway, and now that lion was touching her, hurting her.

He would not kill her!

Kevin rushed to the cell door, grabbed hold of the bars and shouted, "I need out. Now! Someone is going to die if I stay in here another second."

The first of the night guard's laughter echoed off the walls. "Right buddy. We let you out of there and all that's gonna happen is a whole lotta people are gonna die."

Kevin turned to the second guard—a blond man who looked to be in his late twenties. He'd come on shift before Kevin had fallen asleep. Two guards had been assigned to watch him since he'd been brought in this morning, and each new guard was filled in on his being shifter and his supposed murderer status. Unlike the other guards, the blond hadn't looked at Kevin with disgust, or tossed degrading words his way with the news. The blond had looked at Kevin with something closer to empathy.

Earlier he'd taken it to mean the guy simply believed in the words "innocent until proven guilty". Now, he prayed otherwise. Now, Kevin implored to the guard with his mind. *Please, if you are what I think you are, let me out of here. I'm not the real attacker, but I know where the real attacker is, and right now he's trying to kill my mate. Your future queen.*

"What if he's serious, Jack?" The blonde's gaze nervously shifted from Kevin to the other guard.

Jack snorted. "'Bout as serious as all the other bozos we get in here, trying to say they're innocent. Don't listen to a word he says."

Liddy's shrill cry rang through Kevin's ears and he forced himself to concentrate on the blond, on the fact the man had heard his last thought. *Don't listen to what I have to say then, listen to what's in your mind. I'm your ruler, your king. I can prove it to you. I can shift into my lion form if that's what you want. I am not a killer, not unless you make me stay behind these bars while my mate dies.*

Sweat beaded on the blond's forehead as his gaze shifted again, several times. Finally it landed on Kevin and turned accepting. With a nod, he turned back to his partner and raised his gun. "I'm sorry about this, Jack, but I don't have a choice."

Jack's eyes went round. He reached for his gun, then paused at the click of the other man's. "What the fuck are you thinking, Dillion?"

"That he's innocent." He waved his gun toward the corner, and used his free hand to pull the key ring from where it hung at his side. "Move over there while I let him out." Jack looked from Dillion's gun to the corner, and Dillion roared, "Do it already!"

Swearing, Jack moved into the corner. "You know they're gonna catch you, you crazy son of a bitch. They have cameras on us."

Dillion glanced to the ceiling, where Kevin guessed the cameras in question to be, and the sweat seemed to drip off his forehead. "Don't listen to him," Kevin urged, "Let me out, and I'll guarantee this thing ends on a good note for both of us." Not that he actually had the power to keep the promise, but right now he'd say anything to get the man moving.

"Yeah. Okay, yeah." Dillion fumbled the key ring into the lock several times, then finally managed to open it and slide the door free. Before Kevin could thank him and make his get away, Dillion grabbed his arm and tugged him toward the door. "Let me lead, in case anyone sees us walking out. Once we're outside, we can use my cruiser."

Dillion turned back when they reached the door and aimed his gun at the other guard. "Get in the cell, Jack. I don't want to hurt you, man. I really don't."

Jack looked at the gun, then disgustedly between Dillion and Kevin, before moving into the cell. Dillion hurried over and locked the guard inside. He returned to Kevin's side, grabbed his arm and pushed the snout of the gun into his back. "Okay, let's get moving. The surveillance cameras are intermittent, but someone's still going to figure out you're missing within a matter of minutes."

\* \* \* \* \*

Liddy had figured out the only way to avert the lion's claiming of her was by asking him questions, getting him to share his thoughts and reveal why he believed he deserved all that Kevin had.

She whimpered as the male's teeth sank into her neck with another of his fierce bites. Sharing stopped his possession, but not his tormenting. Hidari's large paws and needle sharp claws had swiped at her body and left behind countless lacerations in his attempt to make her stop fighting him. The blood from her wounds stained her snow-white fur and stung against the icy coldness of night. She shut out the ache to concentrate on what mattered, freedom for both herself and for Kevin.

Kevin would be stricken when he learned who Hidari was, why he thought he deserved the title of ruler. And Kevin would learn soon. She'd captured his last thought. He'd escaped the prison and was coming for her. It was that knowledge that gave her the strength to ignore her hurt and press Hidari for more answers.

*I thought a true ruler had to have full shifter blood to claim the title of king. If your mother was human, then you can't blame Kevin for what you don't have.*

The male roared in her ear and his teeth sank more firmly into her neck. The warm gush of fresh blood slid along her neck and the metallic scent filled her nostrils. When it was Kevin biting her, the smell of her blood was consuming, stimulating; with Hidari it only sickened her further.

*You insolent little bitch. It doesn't matter who or what my mother was. All that matters is my father was king.*

This conversation was the wrong one to be having, but she had no more questions for Hidari she believed he would answer. She would rather share thoughts that upset him and endure pain as a result than have him claim her as his and destroy the bond she'd forged with Kevin. *Kevin's blood lines are true. His mother was a shifter. She was married to your father. You're nothing but a bastard, in the truest sense of the word.*

The male's teeth yanked from Liddy's neck, and the blow to the back of her head was solid and hard. Her teeth snapped down around her tongue, puncturing it until blood filled her mouth. Stars danced before eyes and her head slumped forward. She'd always heard lions could kill with a single swipe of their paw, but until now, as pain rioted through her fuzzy brain, she'd never known how true those words were.

Hidari resettled his teeth into her neck, and jerked her head up. *The only bastard is your beloved Kevin. Your soon to be dead beloved Kevin. I have every intention of seeing that happen myself.*

Icicles of rage swept through her, temporarily numbing her to her injuries. No matter what happened to her, she would not let this male harm Kevin. She had to get him to share more, had to get him to reveal all. *How will you see he dies? What power do you have to make that happen? Who are you?*

*Yes. Who are you, you pathetic excuse for life?*

Hidari's teeth tore from Liddy's neck with the thought. Kevin's thought. The ache she'd only just managed to shut out rippled through her skull and then deep down inside her wounded body as she forced her head to turn. Kevin was there, in his lion form, his dark mane and the long dark vee of hair on his chest claiming him supreme ruler. He made the male who held her captive look scrawny, sick.

*You're just in time for the main event,* Hidari proclaimed with a hiss. His cock returned to the crack of Liddy's ass, sliding along her puckered anus. The scent of his excitement colored the air as he guided his shaft down and brushed the opening of her pussy. She closed her eyes and winced at the feel of the fluid coated head positioning to enter her. The thought of the lion fucking her when they were alone had been sickening. The thought of him doing so while Kevin watched had her stomach convulsing and the contents threatening to spill forth.

Kevin's eyes went steely cold. He bared his long, sharp teeth and growled, *Get your paws off her or die!*

*You won't kill me.* Hidari's paw came up and around Liddy's neck. Pressing lightly at her throat, he continued the swipe of his cock head against her sex. *You won't risk coming so close, because you know she'll be dead before you can reach me. You had your chance to prove yourself, Kevin. You lost it.*

*What chance was that?* Kevin returned, his expression no longer fierce, but bland. His thoughts as calm as if they spoke of the weather.

Liddy cried out as the Hidari's cock sank against her sex and rubbed at the lips of her folds, wetting the dry opening with his own fluids. Panic the likes of which she'd never known sliced through her. She implored Kevin to do something with her eyes, knowing if she opened her thoughts to Kevin, they would be free to the other lion, too.

*What chance was that?* Kevin repeated calmly, his sedate expression making it seem he was oblivious to her plight, her silent pleading.

Hidari's cock inched into her body, and her stomach pitched. She reared forward, struggling to escape his assault. The paw at her neck pressed harder, hard enough to steal the breath from her lungs, and the spikes of his teeth clamped down on her neck. Tears of pain, of the knowledge this was the end, filled Liddy's eyes. She closed them, unwilling to look at Kevin when another male claimed her while stealing her life with the strength of his paw. While Kevin stood idly by and let another male kill her!

She'd trusted him, given him her love, allowed him to come between her and Mama. And in return, he was letting this happen.

The heartache that came with the thought, blistered her exceedingly hazy mind, and then was cut short in a heartbeat as the teeth at her neck ripped free and a feral growl lit the night. Hidari's cock ceased its inching into her pussy and his weight lifted from her body. Inhaling long painful breaths of icy air, Liddy opened her eyes.

Kevin still stood in front of her. *I had to make time*, he told her, *I'm sorry, Liddy. I would never let him hurt you.* The compassion and guilt that warred in his expression told her just how sorry he was, and that he hadn't intended to let Hidari harm her. She started to tell him that it was okay, that she understood his actions now when, with a deafening roar, he leapt behind her, where snarls and hisses clashed with the thunder of massive, muscular bodies slamming together.

Liddy's injured body screamed with effort, but she managed to push to her paws and turn around. A third male, the one who had pulled Hidari from her, was thrown from the depraved cat and landed with a sickening crunch of bones several feet away in the snow. Kevin lunged at Hidari, fighting the lion with his teeth and claws. Crimson soon stained the snow around the pair and gashes lined both of their bodies.

She couldn't tell who was winning, who was losing, or if Kevin had even figured out who he was fighting yet. She only knew she wasn't strong enough to go into battle herself, and that if she tried she would only risk getting in Kevin's way. She moved slowly to the other lion, who had yet to move.

Sinking down next to him, she licked at the long gash on his chest, relieved to find it wasn't too deep. The lion lifted his head. *I'm...okay. Need rest.*

*Soon. I promise, soon.* It wasn't a promise she should make, but right now it was one she needed to hear as badly as the lion at her feet, quite possibly more so.

The hellacious howl behind her knocked all thoughts of promises from her mind. She whirled back, oblivious to her aches, and her heart skipped a beat as horror stole through her body. Both Hidari and Kevin lay motionless and silent on the bloodstained snow. Both of the cats looked dead.

Liddy raced to Kevin's side and nudged his cheek with her own. Tears leaked down her face to mingle with her fur while her heart clenched furiously in her chest. *Kevin? Oh God, Kevin please be okay. I would never have come here if I'd known it was a trap. I thought it was pride gathering, one to figure out a way to save you —*

*Liddy.* He shifted slightly, then returned the brush of her cheek and pushed to his feet in a long, graceful move. His beautiful coat was marred with blood and lacerations, but he was standing and to her he had never looked better.

Her heart pounded while the tears trickled all the harder, now of joy. *You're okay?*

*I will be,* he promised with a damp flick of his tongue over her mouth. He nodded toward Hidari then, whose torn body was slowly reverting to its human form. *He won't be. I had to kill him. I had no choice.*

Liddy's joy burst. *Oh Kevin. I'm so sorry.*

*Don't be. He deserved it. For what he did to all those women, and for what he did to you.*

He deserved punishment for what he'd done, but still... Anguish filled her heart, her thoughts as she admitted, *He was your brother.*

Kevin's head snapped back, his gaze unbelieving as he looked at her. *What?*

She nodded, wishing somehow she could bring Hidari back and make him the loyal, loving brother Kevin deserved. She couldn't do that, she could only tell him what she had learned. *He told me tonight. Your father met his mother the year before he married yours. Your father didn't know he had another son. And your brother didn't know that you existed or even who your father was until after he died. Hidari said he was older than you, that he deserved to be king. He came to Hanover to claim his birthright. He…*

Tears clogged Liddy's throat and she looked away in attempt to gather her emotions. The sight of the naked, bloody man on the snow had her gasping instead. *Oh, my God… He's Tanner. I'd considered the detective had something to do with the attacks, had even thought at times he shared similar looks with you, but I never thought —*

*None of us did.* The male who had pulled Hidari from Liddy was now on his feet. He still looked weak as he skulked to her side, but already his wounds were healing as were Liddy's own. The lion turned pitying eyes on Tanner's lifeless body. *I worked with him every day and I had no idea.*

*He wasn't a good man.*

Liddy turned at Kevin's thoughts. He stood next to her, and the shock of learning about his brother had disappeared from his eyes. *Maybe he was family by blood,* he continued, *but not in heart.* He brushed against Liddy's side and nodded at the other lion. *You are, both of you are, and all of the pride. You're my family, and what matters.*

As much as she hated him losing his brother, his words made sense. Kevin wasn't her family yet, and the pride would never be in the true meaning of the word, but they had shown her complete acceptance and that was something she could only pray for with her true family.

She smiled first at Kevin and then at the other lion. *Thank you for coming for me, both of you.*

*I couldn't let my future queen die,* the male responded.

She and Kevin had not discussed their long-term plans, and hearing the way the other lion referred to her now had her heart soaring with hope. The look of complete adoration in Kevin's eyes had that hope floating.

Kevin nuzzled her mouth with a kiss. *I love you, Liddy. And I don't give a damn what your mother says, we're going to get married and have lots of little cubs. With luck, they'll all look like their mother.*

Fresh tears threatened with the happiness that consumed her. She pushed them back. She'd already cried far too much tonight. *I'd like one or two who look just like you,* she thought, returning his kiss with a long, wet one of her own. *I love you, Kevin, and I'm sorry I couldn't promise you as much as you wanted me to this morning. I just knew I had to see you free.*

*We aren't exactly free yet,* the other lion thought from beside them, and Kevin and Liddy both turned to him. *I need to get back to the cruiser and call this in. It's going to take a lot of explaining, but between the three of us and any other shifters we can get to come forward and make their identity known on our behalf, things could still turn out okay.*

*They will turn out okay,* Liddy assured with a certainty she shouldn't feel considering her past with her mama. For some reason she felt that certainty, though, and it gave her the strength to hope her family by blood might soon accept her as completely as her surrogate one did. *I have connections in this town, and it's well past time I used them.*

# Chapter Six

**ฌ**

Liddy had been dreading this day for eight years. She had hoped to break the news of her being a shapeshifter to her parents gently. Instead, she was going to do it while covered in cuts and bruises and accompanied by a white man who looked just as bad or worse.

"Are you sure about this?" Kevin asked from behind her, as Liddy raised her hand to ring her parents' doorbell.

She nodded and pressed the bell. "If shifters and humans are ever going to live in harmony in this town, it needs to start with Mama."

Liddy's daddy opened the door a handful of inches on the second ring of the bell. He was typically a quiet man, who kept his thoughts and feelings to himself while showing a pleasant face to the world. Now his dark, gently wrinkled face held a stern look that clearly had to do with the fact someone would think to come by so late.

Recognition settled in and his severe look faded to worry. He pulled the door open wide and gestured for them to come inside. "Liddy honey, what's the matter? Have you and your friend been in an accident?"

"I'm fine, Daddy—" And she was now that both she and Kevin were safe, and the worst of their body's wounds had begun to heal, "—but I need to speak to Mama. I know it's late, but this can't wait."

He nodded and started toward the second floor staircase as he spoke. "I can see that. Let me get her."

Annette emerged at the top of the staircase less than a minute later, wearing a red satin robe and a matching hairnet. For an instant, her face showed displeasure. Then their disheveled appearances must have sunk in, as her mama rushed down the staircase and to her side, while her daddy followed behind at a more leisurely pace.

Mama lifted her hand to Liddy's cheek. Concern filled her eyes and reflected in her voice. "Baby, look at your pretty face." The concern melted to loathing as she turned her gaze on Kevin. "And you, what are you doing out of jail? You did this to my baby, didn't you?" She looked back at Liddy. "I told you his kind was no good."

Doubt rallied through Liddy's mind with the condemnation in her mama's words, temper attempted to surface. She considered turning back and forgetting all about telling her parents the truth. Kevin's hand folded around hers, large, warm and reassuring, and she knew she couldn't go anywhere until she said what she'd come her to say. From this day forward she didn't want to keep what she was from anyone, and if that meant losing those she loved so dearly forever, it would have to be that way.

"Our kind," she said flatly.

Annette's gaze narrowed, and she gave her head a shake. "What?"

"Our kind," Liddy repeated, louder this time, letting the pride for what she was ring in her voice. "Mama, Daddy. There's something I need to tell you. I've wanted to for a long time, but I was afraid you would reject me once you learned the truth. You already did reject me, because I fell in love with someone who didn't meet your criterion for a suitable match." Her daddy's mouth opened, and she amended, "At least, Kevin didn't meet Mama's."

Annette's breath drew in audibly. She asked tightly, "What are you saying, Liddy?"

"I'm saying that Kevin isn't the attacker any more than he is a killer. The real attacker is dead. He hurt me and—"

"He hurt you." It was her daddy's voice that boomed now, his face reflecting the wrath of God. When he chose to show his defensive side, he did it loudly. "I'll—"

"He didn't hurt me." Liddy sent him a soothing look. "Not really. Kevin didn't let him. Kevin and one of our friends saved me. And now I need to help save them, save their jobs, their lives. Shifters aren't bad people, Mama. They aren't freaks. They are just like everyone else, mothers, fathers, children." She drew a long breath, then added, "Me. I'm one of them. I have been for a long time."

Her mama blinked rapidly while her daddy's mouth opened and closed a few times. It shut a last time and he nodded his acceptance. She'd always known he would be the accepting one in her family. Her mama would be night and day different.

"I know how hard this is for you to take, Mama. But I need for you to think about me, as your daughter. This is the only thing I have ever kept from you, outside of my dating Kevin for a few days. But even that I had planned to tell you about eventually. I was afraid of your rejecting him, because I love him and I want to marry him. I want you both to love him to, to accept him. To accept us for what we are. I need you to accept shifters in general, Mama. To make it clear to the people of Hanover that we aren't wild freaks who go around attacking people.

"If you can't do that… I hope you can, but if you can't, then I have to go away."

Annette's lips pressed into a hard line. Deep lines that Liddy had never seen before etched her forehead and for once made her look her age. She closed her eyes for a long moment, then opened them to reveal the glimmer of unshed tears. Quietly, she asked, "You won't come back, will you?"

Liddy prayed those unshed tears meant her mama was close to giving in, the way she had always told herself she would with the right persuasion. Still, she couldn't allow her hope to surface. "To a town that thinks I and the man I love are freaks?

No. I won't come back to that. I love you both so much, but I have to follow my heart."

Kevin squeezed her hand, assuring her that she wouldn't be alone no matter her mother's decision. "Liddy, we should go. Give them time to digest all — "

"You're not going anywhere with my baby," Mama snapped, all trace of tears gone.

Kevin stepped forward, bringing Liddy into the circle of his left arm. He pinned her mother with a derisive look. "She's my baby now, and I love her just the way she is."

Something flickered in Annette's eyes. As her mama spoke, Liddy realized it was admiration. "Then she's both of our babies, Mr. Montcalm. But you're still not going anywhere with her the way you two look right now." A sheepish look came into her eyes, and she nodded at their bedraggled clothing. "You need to get those wounds cleaned up, treated. Do your, uh, kind go to the hospital?"

Between the way her mouth hung agog and the rush of thankful thoughts that cruised through Liddy's mind, Kevin knew she was incapable of forming a response. He did it for her with the first genuine smile he'd ever given her mother. Clearly, as he'd told those in his pride at countless gatherings, it was fear of the unknown that had shaped her mother's opinion of those who were different from her. Fear that had begun to evaporate and, in time, he hoped would completely fade. "Unless we suffer mortal wounds, we mend very fast. We should be fine by morning."

Annette returned his smile with one of her own, and the years seemed to fall away from her face. She was the vibrant woman she presented herself as on a daily basis now. In the past, Kevin had assumed her youthfulness came with the assistance of surgery. Now he realized it was the natural beauty that came from loving her family.

"Then how about some coffee and carrot cake?" Annette asked. "I made a cake for Sunday dinner, but it seems we have a lot to talk about, so we might as well have it tonight." She turned to her husband. "Harry, can you see to the coffee while I get these two some towels to clean up with?"

Liddy's father nodded agreeably. "Of course, dear."

Beside Kevin, Liddy finally moved, her body brushing his with the subtlest of touches and sending a bolt of heat and lust shooting through him. God, how he'd missed those touches today while he'd been trapped behind bars. Never again would he spend a day away from his mate.

"Thank you, Mama." Liddy's voice trembled as she talked, and tears slipped down her cheeks. "I've hated keeping this from you. I love you."

Annette came to them and pulled Liddy into a hug. "I love you, baby." She set her daughter back at arm's length and wiped at Liddy's tears. "Now enough of these tears. You don't want your man thinking you blubber all the time, do you?"

Kevin's hearted warmed with the acceptance in Annette's voice. He hadn't thought he cared to have it so long as he had Liddy, but now he realized how much getting her parents' approval meant to him. "I don't mind a few tears. Not when I know exactly how strong my Liddy is. It seems I now know where she gets that strength from."

Annette bit her lip and looked away.

Liddy laughed. "Mama you're blushing."

Tsking, Annette waved her hand at Liddy. "Get your backside in the bathroom to clean up before I take your father's belt to it. You aren't too old to take over my knee, you know." With another laugh, Liddy pecked a kiss on her mother's cheek then returned to Kevin and gave him a much longer, intimate one on his mouth. She went off in the direction he guessed the bathroom to be then, and Annette turned to him. "As for you, Mr. Montcalm, it seems it's about time I got to know my future son-in-law better."

"How about we start by you calling me Kevin?"

"Kevin," she repeated, threading her arm through the crook of one of his and gesturing toward the door her husband had gone through moments before. "Annette, or Mama if you prefer. It's a pleasure getting to know someone who cares so deeply for our Liddy. She's a special girl, you know."

"That I do, Mama. And it's just one of many reasons I plan to make her my queen."

"Your queen?" The surprise in Annette's voice was clear. "Is that a title that comes with money? Not that I care about money or anything else, mind you, you could be a pauper so long as you love Liddy, it's just that—"

"Old habits die hard?"

Annette's eyes lit with amusement and a sound Kevin had never heard from the woman came out of her mouth. Laughter. Rich, hearty and lilting in a way that ensured from this day forward life in the city of Hanover, for shifters, for humans, for people of every color, race, ethnicity and class would be a whole lot different. A whole lot better.

\* \* \* \* \*

Kevin pulled Liddy to the center of the conference room they'd been renting for pride gatherings the last months, and she fought off the blush that came with the knowledge all eyes were on her, on them. On their naked bodies.

In the five months since her mama expressed to Hanover that she had been wrong about shapeshifters being freaks unworthy of calling the city home, Liddy had made love with Kevin, in darkness and daylight hours, among the pride many times. However, she had never done so in her human form. It had been her decision to do so tonight, the night of their nuptials.

Mama's disapproval of both shifters and people dating beyond their ethnicity had truly fled. She had openly cried tears of joy through the wedding, while Chenille and Daddy had shown their support for the marriage with their smiles and cheers of congratulations. The reception had been a beautiful affair, attended by humans and shapeshifters alike. Shifters who no longer tried to hide what they were.

It was for that reason Liddy chose to stand naked in the center of the pride as Kevin announced she was their queen to all in attendance. Joining in their human forms, while fur couldn't disguise who they were, somehow seemed more intimate. And, she admitted as she looked around the large room filled with shifters in various forms of transformation, all of whom watched them intently, far more erotic.

Kevin let loose the roar that signified the time for the joining ritual had come, and turned a wide smile on Liddy. His fangs gleamed white in the overhead lighting, showing their razor sharp edges. She shivered at the thought of those fangs sinking into her flesh, suckling at her warm blood as he joined them together for eternity. Her pussy, already moist from all the attention, pooled with a rush of wetness.

"Now, as for you, my queen..." He reached a hand to her, gently cupping her cheek. She titled her face against his warm palm, purring in the back of her throat. "You're so beautiful, Liddy. If I were the jealous kind, it might bother me to have so many other men looking at you, seeing these big, beautiful breasts."

Kevin released her cheek to cup a dark breast in his hand. The nipple, already aroused, tightened fiercely with his touch. The pad of his thumb scraped along the stiff peak, and the roughness of it told her he'd allowed other parts of his body to shift than just his teeth. For her pleasure, Liddy knew, as excitement charged through her body.

"And this belly," Kevin continued, settling his free hand on the rise of her stomach. "If I were the jealous type, I wouldn't want to share this belly with anyone."

One finger dipped into her navel, and she bit back a cry at the unexpected pleasure the simple touch evoked. He worked his finger in and out, and her pussy dampened further, her sex tingling with the loving heat in his intense blue eyes.

His thoughts gave away his next move, before he said, "And your hot little pussy." The hand at her belly moved to her mound, clean shaven just for tonight. "I couldn't stand any other man, feline or otherwise, looking at this beautiful pussy if I were the jealous kind."

Kevin's smile turned feral as he slid a finger the length of her slit. "But I'm not the jealous kind, because I know how much you love me, and how much I trust you."

His finger sank deep, thrusting hard in and out of her sheath. Liddy watched his thick finger fucking her body and couldn't hold in her growl of ecstasy. "Oh yes, Kevin! Fuck me like that, just like that."

Laughter exploded around them, breaking her from the sensual haze that had overtaken her to stare out at the crowd of voyeurs. The conference room had been decorated especially for these pride gatherings. Large couches and chairs dominated much of the place, while tables and platforms took up more of the space. Kevin and she stood on the highest platform, and she gulped with the realization her bare pussy was at the perfect viewing sight. Everyone in the room could see the way Kevin's finger splayed her sex wide, could see the cream leaking from her body. Could smell the scent of her arousal. They could see Kevin's arousal, too.

Liddy turned her attention on the thick length of Kevin's cock jutting toward her. Rigid veins stood out against the pink flesh and her tongue throbbed with the desire to lick over his sex.

The laughter around them faded to the myriad sounds of slapping flesh and grunts of satisfaction. Each one of those sounds reached deep down inside her. Her pussy pulsed with the need to have him buried deeply inside her, but the knowing in Kevin's eyes as she lifted her attention back to his face ruled out her own need.

"Do it, Liddy," he encouraged in a rough voice. "Suck me. Show everyone here how gifted you are with that delectable mouth."

"I want that." The admittance brought power cruising through her veins, making her blood stir to fever pitch. "I want to fuck you in front of everyone."

With a siren's smile, she closed the short distance that separated them, brushing her lips against his mouth once, then dragging her heavy breasts down his chest as she went to her knees. Cupping her breasts, she captured his cock between them, and milked the solid length with the twin mounds.

Kevin's hands fisted in her hair. His growl of approval filled the room, ringing above the sounds of the others.

"Do you like that, Kevin?" Liddy teased, knowing full well that he did. The proof was evident in the cum that leaked from the tip of his penis, and the way his cock twitched between her breasts, jerking in the direction of her lips.

Before he could respond outside of thoughts, she released one of her breasts and fisted his cock in her hand. Tipping her head back to watch his face, she lapped at the tip, savoring the taste of her husband's cum.

*Husband.*

Liddy grinned with the thought. Happiness consumed her as she took his sex fully into her mouth and hummed her elation against his shaft.

"Oh hell, yes Liddy!" Kevin's grip on her hair tightened and his hips jerked toward her face. His face was a tight mask of quiet control.

She reached for his ass, cupping a taut buttock in each hand. *You have the greatest ass*, she thought, unable to share the thought aloud with her mouth full.

That didn't stop him from hearing it. Using his hold on her hair, he pulled her mouth from his penis and brought her to her feet and into the circle of his arms. His tongue filled her mouth, coasting over her teeth, tasting his arousal on her palate. *As do you, and that's where I want to be right now.*

Liddy trembled with the nip of fangs against her tongue and the power of his thoughts. They held the command he showed only on occasion, but that she loved to the fullest. He kissed her several more seconds, his large hands sliding down her body to palm her ass, and then he lifted her in his arms and moved to the end of the platform where a small round table sat in wait.

She had never been taken on a table before. As Kevin settled her against it, her palms flat on the hardwood and her ass thrust in his face, she remembered she had never been taken in her human form in front of dozens of prying eyes, either.

All of the shifters were engaging in sex now, fucking their life partners and those they were partnered with for the night. Many of them kept their eyes trained on the center of the room, on her and Kevin as they moved. Liddy locked eyes with a woman in the crowd. She was half transformed, soft yellow hair dusting her body save for her breasts and mound, both of which were bare, her breasts jiggling, her pussy leaking cream down the inside of her thighs. Her partner was in the same state of semi-transformation as he took her from behind, fucking her ass with long, solid strokes, much the same way Kevin was about to do to Liddy.

Kevin's cock slid along her crack, the damp head nudging her anus, and Liddy trembled with anticipation. The look in the woman's eyes was a mixture of rapture and love, and it was that same look Liddy knew filled her own eyes as one of Kevin's hands came around to palm her breast and the other moved to her pussy.

He teased the bare mound with slow strokes, then pushed a finger into her crevice. His mouth came to her neck, brushing damp kisses on her sweaty flesh. "So wet," he murmured nipping at her ear while he twisted a nipple between thumb and forefinger. "You like being watched this way, don't you?"

She tipped her head back against his mouth, whimpering as his fangs rubbed over sensitive skin. "Yes. It's arousing, but only because you're here with me. I love you, Kevin. Only you. Forever."

His thoughts conveyed that he felt the same for her, but she wouldn't have needed them. The possessive way he sank his fangs deeply into her neck and plunged his cock into her ass was more than proof enough.

Her gaze was still locked on the woman in the crowd and that woman smiled now, sharing a moment of blissful understanding with Liddy. Then the feel of Kevin's large shaft, her body milking him and the heady tang of her blood on the air took over, and the room before her became a haze of thrusting bodies and satisfied roars.

The finger at her pussy moved to her clit, stroking the swollen nub. The push of his cock grew faster, harder into her ass until tension coiled hot and heavy in Liddy's belly. Sweat glided between the valley of her breasts and her heart beat out of control.

Release crashed over her hard, making her grip the edge of the table for support as her limbs shook, threatening to give out. Wary of the roomful of shifters, she cried out her fulfillment, wanting for one and all to hear her love for Kevin and appreciation for the way his skilled hands played her body so beautifully.

Kevin's climax came fast on the heels of her own, his cock pulsating within her before exploding with a burst of silky warm fluid. He pulled his fangs from her neck and, as he had done months before while fucking her among the pride, he growled her name as he came. Only this time when he said it, it was the knowledge it was truly Liddy in his arms.

His mate. His queen. His wife.

## About the Author

∽

Jodi Lynn Copeland discovered her love for writing at an early age and soon after that came an even greater love for the hot, steamy romance — some riddled with humor and fun, others shock full of enough dark and emotional baggage to sink a ship. Jodi is married to her real life hero and has more than a dozen children, though only one of them is human and two-legged.

Jodi is an all-around tomboy at heart, which you can often see shades of in her writing. When she isn't writing or spending time at the day job she likes to pretend she really doesn't have, Jodi can be found in the great outdoors, scrapbooking, watching the discovery channel, CSI or 24, or on any given Sunday sacked out on the couch with her husband and stepson, taking in the latest NASCAR race.

Jodi Lynn Copeland welcomes mail from readers. You can write to her c/o Ellora's Cave Publishing at 1056 Home Avenue Akron, OH 44310-3502.

## *Also by Jodi Lynn Copeland*

∽

# Tiger Eye
## Kit Tunstall

## Author's Note

છ

There are no tigers in Africa, except in zoos. They are indigenous to Asia, but the story wouldn't have worked as well in an Asian setting. Please forgive the artistic license I used to place tigers in Africa.

# Prologue
## *Mekimba, Africa*
## *Thirty years ago*

### ∞

Grant knew his mother wouldn't approve of him investigating, but he pushed on anyway, ignoring the blades of stinging grass that slapped against his bare legs. Absently, he lifted a leg to scratch a mosquito bite irritated by the dying vegetation, his eyes never wavering from the two frolicking tiger cubs in the grass ahead of him. The contrast of black stripes against their pure white fur enthralled him, making his fingers itch to touch them.

He briefly wondered where their mother was, taking time to scan the area surrounding them. When he didn't see her, he moved forward until he was within a few feet of the babies. The larger of the two cubs pounced on its sibling, issuing a growl that was probably meant to be ferocious. A giggle escaped Grant as they rolled together, yowling at each other in playful outrage.

He stepped closer, pushing aside vegetation reaching his waist, to get to the cubs. Fingers extended, he clicked his tongue at them. The cubs broke apart, watching him warily. He dropped to his knees, inching forward. The smaller cub backed away, hissing at him, but the larger cub stood its ground, growling. When he scooted closer still, the cub's bravery fled, and its eyes widened while it backed way.

They were about to flee. In his eagerness to pet them, Grant abandoned caution and lunged forward, catching the hind leg of the larger cub as it turned to flee. A piteous cry escaped it as he dragged it toward him, escalating in pitch as he wrestled with the cub, trying to pull it into his arms. Although only a baby, it put up a good fight, raking his arms with its razor-like claws.

Muttering words he knew his parents wouldn't approve of, Grant finally succeeded in pinning the cub to the ground. He stroked it with a gentle hand, trying to reassure it. He just wanted to pet it, but the wild racing of its heart made him realize he was frightening the cub. With a sigh of regret, he released the cub and watched it bound away.

As he started to rise to his feet, a sound behind him made him freeze. It was now his heart racing wildly as the roar of the tiger repeated. Mouth dry, Grant turned his head to see the angry mother emerging from the dry grass of the veld. His knees trembled when she rushed him, and although he was only six, he suddenly confronted his own mortality as the white tiger leapt at him.

Angie Hayden called her son's name again, ignoring her scratchy throat, worn raw. She walked a few steps farther, paused to scan the veld in the twilight, and screamed, "Grant, answer me." He didn't reply, just as he hadn't for the last hour she and the rest of the village had been searching for him. She prayed Roman would have better luck with his group, which had gone in the opposite direction. Thank goodness the men of the village, and several of the women, had immediately volunteered to help them search for Grant when Angie grew worried he hadn't returned.

To her left, she saw Dobi pushing through the high grass. His body language conveyed a sense of urgency, and she broke into a run to cover the three hundred yards separating them. Her feet crunched through the grass with moderate resistance, and she didn't allow the higher vegetation to slow her down, pushing it aside impatiently.

Even before reaching Dobi, who knelt on the ground, she knew she would find her son injured. Deep down, she had known that from the moment he didn't come back when expected, hours earlier. At first, she had dismissed it as overreacting, but when the village children began returning, and he wasn't in any of those groups, she had listened to the voice in her head telling her to be proactive.

It wasn't a surprise to know something had happened to him, but Angie was unprepared for the shock of seeing him torn and mangled. So much blood had splattered the ground that she didn't think he could be alive. She was kneeling and reaching for him at the same time, even as Dobi lifted the boy. Her heart stuttered, igniting a spark of hope, when Grant moaned.

"He's alive?" she asked in English. At his puzzled look, she repeated the question in Kimbu. In her state of panic, she had slipped into her native tongue, forgetting the language she had spoken almost exclusively for the past two years.

"Yes." His dark eyes reflected his sadness. "Barely."

On autopilot, Angie rose to her feet, extending her arms for her son. Dobi looked like he wanted to protest, but her firm stance must have convinced him she could bear the weight of the boy. In the back of her mind, she knew it would be better to let Dobi carry him. With his muscular build, he could ferry Grant to the village at a run, while she would have to walk. She ignored the voice of reason and took her son, needing to hold him, fearing it wouldn't matter how quickly he reached the village. With no doctor in attendance, and him so injured, what difference did it make? It was better to hold her son while she still could.

As quickly as she could, flanked by Dobi and the other villagers in their search party, all maintaining silence, Angie returned to the village. Tears coursed down her cheeks, but she pressed on, knowing she couldn't fall apart just yet.

To her relief, Roman and his group were returning as they entered the small clearing with its round huts, thatched with grass from the veld. Her husband's posture of frustration changed to horror when she drew nearer and his eyes fell on their son. He rushed toward her, and she was finally able to relinquish Grant, knowing Roman deserved to hold him too in these last precious minutes.

"My God." He cradled the boy against his broad chest, his face pale even in the fading light. "What happened to him, Angie?"

Dobi was the one to answer. "I think a tiger mauled him."

Roman's face contorted with grief. "He is so still." His blue eyes were haunted when he met Angie's. "There's a Red Cross unit two days away, in the Natunde Valley, dispensing vaccinations to the surrounding villages. They have nurses and probably a doctor or two."

She shook her head. "Grant can't ride in the Jeep for two days over that terrain. He'd never survive."

"Then I'll bring a doctor back here," he said stridently.

"Four days...the boy will not survive that long." Dobi touched Grant's cheek, his dark skin a marked contrast to the boy's pallid complexion.

"What the hell are we supposed to do? Just let him die?"

Angie stepped forward, hugging her husband and child. The tears poured from her, and she barely stifled the escaping sobs.

"Come, friend. Bring him to your hut, and we will sit with him."

It remained unspoken, but Angie knew Dobi was talking about the traditional *seteki*, the vigil maintained for the dying. Chants and prayers would be on the lips of every villager who passed through their dwelling, but they wouldn't be for his recovery. No, the prayers would be for him to find his way in the afterlife, for a safe journey there, and admonishments not to be drawn into the darkness, where he would lose his soul forever.

In a daze, the same state Roman seemed to be in, she allowed Dobi to usher them to the small hut the villagers had built for them when they'd come to stay as Roman helped them build an irrigation system, while Angie taught the children. The place had sheltered them for two years, but now looked threatening due to the shadows shrouding the corners of the room. In that darkness lurked demons trying to steal her son.

The thought was irrational, but she found herself hurriedly lighting the kerosene lamps as Roman laid Grant on the grass mat in the corner, where the boy usually slept. He moved like an old man, his actions stiff and jerky. He seemed to have trouble letting go of his son for a long moment, and when his arms finally released, his legs gave out. As he collapsed to the floor, sobs shook his body, and he buried his face in his hands.

Angie's heart broke at the sounds of Roman's suffering, but she couldn't join him. Right then, she could spare no comfort for him, focused as she was on her son's needs.

As quickly as possible, Angie gathered up the basic medical supplies she had on hand and knelt beside Grant. Dobi filled a basin with water, inferring her intent by her activity. She dabbed a square of linen inside the cool liquid, rung it out, and began cleansing her son's wounds. The cloth turned red in seconds, and she accomplished little more than wetting the blood and smearing it around his skin. Still, she kept at the task, working her way through Roman's entire collection of handkerchiefs. It was clearly a losing battle she waged, but what else could she do? Stand by without trying to help her son at all?

Time passed, although Angie didn't know how much. Contrary to the usual custom of the villagers to visit the dying person, most of the members had maintained a respectful distance. The only constant presence besides Roman had been Dobi, who'd hovered behind them, his eyes wavering between Grant's still form and the open door of the hut. He had seemed to be waiting for something.

The air of anticipation fled from the hut when the medicine man entered, arriving so quickly he appeared to have materialized inside the small room. As always, his presence made Angie uncomfortable. There was an aloof manner about the man that made him unapproachable. Although she didn't believe in his practices, he carried himself with an air of mystery and intensity that suggested he dwelt in two worlds—this one, and a spiritual plane others couldn't even imagine.

Without speaking a word, Kafiri walked over to the grass mat and knelt beside Roman and Angie. She watched with pensive eyes as he examined her son, chanting quietly as he did so. When his dark gaze suddenly turned fully on her, she gasped with shock at the confrontation. It took every ounce of strength not to look away from his compelling gaze.

"There is not much time," he said in Kimbu.

Roman nodded. "Anytime now, he'll…" He trailed off, sobs shaking his shoulders, although not a sound emerged from him to betray his outburst.

"You can save him, Kafiri?" Dobi asked as he took up a kneeling position on the other side of Angie.

"Perhaps."

His words stirred hope in Angie and she brushed aside the voice of doubt, the one that had always privately dismissed the services the medicine man provided for the villagers. "How?"

"By drawing the strength of the tiger." A frown rearranged the deep grooves on Kafiri's face, making him look years older than he was. Even his shock of white hair didn't age him as much as that expression. "It is dangerous, and there will be…side effects."

"I don't care. Do what you can." Angie ignored Roman's shocked expression, just as she ignored her own reservations. He was as logical as she was. No doubt he found the concept crazy. Her rational side shared the view, but her maternal side was ready to try anything to save her son. She found the small hope the shaman offered ridiculously easy to cling to.

"But you must understand —"

"Do it," she said in a hard voice. There was nothing to lose by allowing the old man to practice his superstitions on Grant. With no doctor available, and her son dying faster with each passing second, she was willing to try anything.

After a second's hesitation, Kafiri nodded. "I will do what I can, regardless of the consequences."

"Just save my son." Angie gripped Roman's hand as she uttered the request, needing his strength to get through what was coming. The slight optimism she felt was bound to abandon her, leaving her completely despondent when the medicine man's treatment failed. She would need her husband more than she ever had before to get through the trial of burying her only child in a foreign land.

# Chapter One
## *Natunde Valley Nature Preserve*
## *Present Day*

ॐ

Rage swept through Grant, as did stomach-twisting nausea, when he saw the full extent of the wildebeest's fatal injuries. He carefully pushed aside the tarp Manu had wrapped the calf in upon discovering its grisly remains on his rounds through the preserve. The exam table, although to its full height, was just low enough to require Grant to either stoop or sit on a stool during exams. This time, he chose to stoop, knowing there would be no need for full mobility since the poor calf was dead.

"Those goddamned soldiers used this baby for target practice, didn't they?" Manu asked, his rage clearly matching Grant's.

"It looks that way."

"You're the vet. Did they, or didn't they? Was there any possible justification for this?" He waved a hand at the ragged carcass.

Grant looked up, taking a moment to breathe deeply in hopes of controlling his emotions. "Could there ever be justification for this? The bullets are large caliber, probably from a machine gun. They didn't kill it for food, because there isn't enough left to salvage anything. Whoever did this was sadistic."

"I'd like to get my hands on them."

The disturbing glint in his friend's eyes made Grant swallow. He closed his eyes for a second, focusing on remaining in control. Any lapse could lead to disaster. The beast was always threatening to break through his veneer of humanity with the slightest provocation. "I share your sentiments, Manu."

The cool calm in his voice helped him rein in the anger, and the urge to shift gradually faded.

"They're tearing our country apart. Is it not enough to force Mekimban men into their militia, to rape the women, and leave countless children orphaned?" He shook his head, his disgust clear. "Are there not enough human targets to satisfy them? Now they come onto our protected lands to kill this baby."

"Considering the other atrocities the army commits daily against humans, this is nothing for them, Manu." Grant covered the calf with the tarp again, knowing there was no further need for examination. It hadn't died from disease or normal injury, so he had no need to monitor the herd for health issues.

"Animals," Manu muttered.

"No," Grant said in a soft voice. "Animals act on instinct. When they kill, it is not for pleasure." His nature gave him a unique perspective on the animal condition.

Manu sighed. "True, my friend. To call those cretins animals is to insult every creature living on this preserve."

When the silence lengthened, Grant stood up straight, moving to the drawer where he kept his nonmedical paraphernalia to retrieve a roll of tape. Working without speaking, the two of them wrapped the wildebeest in the tarp and taped it closed. Later that night, one of the rangers would see to its cremation. In the interim, they carried the body behind the clinic, leaving it wrapped tightly to protect the corpse from scavengers before it could be disposed of.

With the wildebeest secured, Grant paused to lean against the wall of the clinic. The work of moving the calf hadn't been exhausting. It was the emotional torment associated with the situation that left him with a sensation of full-body fatigue.

It took a second, but he managed to stand up straight and follow Manu back into the exam room of the clinic. He expected the director of the preserve to keep going, so it was with surprise that Grant watched him eyeing the room.

Appearing uncomfortable, Manu cleared his throat. "You have enough space here, don't you?"

He nodded. "Most of the time, the other table is free, as you know." To Grant's relief, most of the animals on the preserve rarely required transport to the clinic itself. Ninety percent of the time, he took a vehicle out whenever there was an injured or ill animal.

"Good, that's good." Manu stroked his goatee, his fingers rustling the crisp curls. "I have done something spontaneously, Grant. I should have discussed it with you first, but I acted without thought."

His eyebrow quirked. "I work for you, Manu. Why would you need to consult me?"

"Because the clinic is your domain, and I have offered its resources to another."

Grant frowned. "You're hiring a second vet?" That made no sense. There were days when he himself had little to do on the medical side of things and spent his time like the rangers, patrolling the preserve for poachers and other problems.

"No. Do you know the clinic two miles from here? Dr. Senghor runs it."

"I know of her."

"The fighting is much too close to her clinic now. She needed a place to bring her practice so she could continue seeing patients." Manu ducked his head, looking like an embarrassed child. "I offered her space here at the clinic."

Grant inclined his head. "That was a logical thing to do."

Manu appeared relieved. "I had hoped you would not mind." He stroked his goatee. "I don't know how I ended up making the offer when I ran into her at the store in Natunde."

"It's fine." Grant's voice emerged steadily, hiding his anxiety. The clinic was his haven, where he could retreat from stimuli that might trigger a transformation. With the doctor infringing on his space, he wouldn't have anywhere he could withdraw to. But Manu didn't know how important his sanctuary was to him, and it was too late to protest. Besides, how could he, in good conscience? The people Dr. Senghor helped were more important than infringement on his private refuge.

A grin split Manu's face, revealing shining teeth. "I am happy to hear that, my friend, because Dr. Senghor will be here within the hour."

Biting back a groan, Grant managed to nod again, while wondering what tasks he could undertake to keep himself away from the doctor. He had to establish a routine that would minimize time spent with her, lest he accidentally reveal the nature of the beast trapped within.


Zinsa engaged the parking brake and shut off the roaring engine of the old truck she had used to convey supplies and patients from her clinic to the makeshift site at the nature preserve. The door creaked when she opened it, and the muggy air settled on her like a shroud. During the drive over bumpy terrain, having the window down had given the illusion of cool air circulating, but she couldn't fool herself any longer. Even the buzzing flies seemed lethargic.

She slid from the truck, letting gravity carry her to the ground. As always, she made a mental note to install a step on the truck, but knew she probably never would. The value of the hulk of metal didn't warrant the investment. Besides, she thought with a small grin, the weight of the addition might destabilize the rusty bolts holding together the wreck on wheels.

The door groaned again when she slammed it, the window vibrating in the frame. Zinsa ignored the racket while simultaneously wondering how anyone unaccustomed to the truck could take no notice of all the noise. She had expected someone at the preserve's headquarters to come out to investigate, but as the dust settled, no one stepped out of the complex of wooden buildings that formed the offices and sleeping quarters of the employees.

"Hello?" she called. Receiving no reply, she moved away from the truck toward the entrance of the clinic, hoping to find someone available to help unload. She and the patients had managed to pack up everything from the clinic, but most were ill and worn out from the trip. It wasn't advisable to have the older patients lifting heavy boxes, which left only her, but she wasn't looking forward to doing all the work alone.

Stepping into the clinic caused a shiver to race down her spine. Not from the air circulated by multiple fans, but from the sight through the open office door of a man hunched over his desk, logging an entry into a ledger. His blond hair was a perfect foil for his dark tan, and the lightly curling locks made her fingers itch to run through them.

Surprised by her reaction, Zinsa walked to the doorway, composing her expression before clearing her throat. He jerked at the sound, and she said, "Sorry if I startled you, Dr. Hayden. I'm Zinsa Senghor. Manu might have mentioned…"

He nodded. Beyond a quicksilver flash of some inscrutable emotion in his green eyes, his expression was bland. "Yes. Would you like a tour?"

Zinsa walked closer to him, stopping before a large fan to pull her sticky tank top away from her skin, letting the artificial breeze waft over her. She sighed with contentment at the sensation, barely forcing herself to turn away to answer the vet. "Sure, but I need to get the patients in first, along with supplies. Care to give me a hand?"

After a brief hesitation, he nodded. "Of course." His chair squeaked when he pushed away from the basic desk.

Her eyes widened as he stood up straight. He was the tallest man she had ever seen. Surely he stood at least six-and-a-half feet. With his height, it wouldn't have been unwarranted to expect him to be bulging with muscles, but he had a trim physique. This was a man unafraid of physical labor, but not one who wasted hours honing his body to its maximum potential. Her mouth watered as he walked toward her and she swallowed, wishing he didn't have the kind of frame she found appealing.

Most of all, she wished she didn't feel this sensation that made her tingle, as if she had been struck by lightning. Was it the family gift—or curse, depending on how one looked at it? Was she finally experiencing the thing her father had described, had promised she would find someday? After thirty-two years, she had assumed it would never happen to her. It couldn't be happening now. With setting up a makeshift practice and seeing to her patients here instead of at her own clinic, she didn't have time for distractions.

At least, not right away, she thought with a mischievous grin as she turned to lead the way to her truck. Give her a couple of days, and he would be fair game. She would discover if what she felt was just instant attraction or something more.

Grant paused in his assigned task of unloading a cumbersome box from the back of the truck to watch Zinsa assist her last elderly patient down. He was probably going to Hell for lusting after her while she performed the altruistic task of straightening the old woman's housedress and bandana, before tucking an arm around the birdlike frame to lead her inside the clinic. He should be overwhelmed with sympathy for the old woman, not noticing the way the sweaty gray shirt clung to Zinsa's full breasts or the way her hips shimmied as she walked with unconscious feminine grace.

Mouth dry, Grant managed to tear his eyes from her form as she disappeared into the clinic, bringing his attention back to the task of balancing the large box and carrying it inside. Three of the rangers, who mysteriously had nothing to do, had also volunteered their services for unloading and unpacking. He resented the way their eyes followed the doctor, although he had no right to, when his were equally glued to her every move.

At the pace they were progressing, with the men unloading while Zinsa saw to assisting each of her four patients with getting settled, they would have her set up in no time. The thought terrified Grant. The fiery, instant attraction he'd experienced upon shaking her hand alarmed him. He couldn't afford to lose control. Why did she have to be so tempting?

"Are you bonding with that box, Dr. Hayden?" Her crisp English accent lent the teasing words an air of seriousness she probably hadn't meant to impart, judging from the grin on her face.

Grant jerked out of his reverie, his face burning with the heat of embarrassment. Mumbling something unintelligible, he brushed past her where she leaned against the door, completely aware of the heat of her body and the appealing scent underlying the odor of perspiration. It wasn't perfume catching his attention. Just her womanly, musky scent that made him salivate.

As quickly as he could, he dumped the box into the area Zinsa would be using and fled to his office, closing the door. Her smell lingered in his nose, or maybe just his memory, and he snorted, trying to clear it.

Realizing he was leaning against the door, his cock throbbing in time with his rapidly beating heart, getting aroused just by the scent of the doctor, he cursed his foolishness and strode to his desk, dropping into the rickety wooden chair. It squeaked under the force of his weight, but held as it always did.

Casting a brooding glare to where Zinsa was now setting up her makeshift clinic, Grant searched for some other thought to occupy his mind. He could be doing inventory in preparation for his monthly order, or he could take the Land Rover out to observe the herds. Many babies would be coming in the next few weeks, and he liked to have an accurate headcount for each of the different herds.

He could be doing any number of things except the one thing he wanted to do, which was pin the good doctor against the wall, bury his nose into the valley between her breasts and take in the scent of her.

At times like this, there was no denying the animal half of his nature, the beast always tenuously held in check. Reacting so violently to a woman was a new experience, but it had to be related to his animal instincts. True, it had been a while since he had made love to a woman, but being horny didn't explain the magnetic pull Zinsa had on him. If only he could rid himself of the beast, he could squash this inconvenient attraction. Since that was impossible, he would just have to avoid her as much as he could.

He found his plan was going to be difficult when he finally left his office a few hours later. He had spent the rest of the afternoon inside catching up on paperwork and reading a novel, all while trying to block out thoughts of how Zinsa might look stripped of her clinging tank top and khaki shorts.

As night approached, signaled by the cry of hyenas somewhere on the reserve, he crept from his office, relieved not to find her in the area of the clinic set up for her patients. The four she had brought with her were resting on cots lined close together against one wall. The mother of the only child in the group was curled uncomfortably on the floor beside her daughter's cot.

None of the patients stirred as he went through the room, pausing to lock up the clinic. He shook his head at the need, thanks to the soldiers in the area. Before civil war erupted, he wouldn't have felt unsafe in the place where he had been a vet for ten years.

After securing the clinic for the night, Grant walked down the hallway to the back room, where he kept all the supplies necessary for the health center. A small room off to the left housed the operating theater, but he kept going into the storage area, tiredness catching up with him.

In mid-yawn, he paused as he entered his sleeping area. The sight of Zinsa curled up on a cot just a few feet from his double bed had him tripping over his feet. His mouth hung open, but he couldn't seem to recover the ability to close it.

She looked up at him, a small smile on her perfect, full lips. "Hello, roomie."

His eyebrow lifted of its own accord, just as his arms crossed his chest in a challenging way. "What are you doing here?"

She waved a hand to the front. "There's no more room up front with the patients, especially if more come in. Manu suggested I put a cot back here." The corners of her mouth turned down. "He didn't think it was a good idea for me to take a bed in the bunkhouse. It would be too far from my patients."

Grant barely bit back a snort. He doubted Manu's concern sprang from the distance she would be from the patients. More likely, he realized Zinsa would be too big a distraction to the workers who slept in the bunkhouse. It should have been heartening to know his friend trusted him around the doctor, but he feared Manu's trust was misplaced.

A full frown had formed now, creating an irresistible crinkle between her eyes. "Is that a problem?"

With a terse shake of his head, he turned to the bathroom. "No. You just surprised me." Taking refuge in the bathroom, Grant sought any excuse to flee his bed, but couldn't think of anything plausible. The last thing he wanted to do was reveal to Zinsa that he planned to steer clear of her, because that would lead to awkward questions. All he could do was bear the situation for however long it lasted. Local news reported the soldiers were close to crippling the uprising, so the war should be over in a matter of weeks. He could survive the ordeal that long. Couldn't he?

Hurrying through his evening ablutions did little to occupy his thoughts or help him ignore the erection tenting his briefs. He left on his T-shirt and shorts, although he normally slept in the nude. When he could put it off no longer, he opened the door and stepped out of the small bathroom, taking a deep breath. Faux courage carried him to his bed, but deserted him when she spoke.

"I don't want to inconvenience you, Dr. Hayden. I'm sure you don't usually sleep in the clothes you wore all day." After a slight pause, her voice seemed to deepen slightly when she spoke again. "I know I don't."

Slowly, he turned his head. He saw the tank top and shorts she had worn minutes before folded neatly on a nearby chair. A light sheet covered her from the breasts down, but everything above was bare. She might or might not be sleeping in panties, but she sure wasn't wearing anything else. He swallowed, at a loss for words.

What could be just a friendly smile, but seemed deliberately sensuous, crossed her face. "Please be comfortable."

With jerky movements, he looked away from his new roommate in all her glory, barely hidden by the thin sheet that rested so well against the curves of her body. He pulled back the sheet and climbed into his bed, curling on his right side, although he never slept in that position. "I'm comfortable." As he fumbled for the light without turning back to her, he swore a breathy laugh escaped her.

# Chapter Two

**ℰᴓ**

With no patients of his own, Grant found himself recruited to assist Zinsa when she reopened her treatment center in its temporary headquarters the next day. Inside an hour of opening for the day, they had a line extending out the door. With nearly one hundred patients awaiting treatment, he wondered how she'd ever coped on her own.

As Grant prepared a syringe with MMR inoculation for the next child waiting, he glanced over at Zinsa, who was palpating the belly of a grizzled old man with a racking cough. "How do you manage all this on your own?"

She spared him a quick look before returning attention to her patient. "I don't normally. I had two nurses and a physician's assistant up until a couple of weeks ago. My PA was the first to leave me, returning home to the States. Then both of my nurses quit within days of each other, terrified of the fighting and deciding they needed to be with their families. They were local women, so I hope they'll come back once they hear the clinic has reopened in a safer area." A grin flashed across her mouth. "Until then, I'm lucky to have you, Dr. Hayden."

"Grant," he said in a low voice, trying to appear offhand with the invitation.

"Grant." She practically purred his name, conjuring all sorts of illicit images to accompany the breathy repetition. Never before had he liked his name so much as he did right then.

The hours passed quickly, with a multitude of patients streaming in and out of the makeshift clinic. Most required nothing more than simple medication, perhaps a bandage, or just someone to listen, but they ended up with two additional inpatients by the end of the night. In awe, Grant watched Zinsa organize everything, somehow managing to squeeze two more cots into the room.

It was only when they left the clinic to sit outside in the coming twilight, glasses of cold tea in their hands, Grant realized how tired he was. With a groan that was a mix of pain and pleasure, he stretched his kinked back and rotated his neck.

She grinned at him. "You held up like a pro."

"I don't know how you do it." His eyes followed a rivulet of sweat as it streaked down her cleavage, disappearing under her shirt. The sight made his mouth water, and he took a long drink of the tea, hoping to distract himself.

When she leaned back, the new pose emphasized her generous breasts. "I'm not usually going it alone, as I said. There have been times, of course. With a clinic like this, you do the best you can."

"How did you end up so far away from home, practicing medicine in Mekimba?"

A wistful sigh escaped her. "This is my home."

He nodded. "I know how you feel. I was four when my parents came here. They were assigned here for four years, but when the term ended…they stayed." They had stayed for him, knowing his new abilities forced him to live somewhere primitive. His control had been even more tenuous as a child and young teenager. It would have caused panic if they had returned to their home in Boston and he had morphed into a tiger running loose through the city. Blinking, Grant realized he had dropped into silence. "I can't imagine living anywhere else now."

"Me either, but this really is my home. I was born here."

He arched a brow. "How did you acquire the English accent?"

"My father is from London."

Grant shook his head. "Amazing. You sound like you grew up there, instead of getting a trace from hearing your father speak."

Sadness clouded her expression. "I did for most of my childhood. Dad came to Mekimba with one of the first missions of the newly established Médecins Sans Frontières—Doctors Without Borders. He met my mother when she came to him for treatment. He says it was love at first sight for both of them." Her expression changed, becoming seductive. "I come from a long line of that. Dad claims every member of his family has met their partners and fallen in love in an instant." She grinned. "He says it can either be a gift or a curse, depending on the circumstances."

Grant chuckled. "A romantic notion."

Her brow furrowed. "You don't believe it?"

"Has it happened to you?"

An odd intensity colored her gaze. "Oh, yes. Just once."

"What happened?"

A shrug was her answer before she plunged back into her story. "When the rest of the team left, Dad stayed behind, opened a clinic, married my mother, and I came along within a year."

"It sounds idyllic." From her sadness upon beginning her story, he knew it hadn't stayed that way and had to resist the urge to reach out to offer a comforting hand.

"It probably was." She set aside the tea she hadn't drunk from. "I think they were happy here. If Mom hadn't died in childbirth, along with my baby brother, I'm sure Dad would have stayed in Mekimba forever."

"I'm sorry."

Zinsa nodded. "I don't remember her, but thanks. Anyway, Dad took me to London within three months, and that's where I grew up. He fed me stories of his time here from the time I can remember." She waved a hand at the expanse of veld that began just a few yards from the complex of building. "I grew up thinking this was as close to Paradise as I would find on Earth, so it was only natural for me to come here after I finally became a doctor. I opened the clinic, and the rest is history."

Unable to resist, Grant put his hand over hers. "Has it been everything you hoped for?"

"Mostly." She turned her head, meeting his eyes directly. "What has been missing seems like it might have been found."

The words were cryptic, and Grant had the strangest feeling she was talking about him. He dismissed the idea with a shake of his head, knowing wishful thinking when he heard it...or thought it.

Suddenly, Zinsa was on her feet, pulling on his hand until he rose from the steps to stand beside her. "Let's walk."

He shook his head, his stiff neck protesting at the motion. "I'm too sore and tired."

With a lighthearted laugh, she dragged him down the steps. "It will make you feel better. Trust me. After a long day of repetitious motion, there's nothing better than a walk in the twilight. You'll stretch your muscles."

He allowed himself to be dragged forward, more because she hadn't relinquished his hand than because he really thought a walk would help his tight muscles. His stomach clenched when she settled into step beside him, keeping his hand in hers.

They wandered without a particular destination, just moving from the clearing where the buildings were into the veld. An occasional acacia tree in their path forced them to detour, but the dry grass didn't reach a high enough level to be more than an inconvenience, even though they both wore sandals.

The companionable silence between them felt natural, and he had no need to break it. Instead, Grant let his senses focus on Zinsa—on the levelness of her breathing, which was slowly increasing in rapidity, on the scent of her body, tinged mildly with female arousal, if he wasn't mistaken, and on the sound of her sandals forging a path through the grass, each of her steps in rhythm with his.

Before he knew it, they had gone quite a distance. When he turned to look behind them, the headquarters of the preserve was a distant blur, the buildings barely discernable. He offered no protest when Zinsa sat on a large rock, breaking the physical connection between them for the first time in probably twenty minutes. Longing for it again, he edged in beside her, his heart racing when his leg touched hers.

Now seemed like the time to talk, but before he could speak, she asked, "How did you end up here?"

"My parents were aid workers—"

Zinsa shook her head. "I meant here at the Natunde Preserve, working as a vet? I'm sure you could have done other things. Modeling, for instance."

"Oh." A flush tinged his face, and he hoped the darkening sky hid it. It was ridiculous to be embarrassed by her casual comment. "I don't think so. I'm more suited to be a vet. I went to university in Mawunyaga, but found the capitol too crowded for my tastes." Those had been tense years, living in constant fear of losing control. Considering those should have been the most sex-laden years of his life, he had failed miserably, managing to get laid only twice, and not caring overly much for his partner either time. Deep affection was a luxury he couldn't afford, lest he risk revealing his secret. Since it had left him feeling dirty to not have an emotional attachment with his bed partners, he had opted for a life of near-celibacy. "After I graduated, I looked for a quiet place to work and found the reserve."

She eyed him thoughtfully. "You'll never leave Mekimba then?"

He shook his head. "I don't remember a thing about Boston, and I have no desire to see it. My parents are still here, living in a village a couple of days away. Everything I know is here."

Zinsa leaned closer, licking her full lips. "Everything you want, too?"

Somehow, he managed to swallow. "Er, yes."

A grin blossomed, displaying the perfection of her teeth. "Good. I know I'll live here the rest of my life." She placed her hand flat on his chest for a brief second, before lifting her palm and trailing her fingers down his buttons. "This could work."

"What could?" His voice emerged as a rasp, affected as he was by nerves.

Her hand moved upward in a flash, and she tapped him lightly on the side of the nose with her forefinger. "Don't be dense."

Grant searched for a way to withdraw, to let her down easy, but discovered he didn't want to. Even knowing he had to didn't help him resist when she tilted her chin up, cupped the back of his head to force his face down, and touched her lips against his.

The kiss was soft and undemanding, with Zinsa offering, not taking. He couldn't withstand the dewy sweetness of her soft lips, the sweet tang of her musky femininity, or the cautious dart of her tongue across his mouth before it disappeared inside hers again. His hands settled on her shoulders of their own accord and he pulled her as close as he could without displacing both of them from the rock.

Desire swept through him, causing his pulse to pound in his ears. His heart raced, and his cock throbbed, straining to escape the prison of his khaki shorts. Grant curled his hands tighter around her shoulders, struggling to maintain control. She whimpered at the pressure and he immediately let go, trying to pull away. Zinsa's hand on his head turned to a steel vise, trapping him, refusing to release him.

Her tongue pushed between his lips, changing from coaxing to demanding, letting him know she wanted everything. Grant's stomach clenched with dread, knowing he couldn't give it to her. He should break the kiss and leave her before things got out of control. Already he could feel the need rising, his control slipping, as her tongue stroked his, exploring the depths of his mouth.

The first drops of rain saved him from losing control completely. They fell from the sky like large teardrops, striking their faces and heads. With surprise, Grant jerked away, looking up just in time to see forked lightning split the sky. Within seconds, the rain became a deluge. He cursed. "It isn't even the rainy season."

Zinsa bounded to her feet, extending her arms. A delighted laugh escaped her. "I know. That makes it even better."

He frowned. "You're enjoying this?"

"I love the rain, and when it comes down like this…" She shivered, but apparently with delight, not cold.

Grant got to his feet, taking one of her extended hands. "Come on. We're getting soaked."

"A little rain never hurt anyone."

She didn't resist when he drew her forward at a rapid pace, his familiarity with the area guiding him more than his sight in the heavy rain. "This isn't a little rain."

"Spoilsport." She had to yell the word to project over another crash of jagged lightning. Silence was more convenient as they broke into a jog, Grant cursing having come so far without thought.

It was a relief to see the clinic come into sight a few minutes later. He was so wet his clothes clung to him like a second skin and his sandals slid around on his feet. The leather was probably ruined, but that was the least of his worries at the moment.

He rushed up the stairs to open the door to the clinic, pausing to look back when he realized Zinsa wasn't behind him. At the sight of her twirling around in a circle in the heavy rain, he shook his head. "Zinsa," he shouted, getting her to look up. She flashed him a disgruntled look, but came out of the rain, walking up the steps to join him. "You're crazy."

She shook her head. "Just spontaneous."

"Spontaneity can be dangerous," he said in a brooding voice as he followed her into the clinic, locking the door behind them. They crept quietly past the area where the patients rested before she responded.

Zinsa gave him a half-shrug, glancing over her shoulder at him. "I suppose, but life would be pretty boring if you followed a rigid set of rules all the time."

Making a noncommittal sound, he walked toward the back room, conscious of her just inches ahead, just within touching distance. His enhanced sense of smell clued him in to her excitement, making it doubly hard to resist the thoughts circulating in his brain.

In the bedroom, Grant stepped aside, gesturing toward the bathroom. "You first." When he flicked on the lamp, her breasts drew his gaze, the nut-brown areoles and nickel-size nipples plainly visible through the cotton. He jerked his gaze away, a blush heating his cheeks.

With a laugh, Zinsa peeled off her tank top. It had become virtually transparent in the rain, but had provided a modicum of modesty. Free of the shirt, standing with her breasts bared, she paused in the process of unfastening her shorts. "Don't just stand there, Grant. You need to get out of those wet clothes. By the time you wait for me to shower, you could get ill."

The words were logical, but the heat in her eyes and purr in her tone left little doubt to her true motivation for trying to strip him. She wanted to finish what they had started before the storm came. It would be dangerous for him to give in to the attraction burning between them. He swallowed the lump in his throat, searching for a way to handle the situation diplomatically. Nothing came to mind, especially since his own body wanted her as much as she wanted him.

Zinsa continued stripping, kicking off her sandals before shedding her panties and shorts. When she stood naked before him, her hands found purchase on her hips, and she clicked her tongue. "You really need to get undressed."

He closed his eyes, struggling to maintain control. The sharp tang of her arousal carried to his nose, the perfume making his rigid cock tighten to the point of pain. "Zinsa, I can't—"

She didn't allow him to finish. Zinsa took a step forward, placing her finger against his mouth. "Then let me."

When her fingers began deftly working at the buttons of his sodden shirt, Grant tried to stop her, but his body wouldn't cooperate, except to relax under her palms when she smoothed them down his chest after opening the garment. The rain on their skin provided a liquid medium for her caresses, making it feel like silk gliding over his chest.

Her hands froze when she encountered the mass of scars on his side. "What happened?"

He examined her expression, searching for a hint of repulsion, but finding only curiosity and perhaps sympathy. "I was mauled by a tiger as a child."

Zinsa traced one of the white ridges, a ropy, meandering line bisecting his tanned skin. "It must have been a terrible attack if the scars are still this prominent. How did you ever survive?"

A lump in his throat forced him to cough before he could answer. "A miracle, I guess."

"Thank goodness for miracles."

His breath hissed between his clenched teeth when Zinsa scraped one of his nipples lightly with her fingernail. A sound of pleasure escaped him, and he abandoned any thought of resisting when her hands moved lower to unbuckle his belt. She removed it slowly, pulling an inch at a time, while deliberately brushing her hands repeatedly against his body as she did so.

A sigh of relief left him when she dropped the belt on the floor, but he drew in another deep breath when her hands moved to the button and zipper, opening them efficiently to let her hands inside. "Zinsa." He clenched his fists, struggling to control his breathing. His senses were hypersensitive, and the beast inside was stirring to life. He brought up a hand to push her away but somehow ended up cupping her breast instead. Her nipples were firm under his fingers, and her moans moved his passion up another notch. She withdrew, and he wanted to protest but couldn't manage to both speak and keep the creature in check.

"Lift your feet."

His mind was hazy, taking a moment to process her request. When he looked down, he saw her kneeling before him, impatiently awaiting his help with shedding the rest of his clothes. He lifted each foot in turn, and then took a moment to kick off his sandals before reaching out to stroke her hair. The rain had caused the ultra-short cut to kink, and a mass of tight curls met his fingers.

Uncertain of how he could maintain control, Grant nonetheless surrendered to her stroking of his cock. He groaned with anticipation as Zinsa's head moved forward, her intent clear. The first bold rasp of her tongue against his cock caused his body to jerk in reaction. He tightened his fingers in her hair, barely holding back from hurting her. It wasn't an urge to harm her he experienced, but rather the need to dominate. Knowing how he could injure her during the process kept the impulse in check.

She wasn't shy about tasting him. In seconds, his cock was in her mouth, the heat and moisture making him spasm. When she suckled him while cupping his testicles in one hand, his hips bucked, inadvertently forcing more of his cock inside her throat. He froze, looking down to check on her. She didn't seem bothered, and her suction didn't change. With a sigh, he closed his eyes, letting his head fall back as pleasure swept through him.

Zinsa's nails dug lightly into the tender flesh of his sac as her teeth scraped his cock. The hint of pain heightened his pleasure, even as it pushed him closer to the brink of transformation. In his head, he tried to remember the anatomy of an elephant, but the thoughts couldn't distract him sufficiently from her ministrations.

Her tongue swirled the length of him, working his cock like an ice cream cone. Grant's cock spasmed when she traced his corona with her tongue, pausing to flick the V of nerves at the tip. When she sucked that section lightly, his cock convulsed, and hot semen poured from him without even a chance to warn her.

She withdrew, discreetly wiping her mouth before smiling up at him. Kneeling before him, she seemed to be submitting. Amazingly, his cock hardened again, and he had to fight the urge to drop down on the floor beside her, turn her on her stomach, and pound into her.

The animal inside was churning to the surface. A fine growth of hair was sprouting all over his body, and his fingernails were visibly lengthening. In a panic, he stepped away from her, turning his face. "Towels," he said in a thick voice.

"What?" Her confusion was clear from her tone.

"Wet...towels." With no time for further explanation, Grant ran from the room, not pausing for towels or anything else. Only the curtain Zinsa had rigged from bed sheets to provide the patients with a measure of privacy shielded them from the shocking sight of him rushing out, bare-ass naked.

Once outside, he continued to run until well out of sight of the clinic. The chilly rain did little to cool his heated flesh and didn't do a thing to bank the fire of transformation raging inside. He dropped to all fours, and when he screamed at the pain of changing, the roar of a tiger left his mouth. Grant tried to fight it, but as always, eventually lost the struggle to preserve his humanity.

# Chapter Three

Although he couldn't be certain, Grant thought about an hour had passed since the time he transformed. When he came to, he had returned to his human form, finding himself just a few yards from where he had changed. He must have run during that time, had probably hunted even, but had no memory of anything he had done. That indicated he had fully lost control, which was rare for him. For years, he had retained at least a shred of himself on the occasions when transformation became irresistible.

By some instinct, he had made his way back to his starting place. It would make his return to the clinic easier, since he knew precisely where he was. Not that he was anxious to get back. The thought of facing Zinsa after what he had done made his stomach churn with nausea. What was she thinking? No doubt she thought he was a selfish pig, taking pleasure without reciprocating.

Knowing it would do no good to prolong avoiding her, Grant broke into a jog, relieved to find the rain had slowed to a drizzle. Several times, sharp grass or twigs poked his feet, but he kept going, having no choice. It would be too humiliating to wait for rescue in the morning. How could he ever explain being fully nude, *sans* shoes, two miles from the complex?

With a grimace, he acknowledged it might be easier to explain that than to face Zinsa and try to elucidate why he had run away. Certainly it would be easier to traverse the whole country in his birthday suit than do what he had to in a few minutes. Maybe she would be asleep. He clung to the hope, although he recognized it as cowardly. Eventually he would have to offer some explanation. Might as well get it over with.

Zinsa sat on the cot, hugging her knees to her chest. Anger and confusion had kept her from trying to find sleep. Her stomach burned and the gritty feeling in her eyes, from suppressing tears, had her constantly blinking.

What had happened? Why had Grant torn out of the room like that? Had he not enjoyed the blowjob? Was he ill? Was he just a self-centered jerk? His actions supported that supposition, but it didn't feel right. There was something more to it, and she was determined to find out what.

As she saw Grant coming down the hall, moving with silent grace, she took a deep breath to prepare herself. Thoughts of confronting him nearly abandoned her when he stepped into the room, the sixty-watt bare bulb giving his body a golden sheen. Her mouth watered anew at the sight of him, as her pussy clenched with need. It took much self-discipline to hide her reaction behind a cool expression. "Grant."

He couldn't seem to meet her gaze. First, his eyes danced around the room, finally settling on her neck. Grant's fidgeting betrayed his nervousness, the way he shifted his feet and constantly ran his fingers through his damp hair.

When he didn't seem inclined to speak, she pressed on. "What happened?"

"I..." He trailed off, clearly at a loss. A loud sigh escaped him before he strode to his bed, sitting on the foot. "I don't know. I panicked, I guess."

A frown furrowed her brow. "Panicked? Why?" Eyes wide, she asked in a whisper, "You aren't a virgin, are you?"

A small laugh escaped him. "No, not quite." Finally, he seemed to find the strength to meet her eyes. "You made me panic, Zinsa."

"Why?"

"The way I reacted to you. I'm not used to that. You make me feel things...lose control."

A surge of happiness swept through her at the admission. *She* had been the reason he ran away, but not because of something dire. His own emotions overwhelmed him, provoked by his reactions to her. She struggled to suppress a grin. "That's a bad thing?"

His serious expression killed any hint of amusement. "Yes." Without elaborating, his body language made it clear losing control terrified him.

"I see." She tilted her head, thinking. Her body still burned for Grant, despite the turmoil of the last couple of hours. She wanted him, needed him in a way she hadn't with any other man. "What can I do?"

"Stay away from me." The words were delivered in an uncertain tone, contradicting the request.

Bolstered by the conflict in his eyes, Zinsa rose from the cot to walk over to his bed. Grant didn't withdraw when she stood before him, reaching out to cup his cheek with her palm. She knelt slightly to look into his eyes. "I can't do that. I need you, Grant." He drew in a breath when she trailed her fingers across his chest. "You need me too. Someone has to help you loosen up." She grinned at him to show she was teasing, as her hand drifted down his stomach to brush lightly against his cock. "Or maybe just to get you hard."

"Zinsa." The way he said her name sounded like he was being tortured. If his desire was as urgent as hers, he probably was. At least he'd found release earlier.

She grasped the length of his shaft. "Do you still want me to leave you alone?" While asking, she put a knee on the bed, by his thigh. "Should I stop?" The pressure she applied made his cock spasm in her hand.

"Never."

At his surrender, Zinsa put her other knee on the bed to straddle his lap. After he left her, she had dried off and put on a T-shirt, but she discarded it quickly, returning her hand to his erection in a matter of seconds. The thick length made her yearn to have it in her pussy, and it took an act of will to keep from guiding him inside, eliminating the few inches separating them.

She groaned with the frustration of holding off, knowing completion would be that much more satisfying if she prolonged the process leading up to it. Grant must have been of a similar mind, because his hand slipped between their bodies to take hers from his cock, instead placing it on his chest.

Leaning closer, Zinsa rested her cheek against his chest, breathing in his scent. He smelled of rain and wild things. It was exotic, and she responded instinctively. A sound like a purr escaped her when he cupped her breast, rolling the turgid nipple between his thumb and forefinger. It was a delicious sensation, but not so much because of the physical pleasure. Rather, it was being so close to him, hearing his ragged breath as he touched her. They were so close to being one, if only for a short time.

She tangled a hand in his wet hair to force his head down the required inches to meet hers. His mouth was open and his tongue met hers, pushing it back to investigate her mouth. A hint of metallic flavor sharpened his taste, making her draw back for just a second. Seeing his uncertainty, she leaned forward again, capturing his mouth, determined not to give him time for second thoughts. If she didn't come soon, she was going to explode, and only Grant could give her true fulfillment.

Pressed against him, his skin seemed to get hotter by the moment. Or maybe it came from her, as her need rose to a fever pitch. She couldn't distinguish the source. Perhaps they both generated the fire consuming them. That would be appropriate.

Her thoughts turned hazy when Grant lay back on the bed, pulling her on top of him. With seemingly little effort, he grasped her around the waist and lifted her higher, bringing her breasts to his mouth. For a second, he nuzzled the sensitive skin between her breasts, but soon his tongue was on a quest for a ripe nipple, taking a leisurely route around her breast, pausing to trace the outline of her areola.

Zinsa tossed back her head and arched her back, trying to force her nipple against his lips. A chuckle issued from him before he accepted the invitation, first flicking his tongue across the tip before drawing the bead into his mouth to suck lightly. The contact was like lightning striking, searing her whole body as the sensation radiated from the point of contact. The suction he initiated seemed to draw every nerve in her body to her breast. He flicked his tongue across the tip again, swirling the hardened peak and making her gasp. She arched her hips, seeking relief by rubbing her heated flesh against his stomach. It was a poor substitute for his cock, with the light dusting of hair serving only to inflame her even more.

She grasped his chest with her hands, seeking support, as his mouth sent her reeling. The brief respite as he switched to her other breast didn't clear her head. She didn't know why he feared losing control, but she could sense it in the way he held himself slightly separate from her. Zinsa could relate to Grant's dread as the frenzied passion consumed her.

His mouth was alternately gentle and rough at her breast, first biting, then soothing. The constant contrast made it impossible for her to find her way out of the seething storm of desire encompassing her. She was at his mercy, despite being the one on top.

A groan escaped her when Grant scooted down her body. Sure of his intent, knowing she would need an anchor if she didn't want to fly apart, she reached for the metal headboard, bracing herself while his tongue forged a path down her taut stomach. The first breath against her pussy was hot, but not as heated as the flesh it caressed. She arched her hips, straining to reach his tongue.

In response, he brought a hand up to cup her buttocks, holding her still so he could control the pace. Zinsa wanted to scream as his hesitation seemed to stretch to years. Knowing he was going slowly only to heighten her pleasure didn't ease her frustration.

When his tongue finally swept inside her slit, seeking out her clit with confident strokes, she shuddered. "Grant." Her throat seized when she spoke his name, making it come out as a guttural growl. She squeezed the bars of the headboard when Grant swirled his tongue around her clit, his hand still holding her bottom to prevent her from either withdrawing or pressing closer. Each teasing flick of his tongue, followed by a strong surge against her clit, drove rational thought from her mind.

Zinsa became a creature of sensation, held captive by expectation of his next move. She lived for the touch of his tongue, the wisp of his heavy breathing as he consumed the juices of her passion. A scream threatened to tear from her throat when his tongue plunged deep into her opening, exploring the moist cavern where his cock would soon venture. Only knowing the patients in the other room would hear kept her from giving voice to her pleasure.

Deep inside, convulsions began in her womb, emanating outward, as if trying to trap his tongue. Her clit ached for release, and as his tongue thrust in and out of her, her pussy tightened. What little control she had left fled as an orgasm swept over her, inducing her to cry out. Although vaguely aware of Grant's hand clamping over her mouth, she couldn't stifle the cries of pleasure as release freed her for the moment from her body, casting her spirit adrift into a universe of velvet sensation.

Gradually she regained control and was able to stop making the animalistic sounds of joy. When his hand moved from her mouth, she managed a smile, but words were beyond her while she struggled to breathe normally.

His hands moved to her hips, holding her up a few inches as he moved higher, until his head was against the wall, his back cradled by the pillow against the headboard. The new position brought his cock against her slick pussy, and she shifted slightly to cuddle the head inside her folds.

A scarlet flush scorched his face, indicating he wasn't unaffected by the moment. It took him a couple of deep breaths to be able to speak. "I don't have any protection. It's been ages since I needed it..." He trailed off, looking hopeful. "Do you have condoms in your stash of medical supplies?"

"Um hmm." She stretched forward sinuously, brushing her nipples against his chest. "Too far away, though. I need you now."

A wrinkle of worry marred his brow. "We shouldn't—"

She touched her fingers to his lips. "It's fine. Really. I'm protected, and I'm clean." Her lips twitched. "Since it's been ages, I assume you are, too?"

Grant's affirmative turned to a gasp when Zinsa sat down fully, taking his cock deep inside her. She uttered a gasp of her own at the stretched sensation filling her, the slight burning that was almost painful. For just a second, she thought she couldn't take his girth, but a slight shift forward eased the way, allowing her sheath to clamp around him.

"God. You're so tight." He forced the words through clenched teeth. A rapidly pounding vein in his forehead betrayed his struggle for control, making her all the more determined to send him over the edge as he had done to her.

Slowly, she circled her pelvis while rocking up and down. A smothered curse proved she was having an effect, and she increased her pace. Doing so caused a new wave of pleasure to sweep through her, scattering her thoughts. She grasped his shoulders and rode him at a furious pace, striving to take in every inch of him. His heavy breathing mirrored hers, and the way he uttered her name several times told her he was close to coming.

Zinsa lost herself in the rhythm of their thrusts, the flex of her pussy around his convulsing cock, and the pleasure sparking through her body. Time lost all meaning as she straddled him, straining for completion. It might have been seconds or hours later when she cried out as her climax overwhelmed her. Reflexively, her hips kept rocking against him as her pussy convulsed with release, prolonging the moment. A gray fog blurred her vision, and she slumped forward, aware of Grant's arms enfolding her tenderly as she lay against his chest.

Awareness returned slowly as Grant disengaged their bodies and turned them onto their sides, keeping her held close to him. The aftermath washed her in a golden glow of peace, and she recognized the holistic completion of all of her. What had been missing wasn't any longer. Grant had filled the vaguely aching void inside her. Not just with sex either. It went deeper than that. Her brain fluttered cautiously around labeling the emotions she experienced, not quite sure if she could really believe in love at first sight, but also convinced this was more than just an intense sexual attraction.

The events of the day caught up with her, weighing Zinsa's eyelids. Sleep stole over her, and it was just as she was about to surrender to its embrace that she realized Grant hadn't come. His muscles were still knotted with tension, and he didn't seem to have the air of contentment she'd found. She wanted to analyze the moment, but sleep caught her in its net, dragging her down. As she slipped away, Zinsa realized there was still something missing. The emptiness was between them, not inside her.

# Chapter Four

೫

Grant's behavior the next morning reinforced Zinsa's conclusion. He was distant and withdrawn. He could barely contain his relief when a call came in on the radio set in his office requesting him onsite at an injury. Taking a bit of perverse pleasure from doing so, she went over to him after he signed off, saying, "I'll come with you. I've already discharged two of the patients, and the clinic isn't open today. I want to see you work."

"Uh—"

She trailed a hand up his biceps, encased in a thin white T-shirt. "Unless you don't want me?"

He swallowed audibly. "I'd be happy to have company."

Zinsa winced at his words, reading more into them than perhaps he meant—as if anyone would do, and she was nothing special. Her heart hurt contemplating that, because after last night, she wanted to be very special to Grant. She just had to get past the wall he had erected between them first.

They took the Land Rover. Settled beside Grant as they bounced over the sometimes-rough terrain, following the worn tracks when they could, while navigating through the veld when they had to, she regretted coming. His silence repudiated her, just as the set of his shoulders and general body language communicated his withdrawal. Whatever she had hoped to accomplish when she'd had the inspiration to tag along seemed doomed to fail, especially since she couldn't clearly identify her objective.

"Brace yourself."

She blinked with surprise at the first words he had uttered in ten minutes, barely getting over her stupefaction in time to grasp the handle above the Land Rover's door as they splashed through an opaque stream, which cut through the grassland. The tires seemed to protest navigating the muddy banks for just a second before getting traction and conveying them safely to the other side. The resulting jolt made her teeth snap together and induced a small headache.

"I wasn't expecting it to be so rough." She had known most of the preserve was untamed, populated by wild herds and their predators, but only in an abstract way, having never spent much time driving through the rough and wild areas of Mekimba. Her clinic was on the main road leading from Natunde, the nearest town. It was a five-mile drive down well-worn paths, deep with tire ruts. She'd had no reason to venture off the trails, until now.

He glanced briefly at her before returning his attention to the veld, following the faint path a vehicle had forged previously. "Are you sorry you came?"

Instead of answering, Zinsa turned her head to look out the window, staring at the golden grass without really seeing it. She refused to answer, because she didn't know her reply. It appeared to be futile to tag along today, but his question seemed to be probing a deeper issue. Was he referring to last night, when she came, but he didn't? Well, not after his blowjob, she silently amended. It shouldn't bother her so much that he hadn't climaxed again. Physiologically, it wasn't that unusual. It was the accompanying emotional withdrawal that had her so confused.

If he thought her lack of reply strange, he didn't say so. The silence lapsed again, lasting until they rounded the bend and came upon a herd of impalas. Nearby, one of the rangers stood beside his Jeep. He lifted an arm to flag them down, and as Grant parked behind his Jeep, Zinsa saw two other rangers on ATVs off to the side. Her brow knitted with confusion as she climbed from the Land Rover, wondering what was happening. All Grant had said was there was an injured animal.

After retrieving his black bag from the back seat, Grant walked over to James. Uncertainly, she trailed behind, hovering near them while doing her best not to intrude.

"What do we have?"

"An injured impala, Doc." James pointed in the direction of the herd. "See the little one there? It hasn't gotten up in at least an hour. I've seen it move, but I can't assess the injuries." He moved his hand to indicate the two rangers waiting on ATVs. "I couldn't segregate the calf from the herd until they arrived, and they only beat you by a couple of minutes, so we decided to wait."

With a terse nod, Grant turned toward the herd. He glanced over his shoulder. "Stay back, Zinsa. Impalas are usually placid, but you never know when there's been an attack. The herd is skittish."

At his words, she looked more closely at the herd. At first glance, they were little more than a blur of chestnut-brown and white, but when she peered closer, she could see the restless shifting of the members. Their noses twitched and their postures suggested they would bolt at any moment.

Their air of fear increased when the ATVs roared to life, heading straight toward the herd. Outraged on their behalf, Zinsa almost spoke up, until she realized the two rangers were only culling the injured calf from the herd by forcing the other animals to move back. To her surprise, the impalas scattered, but didn't flee with panic. They must have been through the procedure before.

When Grant walked toward the calf, she couldn't contain her curiosity and followed. As he knelt by the injured animal, she stood a few feet away, close enough to observe, but far enough back to keep out of his way.

The calf made a low bleating sound when he reached out to touch it. Her stomach clenched with an indescribable emotion at the gentle way he caressed the baby while speaking to it in a soothing tone. His movements were careful and slow as he reached into his bag for a stethoscope.

Emboldened, Zinsa moved closer to stand beside James, who was splitting his attention between the herd, the frantic calf, and a lone female who had split off from the others. "Is that the mother?"

He nodded. "How did you guess?"

"She hasn't torn her gaze from Grant and the baby. Her fear is different than the others. She seems more worried about the little one than herself." She shrugged. "I've seen it countless times with my patients." Zinsa gestured to the baby, who seemed to have calmed after its initial fearful reaction to Grant. "What happened to it?"

"It was attacked." James took a step closer, hunching slightly to point out the gaping gash on its side. "Looks like a big cat...lion or tiger, maybe."

She frowned when Grant flinched. "Is everything okay, Grant?"

He nodded, not looking up. "I think the baby will be fine." He sounded choked, and his movements were jerky when he removed a bottle of antiseptic and a roll of gauze from the bag. As soon as he started treatment, his hands became steady, and the moment passed.

Within minutes, he had cleaned the wound, stitched it up, and administered a shot of antibiotic, saying in an offhand way, "There's no point in bandaging. The little one would have it off in no time."

Finally, he got to his feet, closing his bag as he did so. The rangers on the ATVs must have realized he was finished, because they revved their engines in preparation to move away from the herd. The calf cried out as it tried to get to its feet when the ATVs came closer.

Apparently, it was too much for the mother. With a cry of her own, one of angry desperation, she came running toward them. As she did so, a large male broke from the herd, falling into place beside her, butting her with his body. His intent was ambiguous, but their path wasn't—they were headed straight for the calf and anyone in the way.

Seeing them bearing down, Zinsa ran, as did the others. From the corner of her eye, she saw James going in the opposite direction from her. The rangers on the ATVs had driven out of range. She froze, whipping around in search of Grant. Her heart swelled with relief when she caught sight of him, but a gasp of horror escaped her when she realized he was still with the calf, trying to get it to its feet and out of the way of the approaching male and female.

It happened almost too quickly for her eyes to follow. One second, he had the calf on its feet, slapping its haunch to get it running, and the next, he was flying through the air, propelled by the antlers extending from the male's head.

As quickly as it began, it was over. The male herded the female and her calf back to the others, losing all interest in Grant. Even as the impalas were still near him, she was running to reach Grant, uncaring if it was safe yet.

At his side, she dropped to her knees. She winced when she saw the wound. The male had gored Grant's shoulder, his antler going in at least three inches. Blood flowed freely, soaking his white T-shirt. Managing a shaky smile, she asked, "Are you with me?"

A groan escaped him, and his eyes opened. "Damn, that hurt."

His color seemed good in spite of the blood loss, and she was encouraged by his ability to sit up on his own, albeit with a few more curses. Zinsa reached for his bag and unsnapped it. A quick look revealed a pair of scissors and a fresh roll of gauze. Other treatment would have to wait until they got back to the clinic.

"This might hurt." As gently as possible, she pulled the fabric from the wound, using the scissors to trim a circle in the cotton. The wound looked awful, although it could have been much worse. He would certainly need stitches and an antibiotic to prevent infection, since puncture wounds could turn nasty in no time.

"How bad is it?" he asked in a raspy voice.

Zinsa unwound a handful of gauze, clipping the appropriate length. "You'll live, but the trip back isn't going to be fun." She paused in her ministrations to push the hair off his forehead. "Do you have something for pain in your bag?"

"Just morphine." Teeth clenched, he shook his head. "I don't want that."

Gently, she pressed the crude square of gauze against the wound. His face paled, and he expelled his breath with a gasp of air. "Are you sure you don't want it? The ride back to the clinic won't be easy."

A brittle smile eclipsed his lips. "I'll be fine. I hate being drugged. It's a control thing."

Zinsa let a long sigh be her only response to indicate she disagreed with his decision. At her nod, James and one of the rangers she hadn't been introduced to came forward, kneeling beside Grant to help him to his feet. With his teeth clenched so hard his lips bowed outward, he got upright without crying out. His color didn't improve, but he didn't pale any further. To her relief, he managed to walk to the Land Rover with only some minor assistance from James on his uninjured side.

She followed behind, carrying his bag, while doing her best to hide her fear. His injury wasn't what frightened her. She had seen and dealt with worse. What kept her heart pumping was replaying the scene in her mind over and over, with each rerun having more dire outcomes than the one before. By the time she reached the vehicle, her hands were shaking, and she had to stand outside taking deep breaths to gain some measure of control before opening the driver's side door to slip into the plush leather seat.

James settled Grant into the passenger side, keeping his elbow braced on the armrest between the seats. Perspiration dotted his forehead, and his eyes were closed. His breathing was deep and regular, so she wasn't worried about him as much as she might have if the wound was lower. What frightened her most was the amount of blood he already lost and would continue to lose during the ride back to the clinic.

Focused on Grant as she was, Zinsa started when James leaned his head in her window. She bit back a cry of shock and tried to force a smile. "Thanks for helping get him in."

"No problem, Doctor." He nodded to Grant. "I'll follow you back to the clinic and help you unload him."

"Thanks, that would be great." With a nod, he turned and started toward his Jeep. "Oh, wait." James paused, turning in her direction. "Could you go first? I'm not certain I remember the way back."

His wide smile highlighted the sparkling white of his teeth against his matte black skin. "Of course, but if you get lost, just follow the recent tire marks."

Zinsa nodded and started the Land Rover, waiting until James had climbed in his vehicle and started forward before turning the wheel to follow him. Almost immediately, she hit a bump that jostled the car, provoking a groan from Grant. "How are you?"

"Fine," he said without opening his eyes. It sounded as though he spoke through gritted teeth, and when she glanced at him, he seemed to be using every ounce of his strength to get through the journey. She decided not to make him use any reserves to answer questions unless his condition took a turn for the worse.

Somehow, she managed to divide her attention between the crude path and Grant as she followed James's Jeep back to the clinic. What had been a rough ride before now seemed a never-ending series of hurdles to cross, with each one designed to wring the maximum amount of pain from her silent passenger. Her nerves were stretched to the breaking point by the time they left behind the rough veld and emerged onto the paved path that extended about a mile past the compound.

The last mile passed quickly, without the jarring that plagued the earlier part of the trip. When she shut off the Land

Rover in front of the clinic, Zinsa wiped a hand down her sweaty face. She took a moment to breathe deeply to restore calm before unfastening her seat belt and opening the car door. By the time she slid from the vehicle and walked around to Grant's side, James had assisted him from the Land Rover and had him on his feet. Together, with her walking on Grant's other side for added support, they led him inside the clinic.

"Where do you want him, Doctor?"

Zinsa cast a glance around the small treatment room, already crammed with patients. The exam table reserved for her was free, but he would need to rest after the treatment. With a decisive nod, she said, "His bed, back this way. It's where he'll be most comfortable." She angled her body in the right direction, somewhat taking the lead, while still assisting Grant.

Once James helped her settle Grant on the bed, he took his leave with a nod. Zinsa followed behind him to fetch supplies from the front of the building. On the way back, she took time to close the door separating the living quarters from the clinic. It would assure a measure of privacy while she treated him, which she needed. Having her patients see her shaken state wouldn't bolster their confidence in her. Revealing any hint of weakness would drive away the people she was committed to helping, but she couldn't hide her vulnerability when it came to Grant. Even knowing the wound wasn't life threatening, save for the blood loss, she couldn't get a handle on her emotions.

But she didn't have the luxury of indulging in her weakness right then, she reminded herself. He needed a physician. Later she could become the weepy girlfriend and indulge in gruesome visions of all the dire outcomes that could have happened.

Girlfriend? Was that the right word? As she mulled over the question, Zinsa checked Grant's pulse, finding it stable and strong. His breathing was even, and his color had improved again since he was liberated from the vehicle and laid on the bed. At the touch of her fingers on his forehead, his eyes fluttered open, temporarily clouded with confusion. When he blinked, he seemed coherent again. "You're back." The steady pitch of her words pleased her, indicating she was regaining control.

"When was I gone?"

She assessed his condition to make sure he wasn't suffering from confusion and determined he was trying to tease her. "I guess you weren't, but you had me worried." Going through the familiar motions, such as stripping off the T-shirt and examining the wound more thoroughly, restored the rest of her professionalism, allowing her to do the job at hand.

"Sorry." He grimaced when she irrigated the wound. "Didn't mean to worry you."

Zinsa looked away from the injury to meet his gaze. "I don't want to lose you, Grant." Quickly, she dropped her eyes back to his shoulder, disconcerted by the intensity of her words. Now wasn't the time to delve into relationship matters.

To her surprise, he tipped up her chin with the hand of his good arm, locking eyes with her. "I don't want to lose you either, Zinsa." A deep sigh escaped him, and he released his hold. "Seems inevitable though."

She wanted to pursue the subject, but it was clear he didn't have the strength to discuss the matter thoroughly. He was already fading, and by the time she gave him an injection to help him rest and ease the pain, he would be out for hours. She would just have to wait until he woke up to assess his condition. If he was stronger then, they could have a talk. Her impatience had to take a backseat to his welfare for the moment.

# Chapter Five

જી

Zinsa was trying to immerse herself in a novel, but having little luck, when Grant awakened three hours later. As soon as his eyes fluttered open, she dropped the book and hurried to the bed, immediately touching his forehead. To her relief, he was cool, and his color had improved dramatically. "How do you feel?"

"Better." A groan escaped him when he shifted into a sitting position, bracing his back with pillows propped against the headboard.

She peeled back the pad to examine the wound. There was a bit of seepage around the stitches, and it had taken on a reddish tint, but the antibiotics she had injected into him should keep an infection from forming. As long as he healed cleanly, there was little to worry about. "Can I get you something? Food, water?"

"I'm starving." His free hand clamped around her forearm, drawing her down onto the bed beside him. "For you."

An undignified giggle escaped her when Grant nuzzled her neck, finding a ticklish spot. The physician in her tried to take charge, and she wriggled far enough away to avoid his teasing lips. "We shouldn't. Your shoulder—"

"Has nothing to do with my cock." His voice dropped as his hand moved from her arm to between her thighs. "Or your pussy."

Uncertain, she drew back to look into his eyes, finding them dark with hunger. The injury didn't seem to have slowed him down, and surely he would know whether or not he was capable of making love. "As your doctor, I still say we shouldn't do this." She relaxed, melting into him, and sighing when his lips brushed her neck. "As your lover, I'm all for it."

His breath washed over her neck when he chuckled, heightening already sensitive nerve endings and sending a shiver down her spine. She curled as close to him as she could while still avoiding his shoulder. Grant placed his injured arm around her, and the warmth of his hand seemed to burn through the thin fabric of her T-shirt.

Grant's lips drifted down the column of her throat, seeking out the sensitive spot where her neck and shoulder met. Zinsa yelped with surprised pleasure when he nipped the area forcefully, drawing skin into his mouth to suckle. A rush of moisture flooded her pussy as he sucked, and she writhed against him, trying to turn her body to more fully press against his.

His groan of pain made her freeze, and she looked up at him, too turned on to be completely objective. "Do you need to stop?" Please, no. She needed him too badly.

A shake of his head filled her with relief, and she stretched upward, straining her neck to reach his mouth. He met her partway, dipping his neck, and their lips met with explosive intensity, tongues dueling for entrance to the other's mouth. Satisfaction swept through her when she yielded to him, and his tongue invaded her mouth. Each dart and thrust ignited pulses of electricity throughout her body. Submission wasn't a bad thing, she decided, as Grant shifted positions, bringing her onto her back so he could lie on top of her.

By some magic of motion, Grant managed to keep his lips locked with hers, his tongue constantly stroking, while his hands pushed up the hem of her T-shirt above her breasts. Wowed by his dexterity and heated kisses, Zinsa couldn't seem to find the impetus to help him with the bra.

Not that he needed any assistance, as evidenced by his smooth unhooking of the front clasp. When his hands cupped her breasts, as his legs supported his weight to keep from crushing her, she was thankful she had selected the front-opening bra. It made instant access so much easier.

Grant turned his head slightly, his mouth leaving hers. Zinsa's lips pressed against his cheek, and she licked the skin offered to her, pleased to feel him shudder at the sensation.

"I love your breasts. They're perfect." He squeezed lightly for emphasis, rubbing his thumbs over the plump nipples. "Like firm melons, with juicy berry nipples."

Amid laughter, Zinsa asked, "Are you going to eat me or fuck me?"

He turned his head again to look into her eyes. "Both, love."

The husky promise made her pussy convulse with anticipation, and she wrapped her thighs around his legs, arching her hips in search of relief. "Get to it then."

A grin slipped over his face, visible for just seconds, as his body slithered down hers. "Yes, ma'am."

Her nipple hardened to the point of pain as his mouth reached it, his breath fanning over the taut peak. Restlessly, she lifted her back, trying to find his mouth, but he hovered just out of reach. She groaned, frustrated at his teasing, and then jumped with surprise when he licked her nipple. That sensation had barely been processed when he blew on her bud again, making her cry out. It was exquisite, causing shudders of pleasure to rack her body. Giving her no time to assimilate or recover, Grant repeated the process several times, until she was a wriggling mass of pure sensation, aching for his cock.

"Do you like that?" he asked against her breast, his lips tickling her nipple.

"It's wonderful." Zinsa brought up her hand to cup her ignored breast, offering it to him. "But this one feels neglected."

Grant gingerly lifted his torso, switching his angle to bring his mouth to the needy breast. A grimace of pain flashed across his face, but disappeared as he dipped his head. "We can't have that." His mouth engulfed her nipple and a good portion of her breast as he sucked with enthusiasm, each rhythmic tug of his mouth on her nipple causing her body to lift from the mattress in frantic arches.

Zinsa buried her fingers in his hair, holding his head securely against her, relishing the careful attention of his diligent tongue as he nibbled, flicked and swirled his way over her areola, moving toward the valley of her breasts. When he reached the area, Grant paused, drawing in the scent of her. Instinctively, she mimicked the motion, drawing in a deep breath, cherishing his richly masculine aroma.

His tongue traced an elaborate pattern over her skin as he inched his way downward, taking time to explore every inch of her chest as he went. With his mouth busy at her stomach, blowing gentle breaths across damp trails left by his tongue, Zinsa's tummy quivered continuously and her pussy soon picked up the rhythm, convulsing in time with his breaths.

One of Grant's fingers traced her rib cage, taking time to become intimately familiar with the shape and length of each rib. It shouldn't have been erotic, but it was, feeling even better than his soft kisses and light nibbling near her belly button.

Her breath caught in her throat when he finally went lower, his breath caressing her mound, as his hand left her ribs to stroke the neatly trimmed hair shielding her pussy. Arousal flowed from her in torrents and she marveled at how her body could continue to react so vigorously to the prolonged foreplay.

Any thoughts of biology fled when Grant buried his face between her thighs, his tongue squirming inside her slit to taste her with broad strokes. Whimpering with need, she bucked her hips against his face, crying out each time his tongue touched her clit.

His strokes started randomly, but soon he had narrowed in on the space between her clitoris and opening, taking leisurely swipes up and down the sensitive area, just barely flirting with her clit or teasing her opening before repeating the process. She was close to screaming with frustration, made all the worse by his other hand on her hip that restricted her ability to arch her hips.

"Please, Grant, I need your cock."

He didn't reply, but his tongue thrust into her opening to sweep the walls of her pussy as it contracted. Without thought, Zinsa tightened her hands into fists, eliciting a sound of protest from Grant when she accidentally pulled his hair. Good, she thought with a twinge of satisfaction. If he was going to keep her in this constant state of pleasure, bordering on pain, he deserved an equal measure. If she were more coherent, she would figure out how to do that, but her brain was mush under his passionate ministrations.

A gasp left her when Grant's tongue surged upward to caress her clit just before he sucked it into his mouth. "Oh, God, more. I need you inside me."

In response, the hand that had parted her lips shifted, and two of his fingers plunged deeply inside her wet heat. At the same time, he eased his hold on her hip, allowing her to thrust freely as she writhed against his face, wanting as much of his fingers as she could take, while shuddering under the onslaught of his tongue on her clit.

When a third finger entered her, Zinsa's thrusting took on a frenetic pace. She couldn't breathe, needing to come so badly. Her pussy convulsed, and she was on the edge of release when Grant's fingers left her opening. If she'd had voice to protest the withdrawal, she would have, but could only ride out the tumultuous sensations storming through her, waiting to see what he would do next.

She hoped he was finally going to fuse their bodies, but instead his fingers, slick with her arousal, slid lower, seeking out her anus. Without thought, she clenched her anal muscles, babbling an incoherent sound to object. Either he didn't hear her or he decided to make her say no plainly, because his middle finger probed her anus, circling gently. It was so foreign, but his massage felt good, and her muscles relaxed enough to permit his finger to slide inside an inch. Zinsa groaned at the invasion, expecting pain, but receiving pleasure instead.

"More." The request was a guttural expletive more than a real word, but he must have recognized the syllables, because his finger penetrated her fully, having easy passage once he had passed the tight seal of her sphincter. His rate was slow, in contrast to his greedy mouth devouring her clit, as he thrust his finger in and out of her.

Zinsa found it impossible to buck her hips with his mouth on her pussy and his finger in her back passage. She was forced to lie still under the ardent blitz, surprised to find it so pleasurable to be at his mercy. Within seconds, her orgasm had peaked again, and she trembled on the edge of coming. When Grant's thumb plunged inside her pussy to fuck her in concert with his finger in her ass, release came in an instant, so potent it almost made her scream. She bit hard on her tongue to hold in her cries of satisfaction as her body pulsed and thrummed with the power of her orgasm.

Tremors suffused her body, scattering all thought or awareness, except for the pleasure consuming her. Never in her life had climax been so intense, and she wanted to revel in the moment. The compulsion was almost as strong as the one telling her to mount Grant and ride him to another peak. The need to have him inside her won out, because as satisfying as the orgasm had been, there was still something missing. She didn't want him leading her to release. She wanted him along with her, as helplessly lost to passion as she had been.

As she came back to herself, Grant shifted to lie beside her on his side, his stomach pressed against her ribs. He brushed a gentle kiss across her sweaty forehead before tucking her close to his body.

A frown furrowed her brow. He seemed to be settling in for the night. The heavy weight of his cock pushing into her hip indicated he was far from release. "Grant?"

"Hm?" He sounded sleepy.

"Don't you want to make love?"

His chin rubbed against the top of her head. "I thought we just did."

"Yes…no…sort of."

His chuckle had a strange edge. "Which is it, love?"

Zinsa sighed with frustration, struggling to articulate her emotions. "You made love to me. We didn't make love."

"What's the difference?"

She grasped the length of his cock in her palm, squeezing lightly. "This is the difference. What you did to me was wonderful, but what about you?"

Releasing a deep breath, Grant said, "I don't feel up to it right now."

On their short acquaintance, it should have been impossible for her to detect that he was lying simply from the slight change of pitch in his voice, but she could. Maybe it wasn't so strange, because she felt like she knew him on many levels, except the most intimate, where he wouldn't let her in. "Your cock tells a different story." She stroked him, and he convulsed in her hand.

Grant's arm slipped between their bodies, and he captured her wrist, moving her hand to his stomach. "My cock would always be ready for you, but my arm is sore, and I think whatever was in that shot you gave me is still having an effect."

With a sigh, she let him have his way. Knowing he was being deceptive and proving it were two different things. It was conceivable the Demerol had left him groggy, and maybe his shoulder was acting up again, but they weren't his primary reasons for avoiding intercourse. No, it was something deeper and much more confusing. She suspected it still had to do with his issues of control, but wasn't up to the long talk she had planned for during the time he rested. Right then, she just wanted to surrender to sleep in his arms, letting her mind pretend everything was perfect, if only for a little while.

\* \* \* \* \*

After sleeping fitfully, Grant sneaked out of bed early the next morning when the first streaks of dawn lit the sky. Not wanting to wake Zinsa and face the questions he could practically feel hanging between them, he dressed in a hurry, wincing at the stiffness in his shoulder. He spared only a minute to scrawl a note for her, using the pretext of checking on the injured impala to explain his early departure, before heading off to the bunkhouse's communal showers.

The shower refreshed him, and turning the knob to cold for the last few seconds had finally eased the constant ache in his groin that had assaulted him last night, when he refused to come. The pain had been nearly unbearable for a few minutes there, and only the fear of transforming in front of Zinsa stopped him from plunging his cock inside her throbbing pussy, so slick with her arousal.

He bit back a groan as he walked to the Land Rover, sliding into the driver's seat in an awkward step up, careful to keep pressure from his wounded arm. He mentally thanked Manu for having at least one automatic vehicle on the preserve as he put the key in the ignition and fired the engine. Shifting would have been impossible in his current state, making escape that much harder.

Grant tried to ignore the voice in the back of his mind calling him cowardly as he drove down the lane, hoping to have an easy time finding the impala herd. After checking on the baby he had injured in his wild state, he would try to figure out what to do about Zinsa. Telling her the truth was an option that didn't even enter into his brain.

\* \* \* \* \*

After his strange behavior the night before, she wasn't taken aback by waking alone, but was surprised he had taken time to write a brief note. The explanation was terse, and he hadn't bothered to sign his name, but she supposed she should feel grateful he had acknowledged she would wonder about his whereabouts.

Zinsa wasn't feeling particularly grateful when she left the bed and padded to the shower, immersing herself in a tepid spray as her anger simmered, slowly reaching a boil. Was it silly to feel used when he was the one who hadn't climaxed? All the pleasure had been directed toward her, but in the cold light of day, it all seemed clinical and detached on his part, as if he had deliberately seduced her to forestall talking.

The rough towel left marks on her skin from her rubbing so hard, caught in the grip of her annoyance. For lack of a better target, she tossed it on the floor and kicked it away once her skin was dry. Glaring into the small mirror, Zinsa saw Grant's face the way it had been last night, instead of her own. There hadn't been any mistaking his withdrawal from her, despite the close physical proximity he had maintained until she fell asleep. After that, who knew? She had rested more deeply than she could recall in recent months, but any sense of peace she had garnered from the sleep had fled upon waking alone.

She dressed without paying much attention to clothing choices, her hands automatically opting for comfortable favorites, while her mind whirled with confusion. What was she going to do about Grant? Chances were good she would soon be able to return to her clinic, since the news was reporting the guerillas were withdrawing from the area, with the army in pursuit. Should she pretend that nothing had happened between them, that she hadn't inherited the family "curse" of instantly recognizing her soul mate? Was that even possible?

Taking several deep breaths, Zinsa calmed herself, knowing she couldn't be an emotional wreck and give optimal care to her patients. The simple truth was, she couldn't make any decisions on her own, at least not yet. First, she had to talk to Grant, really talk to him, to see how he felt. If he didn't share her emotions, she would have no choice but to withdraw. But if he did, he better have a damned good reason for the way he was acting.

\* \* \* \* \*

The patients made it easier for Zinsa to forget her angst, and she immersed herself in their care, doing her best to juggle all the tasks single-handedly. About an hour after opening the clinic for the day, Amani, the mother of the only child among her patients, offered her services in a quiet voice. Although she had no formal medical training, she wasn't afraid to help lift patients, clean messes or fetch supplies.

As they worked together, Zinsa made a mental note to offer Amani a position when she reopened the clinic, knowing the woman had no other source of income. Her husband had been one of the men killed in a village raid by the national army a few miles away. During the attack, a stray bullet had caught her daughter in the thigh. By the time Amani had carried her to the clinic the next day, a serious infection had set in, requiring massive doses of IV antibiotics and constant care.

While Hasina was being treated, Amani had found little time to worry about the future, but Zinsa knew it weighed heavily on her and hoped the offer of employment would ease her mind a bit.

The stream of patients slowed to a trickle abruptly. One moment, there were twenty or more people in line, and when she looked up a couple of minutes later, there was only a young man left, waiting for her to finish vaccinating the boy on the table. A deep gash across his check wept blood, and she gestured him forward as Amani lifted the boy from the table and passed him to his anxious mother. In a flash, the woman propped him on her hip and rushed out the door.

"What in the world?" Zinsa shook her head, exchanging a concerned glance with Amani.

"Soldiers are coming, Mrs. Doctor," said the young man, surely no older than fifteen, as he stepped forward. "I saw them a mile or so back and ran away." A visible shudder racked his body. "I do not want to fight for them."

Zinsa nodded, changing her gloves as the boy climbed onto the table. It didn't matter if the boy had seen guerilla warriors or national military. Either group was as likely to co-opt him into service, with or without his consent. "What happened to your face?" The wound bled copiously, but didn't look as deep as she first thought upon closer examination.

A sheepish expression crossed his face. "I ran so fast I fell."

She chuckled. "Good thing you found your way here."

His eyes reflected his fear. "I came to warn everyone. Batonga's forces are sweeping all the buildings in search of guerillas and sympathizers. The president is determined to eradicate all of them." His voice lowered an octave, and his eyes skittered around the room before he said, "My father is a soldier fighting for Batonga's displacement. Early yesterday, he and his regiment pulled out of the area. Do you think he will be all right?"

A sigh escaped Zinsa as she searched for an answer to placate the boy without offering false hope. "As a soldier, I'm sure he knows how to take care of himself."

The boy nodded, looking thoughtful. His expression changed to a grimace when Zinsa daubed the wound with antiseptic. "The stinging eases in a second."

"I don't feel anything," he said with transparent bravado.

She barely smothered a grin at his typical teenage male attitude. "Good. Are you afraid of needles?"

His dark complexion seemed grayer when he said, "Of course not," in a higher pitch.

"Amani, could you hand me that tray?" Zinsa took it from her, selecting a syringe with a small needle. "I'm going to numb the area, and then I'll get you stitched up."

He didn't protest, although Zinsa thought he might pass out when she brought the needle closer to his face. Once past that hurdle, he seemed fine, and she had him lie back while she stitched up the wound. A few minutes later she affixed a bandage and stepped back, peeling off her gloves. "All done."

"Thank you." His voice was reed-thin, but he sat up and stood without falling. Appearing a bit shaky, the boy reached into his pocket. "This is all I have, Mrs. Doctor. Will it be enough?"

A lump clogged Zinsa's throat when she took the delicate locket from the young boy. The gold was tarnished, and it was obviously cheap, but the way he held it indicated it was of great value to him. She turned it over, and the weak latch popped open, displaying a picture of a young African woman with a beautiful smile. She held a little boy on her lap.

"It was my mother's."

She cleared her throat to speak. "I can't take this."

His mouth firmed. "I must pay my debts, Mrs. Doctor."

Zinsa forced her emotions in check, nodding firmly. "Absolutely, but the locket is too valuable to cover a paltry stitching." Seeing the hope shining in his eyes, she extended the locket while searching for a way to allow the young man to settle his debt. "If you're agreeable, the clinic needs cleaning. If you will mop the floors, that will be sufficient."

"I would be happy to." His eagerness dimmed when his eyes moved to the door. "What about the soldiers, Mrs. Doctor?"

She patted his arm, forcing herself to sound confident. "If they come to the preserve, they will look in the buildings and be gone as soon as they realize there is no rebel army here."

"Yes, Mrs. Doctor."

"Zinsa."

Looking uncertain, he nodded. "I am Kumi."

"Come along, Kumi, and I'll show you where to find the mop." Zinsa led him to the cleaning supply closet and set the boy to work before going to the door of the clinic to put up her handwritten sign, informing prospective patients she would be closed the rest of the afternoon. Surely by tomorrow the soldiers would be out of the area, and business would again be brisk.

# Chapter Six

ॐ

Unspoken fear of the soldiers hung in the air and it was almost a relief to see them march into the complex an hour later. Zinsa watched through the window as the group of approximately thirty broke off into six smaller units to search each building in the complex. Her stomach curled with dread when a cluster of five men, all wearing the red and gray militia uniform, headed toward the clinic. Each man had a sidearm in his hip holster, and two carried machine guns. Knowing the damage any of their weapons could do, she wanted to get them in and out as quickly as possible.

She was on her way to unlock the clinic door when the men reached the porch. Their boots thundered over the solid frame as they rushed forward, and something solid slammed into the door seconds later. Zinsa opened it, barely concealing her fear when she saw a tall man standing before her, the butt of his gun inches from her. That must have been what he pounded against the door. "Yes?" To her credit, her voice emerged steadily, sounding only mildly interested, not terrified.

"By order of President Batonga, we are here to search the premises for any insurrectionists." His eyes gleamed when he scanned her. "They will be executed on sight."

She stepped back, holding open the door to let them enter. "You won't find any here."

He made a gruff sound in his throat, one that might have been an expression of disappointment. With terse hand movements, he directed the others with him to enter and fan out. As they did so, he went to the main room, throwing back the sheets she had arranged for the privacy of the patients to separate them from the treatment area. "Who are these people?"

Zinsa stepped in front of him. "They're my patients."

His eyes narrowed. "Why do you have human patients on an animal preserve, vet?"

"I'm a doctor. Until the fighting got too close, I ran a clinic a few miles down the road. My friend offered me a place to treat people. There is never a shortage, thanks to the war." Zinsa bit her tongue to quell the tirade she wanted to launch into. He didn't seem like the kind of man who would accept a dressing down from anyone, especially a woman.

A grunt left him, and he pushed her aside, approaching the beds. His finger stayed on the trigger of the machine gun as he examined each patient in turn, starting with the old man incapacitated by pneumonia. His eyes dismissed him and the older women, but sparked with interest when lighting on Amani, who had curled onto the bed beside her daughter, holding her close. He uttered an ambiguous sound, but was distracted from whatever he was thinking by the arrival of his troops.

Zinsa barely caught back a gasp of horror when she saw one of the men dragging Kumi forward, shoving him to the floor at the leader's feet.

"I found this one in the bathroom, Major Natufa."

Natufa nodded, eyeing Kumi with cold eyes. "Why were you hiding, boy?"

Kumi shook his head, his eyes staying glued to the floor.

"Speak." His boot tried to provide motivation by connecting with Kumi's thigh.

"Stop it." Without thought, Zinsa surged forward, placing herself between Natufa and Kumi. "He's frightened."

"What does he have to be frightened of? We are the military of the people." He spat in Kumi's direction. "Only the dissenters need fear us, the cowardly lot."

"They aren't cowards," Kumi burst out, lifting his head. His eyes gleamed with anger. "They fight for the people, while your president cares for nothing but himself."

"Kumi—" Any words of caution she might have issued were lost when Natufa shoved her aside so he could lift Kumi to his feet. She tried to get between them, but one of the other soldiers came forward to hold her arms. "Don't hurt him. He's just a child."

"He's plenty old enough to fight. Meleche, we have a new recruit." Natufa drew the boy closer, pressing his face against Kumi's. "You will soon learn to respect the president. We will teach you everything you need to know." With a laugh, he pushed Kumi toward the soldier Zinsa presumed was Meleche.

"You can't take him."

Natufa turned to her, and she shivered under the intensity of his gaze, fearing she was now the center of his attention and knowing she was better off when he had ignored her.

"I may take anything I want." His words were arrogant, and his eyes were lustful when they settled on her breasts.

"Your unit is leaving," said Amani from the window, where she was pointing to the men assembling in the clearing.

"We'll catch up." Natufa nodded to one of his men. "Secure the door."

"What about the men?" Meleche asked.

A hearty laugh left Natufa, giving a glimpse of his yellowed teeth. "What men? A boy and an old man? They will be no problem."

Kumi had been struggling in Meleche's arms, but now he renewed his efforts, breaking away with a surprising kick into the soldier's knee. He stood uncertainly for a moment, eyeing the door.

"Run, Kumi," Zinsa urged. "Get out—ouch!" Her advice to escape faded to a cry of pain when Natufa jerked her against him, his fingers biting into her upper arms.

"Run, boy, and I will have you shot."

For a second longer, Kumi hesitated, looking to Zinsa for guidance. Her stomach heaved when she had to shake her head to counsel him not to run. His thin shoulders sagged with defeat, and he relaxed his posture from one poised for flight. Meleche shoved him across the room, forcing the boy to stand there with his palms flat against the wall, his back turned on the rest of them. He kept his pistol against the back of the boy's head, ensuring Kumi wouldn't try anything rash.

Zinsa was briefly grateful for that as Natufa's eyes stripped her bare, not wanting the boy to witness her humiliation and feel like he should have acted. His hands weren't far behind, tugging at the neck of her T-shirt. She struggled against his hold, elbowing him in the stomach. Other than a grunt as his breath escaped, he gave no indication it affected him. He was almost as tall as Grant, with bulky muscles, and he had little trouble lifting her into his arms.

From her precarious position, with her head pointing toward his heavy boots, Zinsa saw the other two soldiers not assigned a duty by Natufa turn their attentions to Amani. The first reached for her, and she slapped away his hand, earning a cuffing from the other one. Upon witnessing that, Hasina began wailing loudly, while the old women shouted at the men to release Amani and Zinsa.

She lost her vantage point when Natufa dropped her on the exam table, pinning her down with his elbow pressing into the small of her back. Zinsa sat up as far as possible, lunging forward to bite his biceps as hard as she could.

Curses accompanied his hand against the side of her head, forcing her to let go. His aim hadn't been true, or she would have been knocked unconscious, judging from the size of his hands. As it was, she saw stars and couldn't muster the ability to continue struggling even though her brain urged her to. The only motion she managed was to crane her neck to see Amani and the patients.

"Enough." Natufa rounded on the patients, pointing the machine gun at them. "Not another sound, or I'll silence you all permanently."

Immediately, the older women broke off their haranguing, but Hasina continued crying noisily. Natufa's rifle zeroed in on her, and he jerked his head at Amani. "Shut her up, or I will."

The men holding Amani released her with obvious reluctance. Zinsa was so proud of her newfound friend, watching her walk proudly while modestly covering her exposed breasts with the shreds of her shirt. She knelt by Hasina's bed, stroked the girl's forehead, and whispered softly to her. After a moment, she stopped crying. Amani hugged her tightly, looking for all the world as if it would be her last chance. It probably was, Zinsa acknowledged grimly, having seen the worst these soldiers could do to the civilians caught in the middle of their conflict.

With utmost composure, Amani stood up, drew the makeshift curtain to shield her daughter, and walked back to the men. Quiet defiance emanated from her, but she seemed to have accepted her fate in order to protect Hasina. Zinsa drew courage from her and vowed not to scream. It was vital the little girl not become upset again.

As Natufa started to turn back to her, Zinsa's eyes fell on the tray holding the supplies she had used to treat Kumi's wound. As of yet, she hadn't disposed of the syringe and needle. She judged the distance, determining she couldn't reach it in her current position, on her stomach. Only on her back would she be able to reach it.

Considering her options took a millisecond, and she decided the instant Natufa's hand settled on her buttocks, caressing them. "I want to be on my back."

His hand froze in its quest downward, and he regarded her with cold eyes. "What?"

She swallowed to clear her throat and aimed for a seductive purr, finding a measure of success. "I want to see you."

"Why?"

Zinsa lifted a shoulder in a half-shrug. "I clearly have no choice, and I don't want it to hurt. If I'm not going to fight you, I might as well enjoy it."

Although Natufa still appeared suspicious, he lifted his elbow from her back, clearly poised to grab her if she tried to run. She had to fight the compulsion to try, forcing calmness she didn't feel while shifting onto her back. Her smile felt shaky, but he didn't seem to realize when he loomed over her, his eyes on her lips. She licked them to entice him, even as her stomach churned with nausea. "Do you have a big cock?" Ignoring the roiling waves in her gut, Zinsa stroked his arm. "You're such a big man. You must be well endowed everywhere, right?"

A smile of pure delight flashed across his sharp features. It might have made him less threatening if it hadn't emphasized the cruel set of his eyes and grotesqueness of his stained teeth. "You can be assured."

Somehow, she managed to sound excited when she said, "Will you show me soon, Major?"

"Very, my sweet." His large hand cupped her breast, squeezing roughly. "First, I want to taste you."

Again, Zinsa licked her lips, holding her breath as his head descended. She squeezed shut her eyes when his mouth settled over hers, his halitosis nearly overwhelming her. When his tongue violated her mouth, she lifted her hand from his arm, stretching for the syringe. He didn't seem to notice the movements, and she ensured he remained distracted by caressing his tongue with hers, barely suppressing the gag reflex.

Her fingers fumbled with the plunger though she had used a hypodermic countless times. Carefully, she pulled on the plunger, hoping the syringe would roll toward her. It did, and she nearly sobbed with relief when it was in her hand. Suddenly infused with dexterity, she flipped the syringe so the needle was pointed aloft. With all of her strength, she drove the hypodermic upward, forcing it deep into Natufa's carotid artery.

A strangled gasp escaped him, and he reeled away from her, allowing Zinsa a chance to gain her feet. He ripped the needle from his neck, clamping his hand over the injury as blood poured from the hole. "Bitch."

If he was trying to use anger to hide his fear, it wasn't working. Unfortunately, she knew it probably wouldn't kill him. The blood would clot before he could possibly bleed out from the small hole. It had seemed like a great plan at the time, but now that she stood facing an enraged man outweighing her by one hundred pounds, with only a metal exam table between herself and his machine gun, she saw the flaws in the idea.

Apparently, Natufa realized he wasn't going to die from the injury. Either that, or he decided to take her out with him. With a roar, he lifted and tossed aside the exam table, storming toward her. Zinsa turned to run, only to encounter one of the two soldiers who had been abusing Amani. His gun rested between her eyes, and the cold steel of the barrel made her freeze. She could almost feel the bullet entering her head, and could definitely picture the damage it would do to her brain.

Natufa was behind her all too soon, his gun against the base of her neck. He must have abandoned rape in favor of going straight to murder. Racking her brain produced no ideas, and she was struggling so hard for even a glimmer of an idea that she was hallucinating. She must be, because there couldn't be a tiger tackling the man with his gun pressed between her eyes.

Blinking, Zinsa watched in frozen surprise as a white tiger mauled the man who was threatening her. Everyone in the room seemed equally frozen with shock, as none of the soldiers moved to shoot him.

As if her thought had prompted Natufa, he swung the rifle from her neck to the tiger. With a cry, she launched herself at him, angling the gun away from the tiger and the dying man. Natufa squeezed the trigger as he threw her off, and one of his bullets passed through the soldier who had been holding Amani. Crimson blossomed on his chest, and he wore an almost comical look of surprise as he fell backward.

Amani rushed to her daughter and Zinsa lunged toward Natufa again from where she had fallen, hoping to knock him to the floor. He grunted under the impact as she hit his knees, stumbling, but not falling. However, he dropped the gun, and her heart lurched with excitement.

The machine gun spun toward the tiger, and it batted the rifle back toward Zinsa. Shaking her head as she lunged for it, dismissing the fanciful thought, she grasped the butt and pulled it into her hands. As she swung around, Meleche fired his handgun at her, missing her by just inches. Forced to swallow her squeamishness, she aimed the gun in his direction. Although not certain she could shoot him in self-defense, she definitely couldn't shoot him with Kumi in the way. "Drop it."

Meleche eyed his pistol and the rifle for a half-second before dropping the handgun and running for the front door. Zinsa watched him go, realizing the other soldier posted to guard the door had already taken off.

A blur of motion drew her eyes, and she turned her head in time to see the tiger leap on Natufa, knocking him to the floor. The tiger roared in the man's face before clamping his jaws around Natufa's neck. In seconds, the man convulsed in the throes of death, and scarlet blood stained the tiger's white muzzle.

When the animal climbed off Natufa's still body, it turned to stare at Zinsa. Fear flickered through her, but died when she looked into the creature's green eyes, an unusual shade for a tiger, she thought. Immediately, a sense of calm filled her, though she couldn't explain it. Perhaps it was because any hint of bloodlust disappeared from the tiger, or maybe because the eyes seemed uncommonly intelligent.

Her brow furrowed with confusion and her eyes wandered over the tiger. Her frown deepened when she saw a wound on the tiger's shoulder. At first, she assumed it had been shot when Natufa's gun discharged, but leaning closer, she saw it was a puncture wound, and several hours old.

Zinsa reached out a hand to the tiger, not sure what compelled her to do so, other than the desire to keep it near until Grant could treat it.

Where was Grant? He hadn't returned from checking on the impalas. Was he safe? Had the soldiers found him, hurt him maybe?

Had he turned into a tiger and saved her life?

A sharp laugh escaped Zinsa, and she wondered where the notion came from. Again, her eyes locked on the tiger's, and she gasped upon realizing why the green eyes were so calming. They belonged to her lover. Somehow, Grant was before her in the form of a tiger.

The idea was insane, but she couldn't doubt the proof in front of her. Those were Grant's eyes on the tiger. It seemed impossible the color could naturally evolve in a white tiger, especially one that just happened to come to her rescue. She cast her mind for a more logical explanation, but came up with nothing. The harder she tried to find an alternative rationalization, the more it made sense that he had to be the tiger. It explained so much.

She might have stared at him all day if Kumi hadn't distracted her. He had picked up Meleche's handgun and was easing toward her slowly.

"Stay still, Dr. Zinsa. I will shoot it."

"No." In a panic, she got to her feet, blocking Grant with her body. Zinsa struggled to calm down, making her voice soothing as she reached for the pistol. "It's all right. I know this tiger. He lives here on the preserve." She held out her hand, silently requesting the gun.

Appearing uncertain, Kumi handed it to her, his fear-filled eyes not straying from Grant. With relief, Zinsa tucked the pistol into the pocket of her shorts to remove it from the boy's sight and from Grant's. Then she turned back to the tiger, hoping he knew who she was in this form and could understand her. "Good boy. Go lie down." She jerked her head in the direction of the bedroom. "Grant is in the bedroom. He'll be looking for you."

After a second's hesitation, the tiger appeared to nod. His motions were unhurried and graceful as he walked from the room, headed in the direction of the bedroom. With any hope, Grant would soon return to his human form and join them before anyone could try to track down the tiger.

Once he was out of sight, Zinsa took the gun from her pocket and tossed it on the floor. Turning to Kumi, she put a hand on his shoulder. "Will you find Manu for me? He will be in one of the buildings in the complex. Tell him...say Zinsa needs him at the clinic."

As Kumi ran out of the clinic, skirting the bodies in his path, she turned to her patients, visually confirming they were well before walking over to Armani. Exhaustion seemed to creep over her, and a mind-numbing haze was protecting her from having to deal with the truth of what Grant was. As she lost herself in the process of first treating Amani's cuts and abrasions, then in explaining the events to Manu and deciding how to proceed, one thought lingered with her. Grant had one hell of an excuse for trying to keep her at arm's length. She just had to decide if she could deal with what she had learned, or if she would withdraw as well.

# Chapter Seven

ဢ

Grant awakened on his own bed, naked as the day of his birth, with his head fuzzy. A copper taste lingered in his mouth, remnants of a hunt he couldn't remember. Vague images came to him, chief among them Zinsa staring at him, speaking to him in a soothing tone, but smelling of fear. How much had really happened, and how much was a product of his mind, produced during the time his human side was repressed?

He rose from the bed, intent on finding Zinsa and trying to recapture memories of the missing time from when the Land Rover's radiator exploded, necessitating that he walk back to the complex, and waking up on his bed. By concentrating, he was able to remember approaching the clinic, but everything beyond that was hazy. Had there really been men in uniforms?

Teeth gritted with frustration, he once again cursed the unique ability thrust upon him the day the shaman saved his life by binding his essence with the tiger's. Maybe it wouldn't be so bad if he was either fully animal or fully human during his transformations, instead of living in this hybrid state, always fighting against the beast, inevitably losing, and having little or no memory of events that transpired while he was in tiger form.

As Grant padded to the dresser to retrieve clothes, he heard footsteps coming down the hall. By the time the door opened, he had recognized the gait as Zinsa's, even without her scent wafting to him. He froze in the act of reaching for boxer-briefs when she stepped into the room, closing the door softly behind her. The moment her eyes met his, he realized she knew what he was.

His heart thundered in his ears, and he forgot about clothing himself. Instead, he had to use all his will power to rein in the impulse to go to Zinsa and beg her to accept him. "What happened?"

She must have thought he had some recollection of the events, because she said, "After you came back to the bedroom, I sent Kumi for Manu. He and the other rangers loaded the soldiers into a truck and took them off the preserve. I think they were going to drop the bodies somewhere for the military to find."

He nodded, at a loss for words. How many had he killed? Searching his memory produced a picture of a large black man who had been hurting Zinsa. Grant had the sense he had done what was necessary, but was thankful most of the incident would remain buried in his subconscious mind.

"How do you feel?"

Grant's eyes widened at the question, which wasn't what he'd expected her to say. "Fuzzy. I don't remember much." Why bother with pretenses? The time for pretending he was normal had passed, just as he'd feared it would. This was why he had avoided getting too close to any woman in the past, and none of the women he had known before had made him lose control the way she did.

The ghost of a smile drifted across her face. "Lucky you." Zinsa cleared her throat. "I meant your shoulder. It looks like you tore it open again during the...what happened."

Reflexively, he looked down, finding the bandage he had worn that morning missing. The stitches had loosened, and dried blood smeared his skin. Upon seeing it, fire flared in his shoulder, and he touched it without thought. "It hurts."

"Let me see."

She didn't appear frightened when she walked to him, taking his hand to lead him to the bed, but he could smell her trepidation, just under the surface. It wasn't the sharp aroma of life-threatening terror, instead having the bitter tang of old anxiety. It pained him to know she had feared him, even for a moment.

Her hands were gentle when she leaned him back to examine his shoulder. After a moment of careful prodding, she released him, standing awkwardly before him, as if not certain where to place her hands. "I think you'll be fine. I doubt the stitches will need to be replaced."

"Good." The stilted conversation was killing him, one syllable at a time. The politeness of strangers shouldn't be what they shared, not after their amazing lovemaking. Dreading her rejection, he reached out for her hands, clasping them in his. Zinsa didn't resist, but she didn't leap forward onto his lap either. "I'm sorry."

Her brow arched. "For what?"

"However you found out, it shouldn't have been like that." He dropped his head, unable to meet her clear brown eyes. "I hoped you wouldn't find out at all, but that was wishful thinking. I should have told you."

Her fingers seemed hesitant as they delved into his hair, lightly caressing his forehead. "How did this happen?"

"Do you remember asking me how I could have survived being mauled by the tiger?" When she nodded, he said, "I wouldn't have if the village shaman hadn't performed a ritual drawing on the essence of the tiger. Her strength became mine, and I healed." Grant shook his head. "That wasn't the only thing I inherited from her. I guess the shaman couldn't bind our essences without some mingling occurring." A half-smile lifted one corner of his mouth. "I've often wondered if the tiger had the ability to change to a human after that."

"Who else knows?"

He shrugged. "My parents, of course. I'm the reason they've stayed in Africa all these years. They couldn't risk taking me back to a place where tigers aren't likely to be strolling around freely. Especially as a child and teenager, I couldn't control the transformation. Any time my emotions got out of control, I changed."

To his surprise, a wide smile lit her face. "Is that why you've held back when we've made love? It was because you feared losing control, not because you didn't want to have a deeper connection with me? Not because you didn't want me?"

Seeing the worry in her eyes made his heart ache anew, to know he had caused her to doubt herself. With a sigh, he drew her closer to him, happy when she didn't resist his embrace as he released her hands and wrapped his arms around her waist. "You make me lose control in a way no one else ever has, Zinsa. I wasn't running from you, just myself." He couldn't hide the note of sadness in his tone when he said, "I've been doing that for thirty years."

Her arms came around his back, squeezing gently. "Stop running."

Grant rested his cheek on her stomach, conscious of the heat of her skin through the thin T-shirt. "I want to, but can't."

"Why not?"

"What if I can't change back? What if I surrender to the animal inside completely?" He swallowed, finding it difficult to voice his most private vulnerabilities. "What if I hurt you?"

She took a step back, tipping up his chin with her fingers. Her eyes focused intently on his, and he couldn't detect any doubt in her tone. "You would never hurt me, Grant. You saved my life today as the tiger. I trust you."

When she crouched lower to kiss him, he knew he was lost. Her soft lips, gently exploring his, were a temptation he couldn't resist. With a groan of surrender, he parted his lips so her tongue could dart into his mouth, rubbing against his with ardent strokes.

His shoulder protested when he moved his hands lower, to dispense with her shorts and panties before cupping Zinsa's buttocks and lifting her onto his lap as he lay back on the bed. She squealed with surprise at the unexpected action, but settled comfortably atop him, straddling his stomach.

Grant kept a hand on her hip to anchor her in position, while his other hand ventured to cup one of her breasts, thumbing the nipple through her shirt and bra. His mouth swallowed her moans when he lightly pinched the bud, and his stomach quivered when she rubbed her slick pussy against it.

Zinsa sat up straight, breaking the kiss and dislodging his hand from her hips. She smiled down at him, her eyes dark with hunger. "I'm going to make love to you."

Overwhelmed by the eagerness in her expression, and his own anticipation, Grant didn't protest when she took the initiative. Her head dipped a second before the tip of her tongue traced the line of his jaw in her leisurely exploration, gradually moving south. He swallowed when she nibbled on the column of his throat and barely contained a laugh of surprise when she sucked on his Adam's apple. It was a stimulating sensation, if not sexual.

Zinsa continued downward, swirling her tongue over his chest, as her entire body shifted lower, bringing the apex of her thighs to settle on his pubic bone just inches from his hard cock. In an attempt to distract himself from the thought of taking her right then, he slid his hand under the hem of her shirt and moved upward to free her breast from the cup of the bra. A tremor racked her body and the rhythm of her tongue faltered for a moment, until she regained control. He grinned at the telltale signs of her arousal. Maybe she was determined to make love to him, to push him past the bounds of all self-control, but he wasn't going alone.

When she reached his nipple, Zinsa sucked the small bud into her mouth, swirling her tongue around it. Grant shifted restlessly, his cock inching upward in search of the warm sheath of her pussy. Each tug of her mouth caused a corresponding tingle to shoot through his body, radiating from his nipple but felt everywhere.

He jumped when she scraped her teeth across his nipple as she left it, ready to move on to her ultimate destination. This detour led her to the heaviest patch of scars on his body, at his side. The first time she had seen them, she had touched them, but in a cursory manner. This time, as her dripping pussy slid lightly over his cock while she readjusted her position, Zinsa tasted them, first with tiny kisses across the area, followed by stroking her tongue through the rough mass, before pausing to trace the thickest ropes of scars from their points of origin.

The last scar led her to his pubic bone, and she paused only to straddle his thighs before returning her mouth to the end of the scar, trailing her tongue lower, to the side of his cock. He stiffened when she blew lightly on his heated skin, her lips hovered just beyond his erection. His cock convulsed with anticipation as her lips grazed the side of his shaft, zeroing in on his thick head. When her mouth closed around him, he groaned with pleasure, swearing his cock hardened even more, if that was possible.

Last time she had sucked his cock, Grant had been too consumed with trying to maintain control to fully appreciate her talent. This time he surrendered to the sensations, giving voice to his pleasure with small moans and grunts as she worked with enthusiasm.

Her tongue made broad strokes around his head before tracing the corona. When she reached the bundle of nerves at the V, the hand he'd had balled at his side instinctively reached for her, his fingers plunging into her short, kinky hair in an attempt to hold her there forever. Her breathy giggle sent electricity arcing through his body, and his cock convulsed.

When she scraped her teeth across the corona, it shouldn't have been as pleasurable as it was. The contrast of satisfaction and slight discomfort had him pumping his hips, anxious to bury his cock as deep into her mouth as he could. She accepted the length of him with some effort, taking a moment to adjust to his size before resuming sucking.

Zinsa's head bobbed up and down as soon as she was used to him, maintaining constant suction. Grant swore she was sucking hard enough to draw his balls through his cock, but it was so amazing he wasn't going to protest. Every molecule in his body was threatening to come apart, his control was nonexistent, and the beast was rising, but he couldn't muster the will to care. All that mattered was her mouth on his cock, her legs around his thighs, and the heady scent of her arousal hanging in the air.

She concentrated her efforts on the head of his cock, and Grant's eyes blurred. His cock spasmed and release almost rushed over him. At the penultimate moment, Zinsa withdrew, and he groaned, caught in a gray world between pain and release. "Zinsa." Her name was a raspy plea torn from his throat.

"I'm not cruel," she said, lifting her body higher as she spoke, until their pelvises aligned. "I want to be with you this time."

Somehow he managed a nod, though all he wanted to do was plunge inside her pussy. With gritted teeth, he held out long enough for Zinsa to position herself and sit down slowly, sinking onto his cock. As soon as her velvety folds encased him, Grant put his hands on her back, pulling her down across his stomach, even as he flipped their positions, needing to be able to delve as deeply into her as he could.

Zinsa cried out when he sank fully inside her. He lifted one of her legs and she curled it around his upper back, allowing him another inch of penetration. Sweat dripped from his forehead into his eyes, obscuring his vision, but not to the point that he couldn't see how excited his lover was. Her need clearly matched his, and they pounded against each other in frenzied waves, meeting as if determined to absorb each other, and breaking apart to recover before trying again when their attempts failed.

He was too close to climax to make it last long, but she was right with him, bringing her hand between their bodies to rub her clit as he increased his thrusts even more, trembling on the edge. When he fell over, the cry that left his mouth blended with hers, and he couldn't tell where the spasms in his cock ended and the convulsions in her pussy began. For that instant, they were one being, their hearts thundering in unison.

Blackness swept through him, rising so quickly he barely had time to pull out of Zinsa and roll off the bed. Huddled on the floor, he tried to regain control, but failed as the beast claimed him and the fire of transformation raged through him.

When he was fully transformed, Grant's sense of self was vague, but he knew who Zinsa was. When she got out of bed and knelt on the floor beside him, his tail twitched. Peace filled him when her hands stroked his fur, and his memories stirred. His mind cleared, becoming sharper in a matter of seconds, and before he knew it, he was human again. It was the fastest he had ever found his way back from being immersed in the beast.

Lying on the floor, with Zinsa's hands on his stomach, Grant fought against the shame trying to overtake him. It took every vestige of courage to meet her eyes, and his heart stuttered when he saw nothing but acceptance. "Zinsa?" Every ounce of his uncertainty resonated in uttering her name.

With a tender smile, she leaned forward to kiss his forehead. "My love."

He sniffed, filtering out the scent of their mutual passion hanging in the air, looking for any hint of fear from her and finding none. His brow furrowed, and he regarded her with confusion. "How can you be so accepting?"

Zinsa shrugged before sitting cross-legged on the floor, her thigh pressed against his stomach. "You are what you are, Grant. I've waited too long to find someone to complete me to throw it away because of fear." She brushed a curl off his forehead. "I've been cursed, you know."

For a moment, he had no idea what she was talking about, but then the memory surfaced. "Your family curse?"

She nodded, grinning widely. "I've found my soul mate and knew him instantly."

"There's no curse in my family, but I know you're the other half of my heart."

"Darling, I've decided it's not a family curse." Zinsa stretched forward, her mouth hovering against his. Just before kissing him, she added, "It's definitely a gift."

# About the Author

෨

Kit Tunstall lives in Idaho with her husband, soon-to-be born-son, and dog-children. She started reading at the age of three and hasn't stopped since. Love of the written word, and a smart marriage to a supportive man, led her to a full-time career in writing. Romances have always intrigued her, and erotic romance is a natural extension because it more completely explores the emotions between the hero and heroine. That, and it sure is fun to write.

Kit welcomes mail from readers. You can write to her c/o Ellora's Cave Publishing at 1056 Home Avenue Akron, OH 44310-3502.

# Also by Kit Tunstall

෨

A Christmas Phantasie

A Matter of Honor

Beloved Forever

Blood Lines 1: Blood Oath

Blood Lines 2: Blood Challenge

Blood Lines 3: Blood Bond

Blood Lines 4: Blood Price

By Invitation Only

Dark Dreams

Eye of Destiny

Heart of Midnight

Pawn

Phantasie

Playing His Game

# Hidden Heart

*Kate Steele*

છ

# Chapter One

සා

"Lindy, your two o'clock is here."

"Thanks, Cin, I'll be right there."

Lindy released the button on the intercom unit and turned back to her work table. "Well, big fella, you're going to have to wait for that nose after all."

Her comment was addressed to the large teddy bear that sat on the table in front of her. His eyes conveyed an expectant air as he patiently awaited the stitches that would complete his nose and mouth. Lindy smiled, not at all bothered by the fact that she was talking to an inanimate object. She'd long ago given up feeling silly for doing so and now realized that teddy bear lovers around the world talked to their favorite "friends".

She automatically put away her tools and moved her new creation back from the edge of the table. Tapping the end of his muzzle, she instructed, "You wait right here, I'll be back in a little while."

With a smile she stood and walked to the closed door. Before opening it she stopped to straighten her clothing. She reached under her shirt, grasped the bottom edge of her bra and pulled it down, then did a little shimmy movement designed to shake everything in place. Pulling the hem of her shirt down, she grimaced as she thought, for what seemed like the millionth time, how much she hated having large breasts. Although firm enough, they never seemed to want to remain where she put them. It was as though they were escapees in the middle of a jail break and she was forever recapturing them and sending them back to their cells.

Lindy sighed and opened the door which connected to her office. She walked in to find her two o'clock appointment perusing the glass case that held some examples of Timberlane Teddies' most popular lines.

"See anything you like?" she quipped, then grinned at her use of a line so often used as a double entendre.

"Actually, I see some familiar faces here," he answered and turned to face her, his own smile in place as he indicated the displayed teddy bears. "My niece is quite taken with Jethro and Sam." He walked across the room extending his hand. "Ms. Timberlane, I'm very pleased to finally meet you in person."

Lindy took the offered hand. "Call me Lindy, please. Won't you have a seat, Dr. Walden?"

"Thank you, and it's David," he replied, sitting in the indicated chair.

Lindy walked around her antique mahogany desk and took her own chair. "So, it's that time of year again," she commented as she pulled a checkbook from the top drawer. "How are things going at base camp?"

"Very well, thanks in part to your generosity. We've made great strides in determining how the grizzlies use natural resources and just how important certain things like the white-bark pine trees are to their existence."

"The white-barks provide the last wild food source for the bears before they go into hibernation, is that right?"

"That's right," David answered with a pleased smile.

"I try to keep up on things, even though the teddy bear business keeps me pretty busy." Lindy took up her pen and began making out the check. "So, will you be returning to camp after your business here in town is completed?"

"In about a week, yes I will, and that brings up the reason I came to see you, instead of having you mail the check as usual."

Lindy looked up curiously. "And that reason would be…?"

"I've come to issue an invitation. Over the last few years you've been so generous in your contributions — the added funding has allowed us to really step up our research. We, as a group, would like to invite you to come and see how your money is being spent. We thought you might enjoy a couple of weeks in the woods to get to know the group and see in person just exactly what it is we do."

Lindy was filled with stunned delight. "I'd love that! So I'll have a week to organize things then return with you?"

"Will that be enough time?"

"Definitely. For this I'll make it enough time. You're going to have to tell me what I need to bring as far as clothes and things."

"My wife, Nancy, is way ahead of you there," David replied as he reached into his jacket pocket. "She sent this note and a list."

Lindy laughed. "I see she anticipated my acceptance."

"Nancy's the voice of practicality and reason in camp, she always looks ahead and seems to have an uncanny ability to see what things we might need in the future. Knowing your deep dedication to our project, she was fairly certain you'd want to come."

"Well, she certainly was right there," Lindy said as she finished writing out the check to the foundation. She handed it to David who looked at it, then did a double take. "The business did quite well last year," she explained with a sheepish shrug. "I've increased our other donations as well."

David shook his head in amazement and beamed. "I can't tell you how much this means to us, but then, you know that without all the research we're doing, animals such as the grizzly bear and the wolf might be extinct by now."

"I know," she answered. "And that's something I want to help prevent. My grandparents, especially Grandpa, had a great love for the outdoors and all its inhabitants. They instilled that same love in me. When they died and left their estate to me, I started this business. Between my inheritance and the success I've enjoyed, I've got more than any one person needs." She smiled. "So I decided to spread it around."

"Well, we're certainly grateful you've spread it in our direction."

"Believe me, David, it's my pleasure."

David rose, pushed his glasses back up the bridge of his nose and ran a hand over his tousled brown hair. Lindy studied him briefly, deciding she liked him. He seemed a sensible and sturdy person, just the sort who should be in charge of a research team. There was also an air of gentle humor about him, something that made her relax in his presence. *He has kind eyes*, she mused.

"Well, I'd best be going so that you can get back to work," he commented, putting the check she handed him in an inner jacket pocket. "I'll deposit this right away, so as not to lose it. Nancy would scalp me if I did, and I don't believe I'd look quite right bald."

Lindy smiled appreciatively, he *did* have a sense of humor.

"I'll contact you toward the end of the week to see how you're progressing in your preparations and give you our travel information, flight times, etcetera. If you should need to contact me before then, I can be reached at either of these numbers," he said, handing her a card.

"Thank you, David. I really appreciate this opportunity to spend time with your team," she told him, shaking his hand.

"It's our pleasure, Lindy. And thank you again," he said, patting his jacket pocket. "Goodbye."

Lindy watched him head for the elevator, sighed and closed her door. A big grin spread over her face. "Grandpa, I wish you were here," she murmured. "I'm going camping with the bears!"

\* \* \* \* \*

A week later Lindy found herself unpacking in her very own cabin. She had been pleasantly surprised to find that the base camp was made up of cabins and not tents. David Walden and his wife Nancy, a wildlife conservationist, shared one,

Sandra and Paul DiAngelo, both wildlife ecologists, shared a second, and Rafe Kutter, a wildlife biologist, was in yet another.

The cabins were all of similar makeup. The main room contained the bed, a dresser and a table with a couple of chairs. There was also a tiny closet and a small bathroom. The bathroom was equipped with a shower stall, toilet and sink.

In addition to the cabins there was a larger communal building, the Lodge, that housed a combination kitchen-dining room and several other rooms. One was designated as the library and used to store the research data, another was used for equipment storage and a third was dominated by a large fireplace, and had thickly padded sofas and chairs which one could sink into and spend a dreamy hour or two contemplating the fire. Everyone had to go further afield to actually find their research subjects, but there were tents and other equipment to make overnight or longer trips possible.

Putting the last of her things in the dresser, Lindy straightened and looked at herself in the mirror. She shook her head and through critical green eyes watched locks of her long, honey-blonde hair settle into place. They framed a face she wished could be termed beautiful, but cute was closer to the mark. She turned her head first this way, then that, studying her even, average features. Wrinkling her nose, she stepped back and examined her clothing.

Following Nancy Walden's advice, she'd packed plain, sensible clothing that could be layered for any changes in the weather. At the moment, she wore a pair of her favorite well-worn blue jeans, a smoky-blue Henley topped by an open olive-green chamois shirt and low hiking boots. She turned sideways, liking the way the shirt fell, as it hid some of her more obvious curves.

Standing five-foot-ten-inches tall, Lindy was grateful for the height that gave her size eighteen body a well-proportioned look. Even so, she'd spent her life very conscious of the extra pounds, and had done all sorts of diets in an effort to reach a weight that in the end had proved to be unattainable and truthfully unnecessary. At thirty-five she was ready to admit that this was it, she was never going to be glamour-girl thin, but at least she was healthy and finally comfortable with herself.

She ate reasonably well-balanced meals, walked two or three miles a day, worked out with weights and even had a heavy punching bag installed in her apartment. It was great for those days when the frustrations of work had her tense and on edge. It was especially effective when she pictured it as her ex-fiancé, Richard, who'd turned out to be a two-timing fortune hunter. There was something quite savagely satisfying in pretending to pulverize those haughty, patrician features.

With a wry smile she stepped away from the mirror, walked out of her cabin and headed toward the Lodge. The building was fairly large, with a front porch that was reached by climbing up two steps. A soft breeze whispered through the boughs of the trees that shaded the clearing and brought the fresh scent of pine to her appreciative nose.

Lindy crossed the porch and opened the front door. Peering in, she quickly ascertained that no one was there. She walked in, closed the door behind her and looked around the room. It was very rustic and oddly welcoming. She sighed and relaxed a bit. Running her own business, she'd learned the niceties of meeting new people, unfortunately it didn't make the doing any easier. She was, by nature, a more solitary creature.

Drawn to a pile of papers laid out on a low table in front of one of the sofas, she sat and curiously perused those that were visible. They were obviously someone's research notes and were written in a strong, bold script. A large, open sketchbook lay by the notes. The two visible pages each held a photograph of a grizzly bear, accompanied by a number, a name and statistics. It was what the rest of the pages held that fascinated her.

Beautifully detailed drawings had been rendered of each subject bear as it was engaged in various activities. The drawings were so intricate and realistic one almost expected the bear to move. The artist had captured the very essence of his subjects.

She sat and slowly turned the pages, totally entranced. Lost in her study of the drawings, Lindy didn't notice that she was no longer alone.

"Do you always snoop through other people's personal property?"

She gasped and started guiltily. The question came from behind her, expressed in a deep voice, a silky growl that sent a shiver coursing down her spine—a shiver that unexpectedly caused her nipples to pinch tight.

"I'm sorry," she replied breathlessly, turning the pages back to their original position. "The sketchbook was open and the pictures were so beautiful." She rose and turned to face the speaker. "I just..." She stopped cold, her mouth open.

Standing before her, larger than life, was a flannel-clad God.

Tall herself, Lindy felt dwarfed by his presence. Her gaze slowly traveled the length of his six-foot-six-inch frame. Dressed in hiking boots and worn, faded jeans, with a tucked-in, dark blue flannel shirt, his clothing only served to emphasize the hard-muscled body beneath. His sleeves were rolled up to just below the elbow, and his forearms—lightly sprinkled with dark hair, and wrapped with a few prominent veins—were well-defined. His hands were large, the fingers long and tapered and his skin was dark, not just tan, but brown, a rich, deep color that radiated warmth.

Lindy's heart actually fluttered when her gaze reached his face. The planes and hollows were precisely sculpted, on the verge of being hawklike, yet softened by an unknown ancestor. His face was framed by black hair pulled severely back and bound by a leather tie. His eyes were dark, almost black, two pools of coffee that should have promised heat and stimulation, but now were hard and cold. His full lips were taut, his ire thinning them.

A dark brow rose. "You just...what?" he asked sarcastically.

Lindy blinked at his tone, attraction suddenly replaced by rising irritation. "Look, I'm sorry. No, I don't normally snoop through other people's belongings, but the book was out and open. I have to assume if it was private it wouldn't have been left where anyone could see it. Can we start over? I'm Lindy Timberlane." She stepped forward and held out her hand.

It was rudely ignored. "I know who you are, Miss Timberlane, and I may as well tell you that I don't approve of your being here." The irritable hunk moved passed her and leaned down to gather his papers.

Lindy couldn't help following the fluid movement of his body, her eyes widening at the sight of his hard, tight ass and how it moved under the taut fabric of his jeans when he bent over. She quickly snapped her eyes upward as he straightened and turned, pausing for a moment to study her. She felt her cheeks slowly begin to heat.

Those exquisite lips tightened again and sparks lit the depths of his dark eyes. "We're doing serious work here. We're not here to guide some wealthy dilettante on a camping trip."

"I am not a wealthy dilettante! I work for a living, Mister…?"

"Kutter, Rafe Kutter."

"Mr. Kutter. I didn't donate money to curry any special favors. I didn't ask to come—I was invited."

"Yes, I know. And it was an invitation that was issued in spite of my disapproval. I was outvoted by the rest of the team. They seem to believe that your favor *needs* to be curried or the gravy train will halt."

Lindy gaped at him in disbelief. "Has anyone ever told you how obnoxious you are?"

Rafe opened his mouth to reply but was interrupted.

"I see you've met Rafe, and discovered what a charming fellow he can be."

The two combatants turned to face the speaker. A smiling woman of medium height with short, brown hair made her way to the pair of them. She held out her hand to Lindy, her blue eyes sparkling with amusement. "Hi, I'm Nancy Walden."

Despite her disgruntlement, Lindy made an effort to cordially greet the newcomer. She smiled wryly as she shook Nancy's hand. "Hi, I'm Lindy Timberlane, and yes, Mr. Kutter and I were just getting acquainted."

Nancy laughed delightedly. "You're being quite diplomatic, Lindy. I'm assuming from the battle lines I could see being drawn that he's made you aware of his objections to your being invited, but don't worry, his bark is worse than his bite."

A small grudging smile played over Rafe's lips. "You shouldn't minimize the danger Miss Timberlane is in, Nancy." He turned his gaze to Lindy. "I can be *quite* dangerous."

Meeting his gaze, Lindy could swear she saw a brief amber glow in the depths of his dark eyes. It sent a tingling shiver down her spine. "I'm no coward, Mr. Kutter."

Rafe studied her thoughtfully. "That remains to be seen." He gave them both a quick nod. "Ladies."

Lindy watched him walk out the front door, then turned to Nancy who was looking at her with a speculative gleam in her eyes. "Is he always so...abrasive?"

Nancy smiled. "Somewhat... He likes you."

"What? How could you possibly think that?" Lindy asked incredulously. "You saw what just happened between us."

"Yes, I did, and I know Rafe well enough to know that if you weren't having an effect on him he'd be polite, accept your presence gracefully, and you'd leave here thinking he was a well-mannered, diligent professional. But you've seen a part of the real man—that's something he normally doesn't share with strangers." Nancy cocked her head curiously. "I could sparks flying from across the room. Am I wrong?"

Lindy blushed. "I'll admit he's far from unattractive, but his personality needs a lot of work."

Nancy smiled. "Well, you're going to be here for a while. I think the work could be worthwhile."

Lindy frowned slightly, perturbed by the conversation and her reaction to it. She felt in some ways that she should be offended by Nancy's delving into such a personal matter, and yet there was something about the woman that made her feel immediately at ease with her. It was like having a bull session with an old friend.

"I don't want to sound impertinent, but may I ask why you're so interested in Mr. Kutter's love life?" she asked.

"For the simple reason that he doesn't have one. Rafe is too solitary and he's becoming too serious. He's a good man and I don't like the thought of him being alone."

"Surely, he has women friends. I can't imagine that a man who looks like that doesn't have scores of women throwing themselves at him."

"While that's certainly true, he doesn't bother to catch any of them, not even for a quick roll in the hay."

"Have you considered the fact that he may be gay?" Lindy asked seriously.

Nancy smiled softly and shook her head. "No, I'm sure he's not. My brother, who *is* gay, was here with us for a few weeks. He was very attracted to Rafe, and told me it was such a waste that he was straight. Jeremy would know — his gaydar works with pinpoint accuracy."

Lindy chuckled. "That sounds like my best friend, Rob."

"Maybe we should introduce the two of them."

"That's a distinct possibility."

The two of them smiled at each other in perfect accord.

\* \* \* \* \*

"I don't think that's a good idea."

"Couldn't I go with someone else?"

Lindy and Rafe looked at each other, neither surprised at the sentiments they'd just expressed.

"Now hold on, you two," David replied mildly and turned to Lindy. "Your biggest reason for coming was to see the bears, correct?" Lindy nodded and he turned to Rafe. "Rafe, you're the one who spends the greatest amount of time observing the bears. It's only logical that Lindy go out with you." At Rafe's raised brow, David's lips quirked with a small smile. "You are, after all, our expert on *Ursus arctos*."

"I'm not going to debate that point," Rafe replied, honestly acknowledging David's praise of his abilities. "I just think Ms. Timberlane would be more comfortable in someone else's company."

"You got that right," Lindy muttered under her breath.

Rafe gave her a penetrating glare while Nancy and the others looked on with amusement.

"Be that as it may," David said, his lips twitching with a suppressed smile. "I'd feel we were doing you a disservice by not providing you with the very best we have to offer, which in this case is Rafe."

Lindy received this unwelcome news in silence, her dinner suddenly feeling like a rock weighing down her stomach. The team was seated around the large dining table finishing off the evening meal. Lindy had pitched in to help fix the meal while meeting the rest of the team.

Sandy DiAngelo sat to her left and was a petite soft-spoken woman with big brown eyes and long hair, which she wore in a ponytail. Next to her was her husband, Paul, a tall and wiry man with a dry sense of humor and eyes that sparkled with mischief. At the moment they were focused on Lindy, the twinkle more than apparent as he watched her second skirmish with Rafe unfold.

She *had* been enjoying the meal. The company was pleasant, the conversation casual, relaxed and teasing at times. She'd even managed to ignore Rafe for the most part, though his size and good looks demanded attention in spite of his sometimes surly attitude. The fact that he'd been shooting frequent and enigmatic looks her way during the evening did little to endear him to her. His unwarranted attention made her feel prickly. Like an unruly and resentful child, she wanted nothing more than to stick her tongue out at him.

Now a pregnant silence filled the room as they stared at each other. Despite the mild hostility she felt toward him, Rafe had also managed to stir something else inside her, an unwilling attraction that caused heat to rise inside, heat that spread and caused a melting sensation that flowed, settling between her thighs.

Reflexively, she tightened her thighs against the sudden crazy need to spread them wide and invite him inside. She felt herself moisten and silently cursed her body's betrayal. A fleeting vision of herself straddling Rafe, slowly riding him, filled her inner vision. An involuntary spasm quivered through her pussy and she drew in a sharp, shallow breath as she struggled to keep her expression impassive.

Something in her eyes transmitted a message. Rafe's eyes widened slightly, his pupils enlarging, the dark pools seeming to soften and invite. Everyone else in the room disappeared. Lindy leaned forward, a helpless, infinitesimal movement as she was drawn toward the sensual promise in those two mesmerizing orbs.

In the space of seconds a raging inferno erupted before her eyes and she felt herself drawn into the flames. Her skin reacted to the heat, a gossamer thin sweat breaking out. Rafe's nostrils flared and she could swear he was taking in her scent. A flash of light again lit his eyes, a solar flare that was suddenly, ruthlessly crushed. Rafe had once more erected an icy barrier between them, and she drew back, shivering with the cold.

He stood abruptly, towering over her. "I leave at first light, be ready or I go without you."

Lindy watched him walk away for the second time. "I suppose I should get used to that," she commented, taking a deep, calming breath while wondering if anyone had noticed what had just passed between the two of them.

"Give him time, he'll loosen up. Eventually," Paul quipped.

She gave him a disbelieving look, one eyebrow raised.

"Scout's honor." He smiled, giving her a little salute.

Sandy laughed. "Paul, dear, you were never a boy scout."

"Is it my fault there was no local troop? My mother did try to get me into the Brownies."

Good-natured laughter met Paul's facetious confession and Lindy rose with her plate, taking it to the sink. Not too surprising was the fact that her knees felt a bit weak. Determined to ignore it, she began to gather the dirty dishes, fully prepared to wash them, before Nancy shooed her out.

"If you're going with Rafe, I suggest you go get some sleep. He wasn't joking about leaving at daybreak," Nancy commented softly as they stood side by side in front of the sink. A quiet conversation was taking place between the three left at the table, giving Nancy and Lindy privacy.

"I didn't think he was. I sincerely doubt the man could tell a joke, even if he wanted to."

Nancy grinned. "I've known Rafe since he was a baby. He inherited his stoicism from his father. I swear that man seldom cracked a smile. His mother was also a wildlife biologist and we worked together before her death. She was a joyous soul, she was full-blooded Native American Shoshone. I never saw a person so at home with nature and wild things. She passed those traits on to Rafe. Believe it or not, he used to laugh." Nancy's smile faded away. "When she was killed, the joy just bled out of that boy. Of course, Rafe's father being the way he was didn't help. He withdrew into himself and left Rafe pretty much on his own. It's a hard thing for a boy of twelve to lose the care and guidance of his father, especially with his mother gone."

Lindy bit her lip as she felt her heart twist in sympathy. "How did his mother die?"

"She was shot by a poacher."

"*What?*"

"Even though this is federal land and protected, poachers still come in trying to bag a trophy they can brag about to their friends. The bear, moose, elk—they're all at risk. We do the best we can and work in concert with the park rangers, but there's a lot of territory out there. It's impossible to keep watch everywhere. Mary liked to camp out and did it quite frequently on her own. One night she surprised a couple of poachers who'd just shot a moose. When Rafe found her that morning she was barely alive. The poachers got away. We don't know if she was shot deliberately or by accident, but they left in hurry. They didn't even bother to take their trophy." Nancy's eyes were filled with unshed tears.

Lindy swallowed the lump that had formed in her throat. "I promise I'll try to get along with Rafe."

"I'm sorry, Lindy, I shouldn't have dumped that on you. I just wanted you to know that Rafe has his reasons for being the way he is. And...there's something I want you to do for me."

"What's that?"

"Don't back down, don't let this knowledge make you go soft on him. Whether because of his looks or his size, Rafe is used to getting deferential treatment from others, if they agree with him or not. Your willingness to stand up to him is just what he needs, something to make him take a new look at what's around him. Shake him up."

Lindy smiled. "All right, I promise to continue being a pain in his ass. And what a magnificent ass it is," she quipped, then slapped a hand over her mouth, her cheeks flushing hotly.

Nancy burst out laughing. "Don't tell David I said so, but I happen to agree with you!"

# Chapter Two

**ᔌ**

Rafe lay naked on his bed, the covers crumpled and thrown back from his restless movements. Through the open window he could hear a soft breeze whispering through the pines. Normally that sound soothed and served to ease him into sleep, but not tonight. Tonight his thoughts were filled with a tall, feisty blonde who not only sported a smart mouth, but the *sexiest* mouth he'd ever seen. A mouth he had a definite craving to taste.

He grumbled a resentful curse under his breath. Why did she have to come here? He'd more or less managed to sublimate his need for sex, relying on masturbation to ease his urges. But now, here was temptation thrust right under his nose with a strength and pull the likes of which he'd never experienced.

The woman riled not only his temper, but his libido, and he was honest enough to admit that his resentment was based on his unwilling attraction. He had secrets to keep, secrets that wouldn't stand the fine examination that came with intimacy. *But damn*, he thought to himself, *I'm so tired of being alone.*

Rafe shook his head and sighed, wondering for the millionth time how his mother had gotten the courage to reveal her "gift" to his father. A melancholy sadness filled him as he thought of his parents. As sudden and tragic as his mother's death had been, his father's had been, if not worse, just as bad. A slow death, years spent mourning the loss of a beloved wife.

His gaze came to rest on the framed picture that graced his bedside table, his parents standing together, smiling at each other, with a younger version of himself standing in front of them. His dad was a big, tall and powerfully built man with dark curly hair, deep brown eyes and gleaming dark brown skin. His mother was also tall, with long, flowing black hair and cleanly sculpted features. In the photo, her brown eyes were glowing with love as she looked at her husband. Rafe could easily see, while looking at his own image, that his physical characteristics were clearly a blend of his African and Native American heritages.

He rolled to his back, muscles shifting smoothly under rich cocoa-brown skin. He sighed again, thinking of his father and grateful for the fact that his resentment had turned to understanding and forgiveness. After his mother's death, his father had done the best he could. Rafe had finally come to terms with that fact.

His thoughts again wandered, coming to rest once more on Lindy Timberlane. "Lindy," he whispered softly, testing the name on his lips.

He breathed deeply, her remembered scent sending a jolt through him. He wondered if she had any idea just how damn *good* she smelled. Hers was an elusive aroma, one that teased his senses and tickled his palate until he was sure he could taste her. Attuned to the memory, his breath came a little faster, his heart beat a little harder, and his groin tightened, his cock beginning to firm and grow.

Rafe trailed a hand over the rippled muscles of his abs and downward until long, tapered fingers wrapped around his burgeoning erection. He groaned softly and closed his eyes, seeing Lindy as she sat at the dining table, watching that indefinable something blossom in her eyes as they'd stared at each other. Something he now knew was desire. His eyes sprang open and he stared sightlessly into the darkness of his room, oblivious to the familiar shadows, his hand beginning a slow stroking motion up and down the thick, hard, satin-skinned length of his cock.

Desire. She felt it too. It was the irresistible something that pulled them toward each other. He'd bet his life on it. A slow grin spread over his face, a grin that turned to a grimace of pleasure and another breathy groan as his fingers closed a bit tighter and stroked a bit faster. Perhaps the chore of guiding her around wouldn't be quite as onerous as he thought. Perhaps it was time to make a change, to take some chances.

His inner vision again pictured Lindy. He found it impossible to resist her lush, full figure and the way she held herself so tall and proud. The flash of fire in her grass-green eyes as she stood up to him, both excited and challenged him. And again, her lips, plump and freshly ripe, came to mind—and in his imagination they opened and welcomed his thick, throbbing length, closing over the weeping, plum-shaped head and sliding down as her tongue bathed and massaged the highly sensitive underside of his eager erection.

Rafe groaned, his hips pushing upward, his breath matching the ever-increasing speed of his hand. His balls, full and taut, drew closer to his body. His cock began to swell ever larger, pulsing within the confines of his pumping fist as he came, the pleasure of his orgasm imploding in his gut and bursting free in hot, creamy spumes of male seed. A low, deep groan was torn from his throat as he came.

Slowly and with decreasing strength, the waves of pleasure subsided and he lay relaxed and sated, his breath slowly returning to normal. His hand settled on his midsection and slowly spread the white cream over his heated skin. Head coming up from the pillow, he looked down the length of his body and smiled a rather smug male smile, that of a man proud of the evidence of his manhood.

Knowing he'd regret it if he didn't clean up, he tilted himself out of bed and entered the bathroom for a quick wash. Returning to bed, he flopped down with a contented sigh and this time was easily lulled to sleep by the familiar whisper of the pine needles as they stirred in the cool night air.

\* \* \* \* \*

Determined not to let Rafe get the upper hand or to leave her behind, Lindy was up and ready to go when the sun made its appearance on the horizon. Despite the restless night she'd spent clutching her childhood friend, Humphrey, she'd forced her bleary-eyed self into the shower and was now reasonably awake and aware. As she packed, her mind kept supplying short vignettes of the dreams that had disturbed her sleep. Some left her with feelings of unease—almost as though something inevitable and inescapable was coming—and some left her just plain horny.

Rafe had figured prominently in *those* dreams, and she snickered to herself, thinking that he had a real future awaiting him in porn flicks should he ever decide to change careers. Sobering, she took a final look at the contents of her backpack, deciding it would do.

The pack contained an extra pair of jeans, shorts, two t-shirts, and enough changes of underwear and socks for several days. In addition, she had a rolled-up tent, a sleeping bag, first aid kit, canteen, her lip balm and unscented sunscreen. As per instructions, she carried no deodorants or perfumes. Where there was a possibility of contact with bears, it was smart to smell as "human" as possible. A bear catching the scent of a human would be more likely to vacate the area than to engage in a confrontation.

Dressed in her jeans, Henley and hiking boots, she was also wearing a fairly warm flannel shirt as a jacket she could take off as it grew warmer. Nancy told her that Rafe would bring the necessary foodstuffs, but Lindy had also stuffed some granola trail mix and energy bars in her pack as well.

As promised, with the soft morning light filling the sky, there was a sharp rap at her door, and upon opening it she was greeted by Rafe's familiar scowl.

"Ready to go?" he asked curtly.

"Yes," she replied just as briefly and turned to grab her pack.

Just as she'd ogled him the day before, Rafe's gaze wandered down her back to the nicely rounded mounds of her bottom. His eyes widened and his fingers twitched as he forced himself to look away. His redirected gaze landed on a large, worn teddy bear that sat in solitary state on the pillows on her bed.

"Who's your friend?" he asked softly, restraining the involuntary smile that pulled at his lips. The bear was obviously important to her, as well-worn as it seemed to be.

Unaware of Rafe's previous perusal of her backside, Lindy shouldered her pack and turned with surprise at his gentle question. Given his previous attitude she was somewhat confused as to why he didn't take this opportunity to mock her for having a teddy bear.

"That's Humphrey. He belonged to my grandmother, and when I was seven, she gave him to me. I take him with me whenever I'm away from home... Now that they're not here, he keeps me close to my family, reminds me that I'm loved and that I'm never really alone," she explained candidly, wondering what Rafe's reaction would be.

He nodded with understanding and pulled a necklace from under his shirt. Strung on a leather thong, accompanied by incised beads of turquoise and jet, was a miniature bear, perfectly and intricately carved from ebony stone.

Lindy stepped closer. "That's beautiful," she commented softly. "It's so realistic you almost expect it to move." She looked up, her open gaze meeting Rafe's.

Their eyes locked for a moment and he nodded. "It belonged to my mother." A fleeting moment of mutual understanding passed between them.

Lindy also saw a brief flash of pain in the depths of his — for once — unguarded eyes before he again withdrew. "Time to go," he said briskly and tucked the necklace back under his shirt. She sighed, nodding her acquiescence, and without any further exchanges they set out.

The rising sun shimmered brightly, the sky clear with the promise of a beautiful day. The morning air was pleasantly cool and refreshing and Lindy took deep breaths of the heady stuff.

"Getting winded already?" Rafe threw the question over his shoulder.

"No," she replied tolerantly. "The air is so fresh and clean, it just feels good to breathe."

A noncommittal grunt was her answer. They tramped on for some time and Lindy's gaze wandered everywhere taking in the pleasing sights the forest had to offer. Overhead, birds sang and squirrels jumped from limb to limb chasing each other and occasionally stopping to chatter indecipherably. Sunshine filtered down through the green canopy overhead, dotting the landscape with pools of bright light.

As much as she admired the magnificence of the great outdoors, there was another sight that kept attracting her admiring regard, the compelling male figure that walked ahead of her. Rafe moved with a smooth, confident gait. Like her, he carried a backpack, one she was sure probably weighed twice what hers did, yet it seemed to have little, if any, impact on his endurance. He walked with an untiring rhythm that never faltered and she bit her lip at the swooping sensation that assaulted her insides when her eyes settled on the taut mounds that moved under the seat of his jeans.

"Oh, *man*," she mouthed silently, remembering a line she'd once read in a romance novel, something about the hero's churning backside as he thrust repeatedly between the heroine's willing and widespread thighs. There was no denying it; the man had one fine backside.

Amused at her repeated trips into sexual fantasy, Lindy smothered a grin and admitted to herself that Rafe was stirring her libido from its near dormant state. A heady awareness of male presence, *this* male's presence, was bringing her body back to an awareness of its own sexuality. Things were stirring inside, heat and yearning, the need to touch, to mate.

Wondering at her reaction to Rafe and disconcerted by her near primitive thoughts, she failed to note that he had halted on the trail in front of her until she came near to colliding with him. Sidestepping to avoid running into him, her hiking boot caught on the exposed roots of a young tree and unceremoniously knocked her off balance. Just as she was about to land face-first in a patch of poison ivy, strong arms wrapped around her and pulled her back from the edge of disaster.

Lindy was stunned at the ease with which Rafe rescued her. She stood unmoving in his arms, arms that were wrapped around her waist and pressed firmly against the lower curve of her breasts. She felt a fleeting disappointment that her backpack kept their bodies from meeting more fully, and was stunned at the thought.

*When did I go into heat?* she thought irreverently.

"What are you doing?" Rafe inquired with mild exasperation.

"I tripped."

"I noticed. Can't walk and chew gum at the same time?"

"For your information I was trying to keep from running into you! I...wasn't paying attention. I didn't notice you'd stopped."

"Just a suggestion? Save the daydreams for when you're sitting down. I don't want to have to carry you back to camp."

To Lindy's weight-sensitive mindset, this was a dig at her size, and she began struggling against his hold as familiar pain and helpless anger dug its claws into her.

"Don't worry, I'd rather crawl back than have you carry me."

Unaware that Rafe had detected the hurt in her voice, she increased her struggles until she was panting with the effort and desperate to get away from him. The thought that he found her size disgusting was hard enough to handle without him touching her.

"Let me go!"

Rafe gave her a squeeze that caused her ribs to creak. "Stop struggling! I didn't mean that the way it sounded!"

Lindy froze in horror. Here she stood, held in the arms of the most maddening and attractive man she'd ever met and, after having known him less than twenty-four hours, her biggest insecurity had just been hauled out of its deep, dark closet to be exposed to the pitiless and oh-so revealing light of day.

Her first instinct was to cringe in embarrassment, but years of running her own business and fighting to build her self-confidence came to the fore. She lifted her chin, forced herself to relax, and this time calmly requested that Rafe release his hold.

He did and she stepped away, not looking at him as she silently straightened her clothing and readjusted her backpack. "I'm ready to go on, if you are," she told him neutrally.

Rafe nodded. "A couple more miles and we'll stop for lunch." He turned his back and began to walk. A few feet away, he threw a soft comment over his shoulder. "You're a very beautiful woman, Lindy."

Preparing to take her first step forward, Lindy again found herself frozen, this time with shock. She watched Rafe's retreating form with disbelief. Had he just said what she thought he said? A quick flood of tears filled her eyes and she blinked them back. At that moment she realized that Rafe's beauty was more than skin-deep. He was turning out to be a genuinely nice man, not to mention intuitive. How many other men would have noticed her hurt and divined the reason for it? That, along with his looks, was a decidedly deadly combination.

She frowned as a small frisson of nervousness twisted her stomach. "I will not fall for this guy," she whispered softly, knowing that it was already too late—she was already beginning to slip.

"Are you coming?" Rafe yelled back at her.

"I wish," she murmured, then yelled out, "Yeah, yeah, I'm coming."

\* \* \* \* \*

"I wish you were coming," Rafe muttered. "In my arms, with your legs wrapped around my waist."

He cursed softly to himself as his cock thickened even more. It was a process that had begun when he'd saved Lindy from her fall. Having her in his arms had sent an unexpected explosion of feeling throughout his body. Her scent had swept over him in a wave that created an undeniable awareness of her. It was beginning to drive him crazy. And now, having felt her soft curves pressed against him, his imagination was coming alive with the possibilities.

There was a subtle tension beginning to build between them, and Rafe wasn't sure how long he was going to be able to deny the desire to take her. He took a few deep breaths, dismayed at the swiftness of the building need.

"I am not an animal," he whispered softly to himself, repeating the steadying mantra in his head.

Hearing her catch up to him, he increased the pace, determined to get a grip on his unfamiliar feelings. With that in mind, he again concentrated on the trail and the signs being transmitted by the birds and other wildlife. Although they seemed to prefer the areas closer to the river, occasionally one of the bears would venture into this part of the forest. So far there'd been no sign of one.

Lost in his contemplation of the surroundings, he was startled to hear a subtle growling noise and instantly halted, scanning the wood for its source. Finding nothing, he frowned, then grinned when he realized it was Lindy's stomach.

"I take it you didn't have breakfast?" he asked, turning to face her, finding her standing with her hand lying against her stomach.

"I can't eat that early, it makes me sick."

"Can you hold on for about twenty more minutes? We're almost there."

Lindy nodded and Rafe continued on, eventually leading them to a clearing through which a small stream ran. It emerged from a shallow, rocky grotto sunk into the hillside, the water trickling merrily over stones worn smooth by years of erosion.

"This is natural spring water, it comes from deep underground."

"Is it safe to drink?"

"Sure."

Lindy carefully negotiated her way over the smooth stones and dipped her fingers into the water where it burbled from between the rocks and formed a natural fountain. She found it quite cold and, cupping her hands, brought the water to her lips and drank.

"Mmmm, that's good," she commented and turned back to Rafe.

He stood watching her, mesmerized by her wet lips and the water dripping down her chin. Taken by the sudden impulse to cross the clearing and lick those sweet drops off her face, he realized that he was standing there with his mouth open. He quickly slammed it shut and bent down to his open pack, removing several packets of food.

"Nancy insisted that I bring a good variety so you'd find something you like. Take a look at these," he offered, keeping his eyes on the food packets.

Lindy crossed to his side and knelt down. "Wow, potato corn chowder, chili, beef stroganoff—I didn't know they made stuff like this for camping."

"It beats hauling a bag of flour and a slab of bacon, or existing on oatmeal, although I have to say the oatmeal with cinnamon, raisins and almonds is pretty good."

"Is this any good?" she asked, picking up the chowder.

"*I* think so," he answered, and took a small pot out of his pack along with a couple of metal bowls and spoons. "Have a seat while I heat it up."

Lindy took the folded blanket Rafe offered and spread it on the ground, settling herself cross-legged on it. She watched him as he started a fire and prepared the chowder.

Lindy accepted the bowl he offered and dug in, taking a tentative taste. Her brows lifted and she looked at Rafe. "This is really good."

Rafe nodded, saying nothing as his mouth was full, but silently offered her some crackers, which she accepted. They finished their meal in a not-uncomfortable silence as they simply enjoyed the food and the setting.

Finishing her bowl, Lindy sighed with contentment. Rafe offered her more, but she declined. He easily polished off the rest and after cleaning up, repacked everything.

Lindy had gone back to the stream for a final drink and Rafe was watching her appreciatively when he noticed the sudden hush that had fallen over the woods. The birds had stopped singing. He began scanning the area and quickly found the reason for the silence. Across the stream, mostly hidden by the dense brush, stood a bear, one he instantly recognized as a very large male that occasionally had a tendency toward aggression.

"Lindy, don't move." He spoke the words with commanding calm.

Lindy instantly froze.

Careful not to make eye contact with the bear, Rafe walked slowly to Lindy's side. Upon reaching her, he took her hand and squeezed it, then began to slowly back away, silently urging her to move with him. Just as slowly, the bear began to move forward out of the underbrush. It was huge. Fully eight feet long from the tip of its nose to its rump, the reddish-brown grizzly easily weighed in excess of nine hundred pounds. His feet were enormous and tipped with black, scimitar-like curved claws.

Lindy, who up until this time had not spotted the bear, took in a sharp breath.

"Easy," Rafe encouraged, then began a soft litany of words and sounds that made no sense to Lindy.

To the bear, however, the words seemed to mean something. He stopped his advance, his ears flicking at the sound, his eyes focusing on Rafe as he listened to the rhythmic cadence of the words. Lindy flinched as the bear huffed what seemed like a response and turned its back to them, melting back into the trees. They stood quietly, unmoving, until the birds again took up their song.

Rafe released a deep breath and again squeezed her hand. "Are you all right?" he questioned, noting the increased pallor of her complexion.

"Sure, fine," she replied weakly. "That was a *bear*," she added in a dazed voice.

"Yes, it was," Rafe replied gently and led her back to the blanket. "Sit down a minute," he ordered softly and sat across from her, their bent knees touching.

"That was a really *big* bear," she told him, eyes wide with shock.

"Yes, I know," he told her patiently. "Lindy, look at me."

"Okay," she agreed, sounding like a lost child. She met his warm, steady gaze.

Rafe reached out and took both of her hands in his. They were chilled and curled around his as though seeking a lifeline. "You're all right," he reassured her.

She bit her lip and nodded in agreement.

"The bear's gone."

Again she nodded, mesmerized by the deep, rich brown of Rafe's eyes and the smooth, gentle tone of his voice, a tone that offered safety and comfort.

"You did very well in your first encounter with a bear. Thank you for not moving as I asked."

"I had to stand still, my legs wouldn't move."

"But you didn't see the bear at first."

"I know."

"Why did you listen to me?"

Lindy opened her mouth to reply, paused for a moment, then admitted softly, "I trust you." The words held a kind of wonder, as though she was just discovering how true they were.

Rafe was at first startled, then gratified by her admission. A wave of warmth swept over him. She trusted him even though he'd given her little reason to, considering the way he'd treated her when she first arrived. He couldn't help but admire her honesty when she could have very well given some inane excuse, rather than make an admission that bolstered his ego.

Never one to be physically demonstrative, he surprised himself and leaned forward to kiss her cheek. "Thank you."

"You're welcome," she replied shyly and smiled, her green-eyed gaze sparkling as color returned to her cheeks.

"Ready to go?"

"On one condition."

"What's that?"

"That we don't see anymore bears today… At least not that close up."

Rafe grinned. "It's a deal."

He squeezed her hands and stood, helping her to her feet. They folded the ground sheet and, after packing it away, headed out toward the river, each silently acknowledging a truce to the hostility that had marked the beginning of their acquaintance.

# Chapter Three

ဆ

By the time the final eight miles were covered, Lindy was ready to admit that she was worn out. It was one thing to walk three miles a day, and quite another to cover nearly twenty all at once. She wanted nothing more than to pitch her tent and fall into her sleeping bag. One thing stood in the way of that goal—camp had to be set up.

Fortunately, Rafe was more than experienced in doing just that. As this was a site he was well familiar with, he knew exactly where to begin. He instructed Lindy to set up their tents while he set up a food preparation area, approximately one hundred yards away.

Despite the popular picture of campers sitting in front of their tents while roasting weenies over an open fire, when camping in bear country, they both knew that this would be a foolish thing to do. If a bear did happen to wander into their camp, it would be prudent to have no food near their sleeping area.

Rafe reopened a previously dug fire pit, uncovered the rocks that lined it, then gathered deadwood from the surrounding area. Their campsite was in a wooded area, the front of it facing out across a huge stretch of grassy meadowland. In the distance, the light from the setting sun sparkled on the river.

Suspended by a rope on a nearby tree was a box which Rafe lowered to the ground. Finished with her chore and grateful for tents that were a breeze to set up, Lindy watched Rafe as he opened the box and began transferring all the foodstuffs from his pack into it.

"What's that?" she asked, indicating the box.

"A BRFC, bear-resistant food container. All our food supplies are going in here and we'll keep them suspended from this tree. This keeps the bears from associating campsites with food. We don't want to attract any uninvited guests," he added with a grin.

Lindy smiled, then suddenly remembered the trail mix and energy bars she'd stowed in her own pack. "Hold on a minute," she said and went back to her tent, rummaging through her pack until she'd gathered every bit of food she'd stuffed in it.

She returned to Rafe and handed it all over to him and he obligingly packed it away with the rest of the food.

"I'm not going to suspend this until after we've had dinner. Want to pick something out, or do you want to be surprised?"

Noting the mischievous twinkle in his eyes, she indicated a packet of beef stroganoff. "I think I'll try that," she told him.

"I thought you trusted me."

"Not with that look in your eyes."

"What look?"

"The one that says you might be up to something."

"Believe me, sweetheart, you'll *know* when I'm up to something."

Lindy's insides did a pitching roll at Rafe's use of the endearment and the steady, heated look he gave her. Suddenly nervous and feeling a bit defensive, she backed up a step. "Yeah, well, be that as it may," she replied a bit breathily, "I'll still go with the stroganoff."

"Suit yourself. I *was* going to make wild rice with *savory* mushroom sauce, sun dried tomatoes and chopped jerky. I've been told it's really good. But if you'd rather have the stroganoff..."

"Okay, okay, I give! That sounds delicious and I'm starving. What can I do to help?"

Rafe grinned, told her to get the utensils and cooking pot out of his pack, and they were soon amicably preparing their meal. Sitting cross-legged on the blanket in front of the fire, they ate and watched the setting sun. It was a stunning view, the sky filling with color as the sun sank slowly down toward the horizon.

Rafe broke their easy silence. "Lindy… That's an unusual name—is it short for something?"

"Lucky Lindy, you know, Charles Lindbergh? My dad had a great admiration for the man. He learned to fly a plane and it was one of his greatest joys. He used to take me for rides all the time. It was wonderful." She sighed. "I really miss him. He always took such pleasure in life—it was contagious, no one could *not* have fun around my dad."

"He sounds like a good man."

Lindy gave him an enquiring look. "You didn't say *was* a good man."

Rafe shook his head. "He may not be here with you, but he's still around, and I'm sure he's still the good man you remember."

"That's exactly the way I think about it," she told him incredulously. "I hated it when people would say he was gone, or my grandparents were gone. They're not gone, they've just relocated," she said with a smile.

"I notice you didn't mention your mother, is she still here with you?"

"Yes and no. When Dad died, Mom was hit hard by it. Instead of descending into the role of grieving widow, she ran. She lives in Europe and travels a lot. We speak on the phone and see each other once or twice a year, but we just don't have much in common, you know? And I think the fact that I look a lot like Dad distresses her to a certain extent."

"She's lucky in a way. My dad *did* descend into the role of grieving widower after my mom's death. He just sort of went inside himself and never really came back."

Lindy reached out and placed her hand on Rafe's arm in sympathy. "I'm sorry, it must have been difficult for you." Even through the fabric of his shirt sleeve, she could feel the tension in the hard muscles under her hand.

"Yeah, well, I learned to cope," Rafe replied, slowly relaxing under her soothing touch. "Dad retreated in to his studies and the digs—he was a paleontologist—and I pretty much ran the household. I guess losing himself in his work was his way of running from the hurt."

Lindy nodded with understanding. "Unless it happened to us, I guess we'd never really know how we'd react to losing our mate."

Rafe sent a sharp glance her way at her use of the word mate instead of husband or wife, then chastised himself. She couldn't know, there was no way, he concluded silently.

"Rafe, I've been meaning to ask you—" she continued, "—earlier, when the bear put in his appearance, you started speaking to it. What were you saying?"

Rafe paused a moment as though ordering his words. "I was assuring brother bear that our intentions were peaceful and that we would do no harm to the forest or to those she sheltered."

"Brother bear?"

"My mother taught me to honor all animals as my brothers and sisters. She told me it was our duty to protect them."

"And the language you were speaking?"

"Shoshone, the language of my mother's people."

She nodded and smiled impishly. "It must be nice to be bilingual."

"Not particularly, when the second language is one most people don't understand," he replied with the lift of a sardonic eyebrow.

Lindy squeezed his arm. "Well, I'm sure glad the bear understood!"

It amazed Rafe how quickly that one little touch lit flames inside him. A wave of warmth and desire raced under his skin, a wave that boosted his heartbeat and sent blood pumping to his now throbbing and eager cock as it grew and caused a distinct bulge under his jeans. He looked at Lindy, at that moment wanting nothing more than to lose himself in her inviting green gaze and the full, tempting lushness of her body.

A calm, detached part of his mind wondered what it would be like to be just a normal man wanting a woman, having her, loving her, raising a family with her. Those tempting images swam before his eyes and solidified in the depths of Lindy's.

He leaned toward her, noticing the rosy flush that graced the smooth, glowing skin of her cheeks. His lips parted and, when hers echoed the move, a low, rumbling growl crawled from the depths of his chest. Lindy's eyes widened but she didn't back away, she leaned toward him, her posture broadcasting her willingness.

Her rising scent assaulted his nostrils, tendrils of it winding around his spine, sending an unexpected and eager quiver through his body. The sweet musky aroma of her desire melted into his awareness and electrified every nerve.

Rafe felt the heated, caressing rush of her breath on his lips as he tilted his head, closing that infinitesimally small space between them. Just as his lips made fleeting contact, a movement in the distance drew his attention. Outlined on the horizon by the last of the sun's fleeing rays, a mother bear and her cub were leaving the river's edge for their nightly resting place.

Rafe pulled back and watched them go, mesmerized by a sight he'd seen many times in the past. He turned back to Lindy and found her looking at him with a puzzled expression on her face. At that moment, the differences between them slammed into him like a blow from a sledgehammer. He wasn't a normal man, never had been, never would be, and no amount of wishful thinking would make it so.

"Let's get these things cleaned up and put away. I want to get the BRFC secured for the night." He rose and without a backward glance began cleaning up the remains of their supper.

* * * * *

Lying in her tent, wide awake, Lindy was still worrying about the significance of what happened earlier in the evening. There was no doubt that Rafe had been about to kiss her, a thing she'd decided she very much wanted. But then something had happened. All the heat and want and need she'd seen in his eyes just seemed to drain away, replaced by such a haunted look of loneliness, regret and resignation that Lindy felt her heart pinch with dismay.

It hurt to think that Rafe wrestled with such poignant emotions, and she couldn't help but wonder why. She hadn't refused his advances, she had in fact been on the verge of throwing herself into his arms. The agonizingly slow moments that passed as he'd moved closer had made her want to moan with frustration.

She wanted him. There was no denying it. Her body was making demands, her mind was confirming the need and now, seeing the hurt that filled him, her heart wanted to heal his. Conflicting emotions swirled inside. Mother, lover, friend, she felt the need to be all those and more to the big, quiet man who slept in the tent next to hers.

She restlessly changed positions in her sleeping bag and froze at the sound of something brushing the side of her tent. Listening intently, her tension increasing, the sound came again and she let her held breath out with a whoosh. It was the tall grass at the back of her tent. The breeze had picked up and intermittently set the stuff dancing against the nylon walls.

Slowly relaxing, Lindy sighed and yawned, pulled her backpack into her arms, and hugged it tight. She missed Humphrey, she admitted wryly and yawned again, her eyelids drifting down. Sleep came, and with it, dreams…

*Naked, she lay back against the huge, warm body that curled around her. Dark, soft fur caressed her, sending delightful shivers over her skin. She could feel the strong, steady heart that beat against her back and she ran an exploring hand down a long fur-covered leg.*

*Another shiver shook her as something nuzzled the hair at the back of her neck, and she smiled even as her hand reached a paw.*

*The enormous paw sported long, curved claws and her fingers explored them curiously. A low growl sounded at her ear and she turned her head, her eyes meeting those of the creature she leaned against. A shocked gasp was torn from her lips as she froze in terror, waiting to be torn asunder. The bear simply stared at her, its eyes dark and familiar and filled with patience as it waited. Lindy slowly relaxed and took a deep breath. Puzzlement filled her thoughts as recognition replaced fear.*

"Rafe," she whispered and woke.

She groggily blinked a few times then drifted back to sleep, the dream filed away in her subconscious. Unfortunately, the next dream was not so easily dealt with, and she woke again, this time in a cold sweat, a phantom roar reverberating in her head. Lindy lay shivering for a moment then sat up and crawled to the entrance of her tent. She cautiously lowered the zipper and peered out. Lit by moonlight, their campsite held none of the monsters that haunted her dreams.

All was quiet, except for the soft sounds made by the breeze as it rustled grass and leaves, and the chirp of crickets and frogs in the darkness. She scooted out of her tent and stood shivering as the moisture dried on her skin. Dressed in a pair of jersey shorts and a thin t-shirt, she felt naked as the air easily penetrated her clothes.

The dream was slowly fading, but she still felt an echo of the terror that had filled her in the dream as something large had leaned over her, its hot, pungent breath coating her skin and making it crawl before she was grabbed and dragged across the grass. Her fingers had dug into the dirt as she'd sought for something to hold on to, and a scream had built in her throat.

Breathing hard, fighting the returning fear that washed through her, Lindy forced herself to calm down, and was silently coaxing herself to let it go and relax when a voice spoke softly from behind her. "What's wrong?"

She screamed and spun to face the new threat.

"Damn! What's wrong?" Rafe exclaimed.

"You scared me!" she yelled.

"Well, I didn't mean to, I was just trying to see if you were all right."

"I had a nightmare. I was…scared," she confessed, the last word trailing off softly.

"You were what?"

Lindy bit her lip and looked up to see a teasing twinkle in his eyes. "I was scared, all right? I admit it," she fumed.

"I see. I guess I didn't help matters."

Lindy shook her head and shivered again as the breeze kicked up and rushed over her. Her nipples pinched tight under the thin fabric of her shirt, and for the first time she noticed that Rafe was bare-chested and wearing nothing but a pair of loose athletic shorts that exposed his well-formed legs to mid-thigh.

Lindy's mouth went dry as her gaze wandered the glistening mounds of muscles that sculpted his chest and abs. She'd known he was built, but this was the most beautiful example of the male body she'd ever seen, and when another breeze whispered over them and Rafe's small nipples went hard, she almost groaned at the spasm that quivered through her pussy.

"So are you all right now, ready to go to back to sleep?"

"I don't think I'm going to be able to sleep."

"Still scared?"

She nodded, unwilling to admit that it wasn't fear that was going to keep her awake, but desire. Rafe had definitely gotten her juices flowing. The man was truly breathtaking.

Rafe gave a resigned sigh and went to her tent, bent down and pulled her sleeping bag out. Lindy swallowed hard at the sight of his oh-so tempting backside as it was momentarily presented for her enjoyment. The leg opening of his shorts rose and she could almost swear she caught a glimpse of the firm mounds of his ass. She shook her head, wondering where these new voyeuristic tendencies were coming from. She'd never felt the need to ogle any other good-looking man in this way.

Throwing her sleeping bag over his arm, Rafe motioned for her to follow him to his tent. He ducked inside and Lindy heard a brief scrambling around then he stuck his head out. "Come on, your bed's ready."

Eyes wide and holding back a smile, she crawled inside Rafe's tent and found her sleeping bag laid out next to his.

"Think you can sleep now?" he asked.

Lindy nodded, and laying down on her side, she scrunched some of the bag under her head to form a pillow. "Thanks," she murmured softly and with a deep sigh relaxed into the warm, welcoming darkness.

"You're welcome, now shut up," he grumbled.

Lindy snorted a soft laugh, deciding that this was the best outcome of a nightmare she'd ever experienced. Who'd have thought the thing would result in her sharing a tent with the hunky Mr. Kutter? Granted, she was horny as hell, but there were worse things to be. She was still smiling when a yawn took her, pushing her slowly yet inevitably toward sleep.

\* \* \* \* \*

The bear had returned, and she relaxed into the heat he generated at her back. Lindy wasn't afraid this time and wiggled contentedly in its embrace. She drifted in a half-doze, feeling the soft warmth of the breath that stirred the hair at the nape of her neck. Images of Rafe and the bear intermingled in her sleep-fogged brain. Again, she pushed back into the body that curled against hers and felt something hard pushing against her bottom. The flowing images solidified and she suddenly knew without a doubt that it was Rafe—so warm and solidly real—pressed against her.

She moaned softly and turned over, pushing at him, urging him to his back. Still half-asleep, her inhibitions at rest, she was awake enough to know where she was and what she wanted.

She slid her hand over his taut abs and down under the waistband of his shorts, finding what she sought. His cock. Full and hard. She slid her fingers around it and lightly stroked.

Just emerging from sleep, Rafe groaned and a drowsy smile pulled at her lips in response. Lindy moved down his body and rose up enough to pull his shorts down and over his towering erection, of truly epic proportions, she noted with awe.

Sleep was loosening its hold on her just as she renewed her hold on Rafe's cock and began slowly stroking. Thick and hot, she could see the full veins that wrapped its darkly sleek and solid surface and feel the blood throbbing under her fingers.

His hips moved, pushing his hard, pulsing flesh further into her hand as she bent to him, her tongue flicking out to sweep up the clear, sweet drops of pre-cum that bubbled from the swollen, plum-shaped head. The taste was heady and compelling.

"Unhhh, Lindy," Rafe ground out.

Needing no further encouragement, she opened her mouth and sank down on the smooth, heavy column she held wrapped in her stroking fist. As her mouth and tongue explored, her other hand found his full, round ball sac and gently manipulated it. Rafe nearly rose vertically from the ground, incoherent grunts and groans issuing from his throat.

Gratified at his response, she continued to play, her fingers stroking and massaging his balls while her lips tightened, holding his throbbing cock in her mouth, her tongue laving over the tightly stretched, satiny skin. Rafe's body was taut with need, moving at her direction, and she breathed deeply of the spicy male musk that rose from his heated skin.

The heady aroma worked through her system, pulling at her, urging her on until she felt near-frenzied with the need to bring him to climax. A light sheen of sweat broke out over her body and she leaned into him, rubbing her breasts against him, her hips echoing the rhythm of his as she drove him closer to orgasm.

In her mouth she felt his cock swell ever larger and pulse as his body froze, then bucked. She heard the shout torn from his throat as the first volley of his hot male essence released. Lindy held on and swallowed each spurt of salty-sweet cream that filled her mouth, savoring the unique taste that was Rafe. He shuddered under her, the tension in his body easing, and she slowly released him, licking his skin clean of any stray drops.

Wordlessly, she slid up the length of his body and collapsed against him, feeling his arm move over her shoulders. They lay quietly for a few moments until Rafe easily rolled her to her back and loomed over her.

"Why?" he asked softly.

"I wanted you," she answered simply.

Rafe's mouth descended to hers, their lips opening, each welcoming the exploring tongue of the other. Lindy moaned with pleasure, then gasped as one large hand cupped her breast, gently squeezing. She arched her back, pushing into Rafe's touch, urging him on, moaning her approval when his fingers found and lightly pinched a taut nipple.

He broke the kiss and pulled back, looking into her passion-filled eyes. "You have to be the boldest female I've ever met. I've never had a woman make a meal of me the way you just did."

Lindy smiled and stroked a hand down his chest. "I couldn't help it, you just felt so good and smelled so good, I *had* to taste." She leaned up and licked one flat masculine nipple, feeling it rise under her tongue.

Rafe growled and grasped her wrists, pulling her arms above her head. "It's my turn now, sweetheart, and I'm *very* hungry."

His lips found hers again and he ravished her mouth, feverishly exploring with his tongue before pulling hers into his mouth and holding it prisoner as he lightly sucked. Lindy moaned, then began panting when he released her mouth and went exploring. He roved over her chin and jawline, lightly nipping as he went, and paused at her ear, sucking the lobe into his mouth, his teeth nibbling.

Lindy went rigid under him when his tongue began to slide over the swirled curves of her ear. "Oh God, Rafe, *don't*."

"Have I found a hot spot, babe?" he whispered in her ear, his tongue following the sound inside.

Lindy bucked and groaned, pulling against his grasp, then gave in with a helpless shudder. "I'm getting dizzy," she whimpered softly.

"Just hold on to me, sweetheart, I've got you," Rafe murmured and released her arms, smiling when they wrapped around him and her generous breasts pressed into his chest.

He continued his assault on her ears until Lindy was quivering with need, her body straining against his. Rafe again pulled back, forcing her to release her grip, and reached for the hem of her t-shirt.

"When I saw you last night, standing in the moonlight in this flimsy little shirt, with your nipples hard and pointing right at me, it was all I could do not to throw you down and take you right then and there." The shirt came up and was quickly pulled over her head and thrown across the tent. Rafe stared reverently at her naked breasts. "Beautiful," he murmured. "You have the most beautiful breasts, Lindy, so full and round." His finger traced a path around one taut areola. "And these sweet nipples, just like juicy, ripe berries."

"You don't think they're too big?"

"You can't be serious."

She nodded.

"No, baby —" he assured her, " — they're not too big, they fit you perfectly."

Breathing hard, Lindy watched as Rafe lowered his lips to her impudently pointing nipple and kissed it, then moved to the other to repeat the process. Her eyes closed and she felt the warm heat of his breath mist over her skin a split second before his mouth closed over her. A guttural moan was torn from her as his teeth closed gently around the base of her nipple and his tongue flicked and laved the tip.

"Rafe, *oh God*, Rafe," she moaned as an orgasmic shudder slammed into her. Legs straining and bottom bouncing against the sleeping bag beneath her, she undulated against the hard body above her, then lay panting and shivering in the aftermath.

"I'm going to suckle you now, sweetheart. Come for me again," Rafe ordered softly.

Giving in to the magic his mouth worked, the gentle suction and pressure accompanied by his tongue's insistent caresses, Lindy helplessly obeyed and cried out as another orgasm rocked her quivering core. Blindly lost to the pleasure, she missed the fact that Rafe was peeling her shorts away and sliding them down her long, shapely legs.

"Rafe?" she questioned, coming slowly out of her daze, having lost sight of him.

"Right here," he answered.

Lindy looked down to find him lying between her wide-spread legs. His hands slid over her thighs and her mind supplied an image of warm milk chocolate pouring over sweet vanilla ice cream. The rich brown of his skin was such an erotic contrast to the creamy hue of her own that she shivered.

"Rafe, did you know that you're the sexiest man I've ever seen?" she asked, looking deep into the heated depths of his brown eyes.

"No, I didn't, but thank you."

"You're welcome. Are you going to do what I think you're going to do?"

"Oh yeah. I told you I was hungry. Is that a problem?"

"No, it's just that…well, no one's ever…"

"Never?"

Lindy shook her head, her wide, green eyes revealing a vulnerable uncertainty.

Rafe bent down and kissed her inner thigh, smiling as she trembled under his lips. "I promise you, if you don't like it, I'll stop. Do you still trust me?"

She wordlessly nodded.

"Then lay back, sweetheart. I'm going to make love to your sweet little pussy and set you on fire."

Lindy moaned and felt another rush of moisture heat her already well-lubricated sheath. Before she could take a breath, Rafe's lips made contact, his tongue laving her clit with a sensual slide. She jumped and tightened her thighs, at first instinctively seeking to close them, but Rafe's actions soon had her seeking to open them wider.

His tongue licked, laved and swirled over the sensitive, swollen tissues of her needy pussy. First he'd concentrate on her clit, driving her higher and higher, then he'd plunge his tongue as deeply as possible into her warm, weeping channel and gently fuck her with it. Again and again he repeated the procedure until Lindy was frantically tossing, only Rafe's sure grip on her body keeping her right where he wanted her. Occasionally he'd vary his actions by lightly nibbling on her swollen labia, but soon he was back at her very center, teasing and tormenting her.

Aroused to the point of madness, Lindy began begging. "Please, I need to come, I need to come, *I need to come!*"

Heeding her pleas, Rafe slid a long finger deep into her tight sheath. The walls fluttered and closed around it as though trying to pull it deeper inside. A second finger joined the first spreading her wider and Lindy began pushing into them. "That's it, baby." Rafe looked up and encouraged, "Ride my fingers."

Dipping back down he took her clit into his mouth and began to suck. The effect was spectacularly immediate. Lindy wailed as her climax hit. Her sheath gripped and milked Rafe's stroking fingers as she continued to mindlessly fuck herself on them. Her body spasmodically rocked with the sharp bursts of pleasure that shuddered through her until finally, finally her muscles eased and she slowly relaxed. She continued to utter small sated moans as the aftershocks rippled through her, and Rafe moved up and leaned over her, drinking in the soft sounds and smiling at the flush that lit her pale skin from within. She was glowing like a woman thoroughly satisfied.

Lindy sighed and without opening her eyes, reached up and pulled Rafe down to her lips, kissing him long and deep. She sucked his lower lip into her mouth and tasted herself on his skin, deciding the flavor was not unpleasant.

Releasing him she looked into his eyes, hers half-lidded and drowsy. "That was wonderful," she sighed softly. "Thank you."

"My pleasure," Rafe answered and kissed her again.

He rolled over and stretched out on his sleeping bag. Lindy couldn't help but notice that his cock had recovered and was again standing tall.

"Looks like you're ready for another round," she teased and reached out to softly stroke his erection.

"He always did have a mind of his own," Rafe answered.

"You know," she slowly drawled, "when we first met, my imagination supplied me with an image of riding your beautiful body." She rose up and straddled him, settling herself on his thighs. "You didn't happen to bring any condoms with you, did you?"

"No, and unless you did, it's not going to happen. I'm *not* taking the chance of getting you pregnant," he replied in a no-nonsense tone of voice.

Lindy felt an immediate pinch of hurt in her midsection. She lifted herself away from him and began rummaging for her clothes.

"Lindy," Rafe began softly and sat up. "You're jumping to conclusions again. It's nothing personal. There are things about me you don't know…things I can't explain. But the last thing I intend to do is take the chance of fathering children. With anyone."

"You don't have to explain anything to me, Rafe, we barely know each other," she replied, slipping her t-shirt on. "Getting pregnant is certainly something I'm not looking for at this point in my life. But I have to say that I rather resent the implication that you think I'd be irresponsible enough to have unprotected sex with you or anyone. I don't make a habit of trying to entrap men by getting pregnant. Let's just forget it, okay? How do we go about getting a bath around here? Will the bears mind if we wash in the river?"

Lindy slid into her shorts, grabbed up her sleeping bag and left without waiting for an answer. She could feel Rafe's silent regard as she slipped out of the tent and she just had to get away. Despite his assurances that his words weren't directed specifically at her, she still couldn't help but feel as though she'd been rejected. She was angry, not only at him but at herself as well.

Rapidly cycling thoughts chased themselves through her head. *This is stupid. We were only having fun, right? Why did he have to mention children…and why doesn't he want any? Does it matter? Is it any of my business? It's not like there's anything between us but maybe a growing friendship and some physical attraction.*

She rubbed her stomach, trying to loosen the knots that formed with that last thought. Nothing between them? *Why was that thought so disconcerting*? she wondered as she returned to her tent and dropped the sleeping bag inside. She grabbed a towel, soap and clean undies out of her backpack, picked up her clothes and slipped her feet into her shoes, then she left the tent and headed toward the river. She'd decided that at that moment she'd rather face ten bears than Rafe, especially when his scent still clung to her skin and the memory of his touch was so fresh.

# Chapter Four

෨

The next few days moved slowly by and there was no repeat of the intimacy they'd shared that first morning. Rafe and Lindy were polite to each other, cooperatively working together to fix meals and keep the campsite in good order. They spent long hours quietly observing the bears at the river and Lindy felt most relaxed at those times, especially when Rafe pulled his drawing pad out and sketched the bears.

It amazed her how the drawings seemed to magically form under his hand. The sure, precise strokes of his pencil against the paper produced some of the most beautiful images she'd ever seen. The only trouble was that watching him work, his long, dexterous fingers lightly gripping the pencil, set her imagination on fire. She kept remembering what it felt like to have those fingers so intimately deep within her body, and it made her ache with need.

One afternoon, after a particularly restless evening spent fighting her imagination and the images of that first morning together, Lindy fell asleep in the grass, lulled by the quiet and the warm sunshine. She was unaware of the picture she presented while curled up with her cheek resting on the back of one hand, or that, struck by the sweet innocence of her expression, Rafe felt compelled to draw her.

When she woke, the sketch was completed and tucked away and Rafe was, she noticed, using the camera to photograph a lone coyote that had come to the river to drink and scavenge.

By the time a week had passed, Lindy was ready to scream with frustration. Not only couldn't she deny the physical yearning she felt for Rafe, but she was finally willing to admit that it was much more than that. Those feeling that had begun to form when he'd first let her see the vulnerable man inside were growing.

She found herself watching him when he wasn't looking, yearning for him to say something or look at her in a way that might convey that he was feeling something too. But he never did. Rafe seemed to have stepped into the role of polite coworker, offering nothing of a personal nature.

What she didn't know was that Rafe was on the verge of an explosion. His gut churned with the need to not only touch her and hold her again, but to tell her all the things he was holding inside, all the things that made his life the personal hell it had become. His soul longed for the solace he instinctively felt she could offer, but he was afraid to take the chance. Afraid to see the fear and loathing that might be her reaction to what he so wanted to confess.

How could anyone possibly believe or understand what and who he really was? The idea of it was so farfetched that sometimes he himself was struck by the sheer impossibility of it.

Another day passed in frustrating silence for both of them and after sharing the evening meal, they retired to their separate tents for the night. Lindy lay wide-awake, too worked up to sleep, when a chorus of howls began in the distance. She froze and listened for a moment, then heard a stirring from the tent next to hers.

Quickly rising, she looked out her tent flap to see that Rafe, too, had been disturbed by the sound. "Is that coyotes?" she asked softly.

"Wolves," he answered. "But don't worry, they shy away from contact with humans. Go to sleep."

Lindy, hurt by his curt dismissal, nodded and ducked back into her tent. She lay back down, a cloud of misery settling over her. Something had to change, she decided. She missed the friendship that had been growing between them and if nothing else, she wanted that back. She lay thinking of ways she might accomplish that goal and yawned, realizing that she felt better now that she'd resolved to try to set things right between them.

Snuggling into her sleeping bag, she was just drifting off when she heard the zipper of Rafe's tent in the silence. She reasoned that he was probably just going to use the "facilities", but something about it bothered her and she rolled over and opened her own tent flap just the slightest bit.

Looking out, she spotted Rafe. Fully dressed, he was leaving the campsite and heading out along the line of trees that bordered the meadow. Puzzled, curious and a bit alarmed at the fact that he was leaving her alone, Lindy feverishly donned her jeans and hiking boots and crawling out of her tent, headed in the direction he'd disappeared.

Fortunately there was plenty of moonlight, and reaching the tree line, she saw him in the not-*too*-far distance. Walking as quickly and as silently as possible, she followed. Rafe had a good head start on her and she was soon breathing hard, trying to catch up with him, but eventually she closed the distance and slowed, not wanting to alert him to the fact that she was following him.

He continued on for nearly half an hour until they came to a hill that was covered with some trees and dense brush. Rafe disappeared into the tangle and Lindy closed the distance, afraid she would lose him. The moonlight revealed a lightly worn path and she carefully picked her way through, avoiding the thorny underbrush.

Up ahead she could see the path widen as it trailed out of the woods and she frowned, very much afraid that she'd lost him. Hurrying to the edge of the wood, intent on her search for Rafe, she failed to notice the bundle that lay in her path and tripped, falling to the ground with an *oomph* as the breath was knocked out of her.

Rolling over, she sat up and reached for the bundle that had trapped her unwary feet. As her fingers came in contact with it, she recognized it as fabric. She lifted a piece up and in the faint light she was able to discern that it was a shirt. Bringing it close, she could smell the distinctive scent on it... It was Rafe's shirt.

"What the hell?" she whispered.

*Why had Rafe shed his clothes?* she wondered. Lindy stood and walked toward the edge of the woods, searching for any sign of him. Reaching the outer perimeter, the hill began its downward slope, one that ended in an open valley. Lindy peeked from behind the outermost tree and stared wide-eyed at what was before her.

One lone bear was surrounded by a pack of seven wolves and they seemed to be playing tag. A wolf would rush in and nip at the bear, which would swing around and give chase. The wolves would scatter and romp around, tongues lolling from what looked like grinning faces, as their pack mate was chased, until the next one would take its place and goad the bear into changing targets.

This went on for some few minutes until the largest of the wolves must have gotten in a particularly painful nip that pulled a muted roar from the bear. He abruptly sat down on the injured part. Holding her breath, Lindy expected the bear to become enraged and retaliate, but instead it sat quietly for a moment as the wolf pack gathered around.

The whole group formed a frozen tableau until an odd sort of heat shimmer began to engulf each of the animals gathered. Lindy frowned at the odd blurring that surrounded the group, blinking her eyes in an effort to clear her vision. She could swear there was some kind of movement taking place, but she couldn't make out exactly what was happening until the air cleared and where there once was a bear and seven wolves, now there was Rafe and seven other men, all completely naked.

A wave of dizzy disbelief swept over her and her hands gripped the tree she leaned against to keep from falling. How could she possibly be seeing what she was seeing? And yet there they were, eight undeniably naked, and from what she could see, gorgeous men. Her heart pounded as her head tried to make sense of what seemed totally impossible. She jumped as Rafe's voice carried to her.

"Cade, you bastard, I'm going to have a bruise on my ass!"

The big man who'd once been the largest of the gray wolves grinned and laughed. "Aw, poor baby, you want me to kiss your boo-boo?"

"Fuck you! Are you sure you're a wolf and not a hyena?"

Laughter rang out from the gathered men.

"Ooh, the bear gets in a low blow. You're gettin' soft, Rafe," Cade said, and offered Rafe a hand, pulling him to his feet.

The men moved closer together, and Lindy strained to make out their muted conversation. "So how goes the patrolling?" Rafe asked.

"It's quiet tonight, we haven't found any poachers trying to sneak in. I think they're getting a bit more cautious after those last two were picked up so quickly by park security."

"Thanks to you and the rest of the pack. I know I've said this before, but I'm grateful you decided to settle in this area. You've really made a difference here."

"We're glad to help," Cade replied. "It benefits us, too, you know. It's nice to have a place where we can indulge our inner animal without worrying about getting our tails shot off."

Rafe grinned and laughed. "I can see where that would be important."

At that moment another wolf came running up to the group and again, with growing wonder, Lindy witnessed a wolf turning into a man. She desperately tried to hear what was being said, but the men had moved further away and lowered their voices. She could see the new arrival speaking to Rafe and Cade then he shifted and returned the way he'd come in.

Cade watched his pack mate leave then turned to Rafe. "So is she yours? Eric says she carries your scent."

"No, she's not," Rafe denied flatly.

"Well, in that case—" Cade said seriously, "—since she's seen us, we'd better get rid of her." He signaled two of his men and watched as pure protective rage exploded in Rafe's glowing eyes.

Growling in a low-pitched, menacing voice that would make a lesser man lose the contents of his bladder, Rafe rumbled, "Don't you touch her."

Cade waved his men off. "Why are you denying your mate, Rafe?"

Breathing hard, Rafe forced himself to regain calm. "She's not mine. You know why."

"You deny her because you still won't accept who you are."

"How can I accept this? How can anyone accept this half-life, this curse?"

"This *gift*," Cade corrected.

"Gift?" Rafe raged. "To be an animal? To know there's a beast inside that makes you different from every other man, a beast that keeps you separate and alone?"

"You are alone by choice, my friend," Cade told him sternly. "All of us here have wives and lovers. My own wife is fully human and she accepts me, all of me, even that part of me that is wolf. You just don't get it, do you? Inside every human is a part that is innately animal. *We* are the lucky ones. Our animal has a form, a shape we control. We can let it run and play and *be*. The animal in ordinary humans is trapped and must be denied, for it has *no* physical manifestation and, if released, becomes only a force of destruction.

"Rafe, you're torturing yourself for no reason. This is who you are. *Embrace it.* That woman on the hill, she must mean something to you for you to let her see this part of yourself. You want her acceptance. I have a feeling you are someone special to her as well. Give her a chance to know the real you. You're a good man, if she has any sense she'll see that... And if not, we can still get rid of her."

Rafe shook his head, a wry smile playing on his lips. "You're a pain in the ass, you know that, don't you?"

"Remember that when you're sitting on your bruise. Take care of yourself, Rafe, and your lady."

Cade signaled his men, together they shifted and were once again a pack of wolves who gathered around their leader and, as one, ran from the valley. Rafe watched them go, Cade's words echoing in his head. Trepidation sat like a lead weight in his stomach as he turned to climb the hill.

He found Lindy waiting for him at the top, one look at her expression and he felt a block of lead settle in his stomach. With a resigned sigh, he gathered his clothes and began sorting them out. "So now you know," he ventured.

"So now I know? Is that all you've got to say? Rafe! I saw you as a bear. You can *turn into a bear*! Why? How do you do it? And who were those other guys? Are they werewolves? Does that make you a werebear?"

Rafe frowned at the excitement in her voice. This wasn't the reaction and the rejection he'd expected and he felt a rising irritation inside. "It's a *curse* I inherited from my mother," he pronounced succinctly.

"You call that a curse? Wow, I wish *I* could do that. That's some curse," Lindy enthused. "So tell me about it. How did this happen?"

Rafe kept silent as he pulled on his jeans than sat in the grass to put on his socks and boots. He stood and bent to tie his boot laces, then straightened and slid into his shirt, walking away as he buttoned it, with Lindy hot on his heels.

"Are you going to tell me, or is it some kind of secret?"

Annoyed by her enthusiasm, he grumped, "A little patience, please," and was gratified by her compliant silence. "All I know is what I gleaned from my mother's journal. She hinted at things when I was younger, and I remember her telling me things that now make sense, but she never got the chance to tell me everything."

"Because of what happened to her?"

"Yes. How do you know about that?"

"Nancy told me."

"Should I be flattered that the two of you were discussing me?"

Lindy grimaced at his sarcastic tone. "She was only trying to help me understand why you were such a bastard. Now shut up and tell me more about your gift."

"Curse," he corrected. "So I'm a bastard?"

"Rafe, quit stalling!"

"All right! My mother was supposed to reveal all when I became a man, which by tradition, is when a boy reaches puberty. She was killed before I'd reached that time in my life."

"So how did you learn about it?"

"Very painfully," he replied and, refusing to elaborate further, went on. "Legend has it that a group of Shoshone warriors, intent on proving which of them was the greatest hunter in their tribe, engaged in the meaningless slaughter of more than a few grizzlies. They went against tradition and killed the bears for reasons other than need or survival. Thus, they angered the spirit gods, who decided to have them know, without doubt, what it was to be one of the great bears, and what it was they destroyed by taking their lives. The warriors were changed. They were given the ability to become bears and were entrusted with the protection of their brothers. And so it has been to this day that the *gift* is passed on, and the recipients can trace their line back to those original warriors."

"You don't sound as though you believe that."

"I don't know what to believe, other than the fact that I can't deny this thing that is a part of me. Where it came from, I don't really know, or really care. My only real wish is to be rid of it, but that's a choice I've not been given."

They walked in silence for a while until Lindy asked softly, "So you really think it's a curse?"

Rafe was quiet a moment, as though considering his answer. His voice was low and edged by emotion as he began to speak. "A year after my mother died, when I turned thirteen, my body began changing, I'd reached puberty. You've been through it—you know how difficult it can be to deal with. Not only the physical changes, but the emotional ones as well. I was alone, Lindy. My mother was dead, my father may as well have been, for all the good his being there did me. One night, while he was away on a dig, the curse kicked in.

"My dad said I was old enough to stay by myself—and I admit, it was something that made me proud, to know he thought of me as a man. I had my first wet dream that night and that part was good, but after the pleasure came a whole lot of pain." Rafe struggled for a moment then continued.

"Being physically able to ejaculate was my body's signal to shift. It wasn't a pleasant experience. It took several very painful hours. I later found out from my mother's journal that the first change is supposed to be muted by the administering of some special brew that reduces the first-time shifter's awareness, both physical and mental. I didn't have that. I got to feel the full force of that first change—and not only that. *I didn't know what was happening to me.*"

By this time they had reached the campsite and Rafe stood in front of his tent, his head down as he ran his hand over his hair in agitation. A light sheen of sweat had broken out on his body as he remembered the past. "When it was over, when I had fully shifted, I was compelled to go into the woods. A part of me knew who I was and was terrified, but there was another part that pulled me out and away from my home and into the forest. For three days I fought to return, but the bear was stronger, and so I was trapped, until one night I woke to find that I'd changed back into my human form.

"Fortunately, I was in familiar territory and was able to make my way home. Can you imagine how it felt to be out there alone and naked, a child of thirteen, wondering what had happened and dreading the thought of it happening again?"

Rafe's voice shook with emotion, the remembered anguish clearly present.

"Rafe." Lindy spoke softly and reached for him, but he stepped back out of her reach.

"When I got home I remembered my mother's journal and how she had told me it was important, so I read it and I learned about the curse and I...adjusted."

Lindy stood before him and he watched her warily, hating the look of sympathy on her face. She felt *sorry* for him. Of all the things he wanted from her, pity was not on the list. It seared his pride.

"I can only imagine the pain you went through and how terrifying it must have been, but Rafe, that's all behind you now. Can't you see that you've been given something unique, an ability to experience something that the rest of us can only dream about?"

Rafe stared at her in disbelief. "You don't have the slightest notion of what you're talking about. It's easy for you to say you would accept and take joy in this ability. You don't have to live with it!" Lindy began to answer him but he held up his hand to stop her. "I'm tired, and I don't want to discuss this anymore. I'm going to sleep." With that, he entered his tent and effectively put an end to the conversation. He stood quietly, waiting, then heard Lindy utter a soft goodnight and enter her own tent.

Without undressing, he lay down on his sleeping bag and stared into the darkness as bitterness, anger and frustration churned inside. He *was* cursed, and no one would convince him otherwise.

# Chapter Five

ജ

Lindy emerged early from her tent, bleary-eyed and yawning.

During the night she'd thought long and hard about what Rafe had told her. Determined to help him, she was sure she knew what Rafe's problem was as far as accepting his gift. She just needed to find a way to get him to open up to her and talk about it.

Starting the fire and brewing coffee as Rafe showed her, she watched the flames and formed a plan, sure that she was on the right track. She intended to make Rafe confront himself and his repressed feelings. In the days they'd spent together she'd learned so much about him and realized that somehow, along the way, she'd been slowly falling in love. It was troubling in light of everything that had happened between them, especially as Rafe wasn't exhibiting any signs of a man in love.

It was a sobering and unpleasant thought that in a few days she'd be returning home while leaving a part of herself behind, a part that no one wanted… Her heart. Lost in a melancholy silence, she started at hearing a muted grumble.

"G'morning."

Lindy looked up and instantly hoped that she didn't look as worse for wear as Rafe did. He'd obviously gotten very little sleep. Dark circles marred the space under his eyes, his lids were swollen and his eyes looked a bit bloodshot. Raspy stubble marched over his firm jaw and his hair had definite touches of bed head. She couldn't help but concede that even rumpled, he still looked ruggedly adorable.

"You look like hell," she complimented brightly.

Rafe squatted down and poured himself a cup of coffee. "Mmm, thanks," he muttered before taking a sip of the hot bracing liquid in his cup. "I've decided we're going to move on today."

A frisson of shock ran through Lindy. "But I still have three days," she told him. "I don't want to go back yet!"

"We're not going back, we're just going to change locations. There's a hot spring about three hours walk from here. I figure you've seen enough of the bears, and truthfully? I want a hot bath."

Lindy quirked her eyebrows and gave him a crooked smile while shrugging her shoulders. "Okay by me," she agreed.

After breakfast they packed up their gear, rolled up their tents, and, after having secured the campsite by making sure there was no leftover food and the fire pit was again reburied, they headed out.

Still determined to help him, Lindy decided to risk his wrath. "Rafe, do you resent your mother for giving you this...gift or curse, whatever you want to call it?"

Rafe shook his head giving her a resigned glare. "You are one stubborn woman, do you know that?"

"Yes. Now will you answer my question?"

Rafe continued to walk, then stopped and faced her. "I don't resent her. If anything, I miss her more than I can say. I've never given up hope of someday finding the bastard who took her away from my dad and me." His voice shook with the force of his need.

"How would you be able to do that? You weren't there, how would you recognize him?"

"His scent. He *touched* her, probably to see if she was alive or dead." Rafe's gaze became distant. "I'll never forget his scent, it haunts me."

Shocked by the bleak and hollow tone of his voice, Lindy followed wordlessly when Rafe turned and walked away.

The sky was overcast with clouds, making it cool and the walk pleasant, as most of the terrain was meadowland and low grassy hills. On approaching the springs, the footing turned a bit rocky in places, but they found a fairly flat place that was sheltered by a natural rock wall and cushioned by grass, that was not too far from the spring.

Accustomed to the routine, the tents were quickly set up, gear squared away and food again placed in a BRFC that Rafe had left from a previous trip.

"You have those things everywhere?" Lindy asked curiously.

"In the places we frequent most often. It's convenient," he answered.

They walked to the springs, which consisted of several pools of varying sizes joined to each other by narrow channels that allowed the water to filter down to each successive pool. The last one was the largest, and far enough away from the spring's source that the water was pleasantly warm and not too hot to bathe in.

Rafe allowed her some time to look around and explore, then indicated they return to the campsite, which was just out of sight around some piled boulders. He ducked into his tent and emerged with a towel. "I'm going for that bath. I'd be a gentleman and let you go first, but I feel like shit. I need this *bad.*"

Lindy smiled, waved him off and watched him walk away. A wicked smile curved her lips as a plan began to form. She had a surprise in store for Rafe. Ducking into her tent, she slowly stripped off her clothes and wrapped a towel around herself. She sat down and patiently waited for ten minutes, giving Rafe time to get into the water and to relax before she put in her appearance.

Stomach twisting, but determined to carry out her plan, she walked barefoot to the spring pool. Rafe was sitting loose and relaxed, his lower half hidden by the lightly steaming water. His bare chest had recently been splashed with water and tiny rivulets of liquid trickled over his skin, winding their way over the firm hills and valleys of his muscles.

He'd spread his arms to either side, and the effect was to make his upper body look even wider. Lindy's appreciative gaze traveled over him, taking special notice of the dark hair that was just visible under his armpits, and the trail of similar hair that traveled from between his pecs, over his abs, separating at his belly button and rejoining to disappear below the water line.

Her imagination supplied a remembered picture of what lay beneath the water and she felt herself growing wet with desire. Now she knew what it meant to want someone so bad it hurt. The disconcerting thing was that the hurt was not only physical but emotional as well, a double whammy from which it might be impossible to recover.

Sure that joining him in the water would keep him trapped so that she could get him to open up to her, Lindy silently dropped her towel and slipped into the water. At the splash of her entry, Rafe's eyes opened, widened with surprise, then narrowed with suspicion.

"What are you doing?" he grumbled menacingly.

"I wanted a bath, too. There's no reason we can't be civilized about this, men and women in some foreign countries bathe together all the time," she answered glibly. "And while we're bathing, we could chat to pass the time."

Rafe's scowl deepened. "You want to chat while you're aiming those at me?" he accused, indicating her plump breasts bobbing above the water's surface. "You're tempting fate, woman. You seem to forget what I am. Get...out...*now*."

Lindy experienced a foreboding shiver but held her ground. "Don't be ridiculous," she said nervously, her eyes widening as the plump head of his cock broke the surface of the water. "Don't even think of me as a woman." Her heart began beating faster as it suddenly became harder to breathe. "We're just two friends enjoying a bath and a little conversation."

Rafe came up out of the water with a roar. "Friends!" he shouted and stalked across the pool, his massive, rigid erection leading the way. He reached down and wound his hands around her upper arms, forcefully yet carefully pulling her to her feet. "It's not my *friend* I want to sink my cock into, it's my *woman*! I think that's exactly what you want…and I'm just animal enough to give it to you."

Lindy squealed as Rafe hauled her up and over his shoulder and stalked from the pool. Mindful of hurting her, he placed her facedown on a patch of grass and draped his body over hers. Holding her prone, he growled in her ear. "I'm an animal, Lindy. Say it," he ordered.

"No, you're not." She gasped as he pulled her up on her knees, positioning her soft, rounded buttocks up like an offering.

He slid a large hand over the smooth creamy skin of one cheek then gave it one sharp swat. "Say it, Lindy."

"No!"

A second swat landed on the other cheek. "*Say it.*"

"No, I won't!"

Rafe let his hand travel between her thighs and found her pussy, fevered and swollen. He dipped a finger into the slick, wet heat and slowly fucked it in and out. "What am I, Lindy?"

"Rafe," she moaned, her hands clutching at the grass under her.

A second finger joined the first, spreading her wider, preparing her for his invasion. "This is what an animal does, it takes what it wants," he growled in her ear. "Admit it, you're afraid of me I'm not a human, I'm a beast." He bestowed a stinging nip on her lush bottom and bathed a third finger in the flowing juices of her body. Forming a cone now with three fingers, he thrust them inside her.

Lindy moaned and pushed back into them. Far from hurting her, Rafe's dominant invasion was setting her aflame. Her body was clamoring for more and she could barely reason, but retained enough of her sanity to know that she'd never give him the confirmation he wanted from her.

"You're not a beast. Not, not, *not!*" she yelled and felt him position himself between her thighs.

He withdrew his fingers and she felt the plump, throbbing head of his cock take their place. She moaned at the blanketing sensation of Rafe as he draped his body over her back, his skin hot and moist, the hair on his chest and abdomen rough against her own sweat-dampened skin. "When Nancy said my bark was worse than my bite?" His lips touched the swirls of her ear, his breath misty-moist and warm. "She lied." His mouth moved down to the juncture of her neck and shoulder, his teeth clamping down as he thrust.

Lindy screamed, not in pain but with pleasure. Thick and solid, Rafe's cock filled her completely. She could feel it pulse against the stretched walls of her welcoming channel as he froze in place, unmoving.

"Ah, Lindy. God, baby, I'm so sorry…so sorry I hurt you." Rafe's voice was deep and husky with remorse.

She felt him begin to withdraw and was surprised by the near growl that rumbled from her throat. "Don't you *fucking dare*," she ordered, panting. "You're not hurting me, but I swear if you don't fuck me I'll make you pay, Rafe Kutter. Somehow, some way, when you least expect it, I'll…" Her sentence ended on a gasping moan as Rafe slid back home, hard and deep.

He nipped her earlobe. "*You* fucking talk too much. Shut up," he breathed softly in her ear, and Lindy could hear something in his voice, something new that sent a warm shiver down her spine and brought tears to her eyes.

She wasn't given the chance to analyze it. Rafe began to move. With exquisite and tender slowness, he thrust forward and back, forward and back, again and again. Each forward thrust brought him deep, the swollen head of his cock nudging against her cervix. She eagerly welcomed the contact and ground her pelvis back against him.

"More, Rafe, faster!"

Rafe ignored her pleas and continued his steady pace, deliberately driving them both into a frenzy of need. Lindy's impatience began to show as she struggled under him, but he held her firmly, directing the pace of their pleasure. Eyes closed, every cell in her body was zeroed in on the thick, pulsing rod that pierced her flesh. Slick, wet flesh that shuddered and gripped in an effort to keep the teasing invader from retreat.

Past caring about any kind of decorum and all inhibitions gone, when begging failed to elicit a response, Lindy began a low litany of curses calling him every dirty name she could think of, beginning with asshole and working her way through the alphabet. She'd have cursed with even more vehemence if she could have seen the grin that wreathed his face.

Just when she thought she'd die from frustration, Rafe picked up speed and began a hard, satisfying stroke that steadily increased to a pummeling rhythm that never stopped until it brought her to a howling climax.

Waves of pleasure rippled through skin, muscle and nerve until it seemed that every cell in her body was contracting and shivering with electric spasms that threatened to knock her unconscious from the overload.

Rafe gripped her hips tightly and pumped hot streams of semen into the fluttering welcome of her womb until, with a final pulse, his cock declared itself satisfied and he collapsed, rolling to his back and pulling her on top of him.

Sated and boneless, they lay breathing heavily, slowly recovering their sanity. Lindy snuggled against him, purring like a cat as his hand slowly stroked up and down her back.

Finally feeling as though her bones had solidified, she leaned up and over him. "I told you I was no coward," she said smugly.

Rafe grinned up at her, his hand coming up to stroke her cheek and gently push the hair back from her face. "You're no coward," he agreed. "You're bold and brazen and beautiful…and you've got one hell of a potty mouth," he teased with a chuckle.

A rosy flush lit her cheeks and she ducked her head, resting her heated skin against his chest, feeling the rise and fall of it and the reverberations from his laugh. She lay content and sated against him, rubbing her cheek against the satiny heat of his skin.

"You know what I'd like to do?" he asked in a husky rumble.

"Have more sex?" she asked hopefully.

"That too, but first I'd like to finish my bath."

"With or without me?"

"With, sweetheart, definitely with."

* * * * *

The bath that began as a leisurely exercise in relaxation, became a hot, sensual teasing torture in which they touched and kissed and explored each other's bodies until the temperature in the pool felt as though it had risen more than a few degrees.

Each seemed intent on driving the other insane with need in an effort to see who would give in first. Lindy teetered on the edge when Rafe's clever fingers dived into her ready pussy to tease and torment, but Rafe admitted defeat when she bent down and engulfed the tip of his aching cock in her mouth, her tongue doing a sensual dance over the ripe, swollen head.

Rafe pulled himself from her teasing mouth and rose up out of the water, taking her with him. Scooping her up in his arms he marched to the campsite and deposited her in front of his tent. "Inside," he ordered tersely, and Lindy, fighting the smile that pulled at her lips, scooted triumphantly in to claim her victory.

Aside from necessary bathroom breaks and to rustle up a quick meal, they spent the afternoon and evening making love and sleeping, only to wake in each other's arms to make love again. Having given in to his instinctive need to claim his mate,

Rafe had put aside all his doubts and reveled in the kind of physical closeness he'd denied himself so long.

It was only later that night that his former uncertainty began to surface and took the form of a dream that forced him awake and sent his thoughts down paths he'd avoided for far too long. He rose carefully so as not to wake Lindy, picked up his jeans and left the tent to don them. Gliding silently over the path that led to the spring, he sat down on convenient boulder to contemplate his thoughts and watch the moonlight reflected in the rippling water of the pond.

His thoughts were disturbing and melancholy and brought to the surface a sadness and guilt he'd hoped was long buried. A cool breeze stirred through his hair and he absently brushed it away from his face, too preoccupied to be distracted by such a petty annoyance. He *was* distracted when Lindy appeared at his side.

"Rafe, are you all right?" she questioned softly.

"Sure," he lied, not certain he could share what he was thinking with her.

"You want to talk about it?"

Rafe reached for her and pulled her onto his lap, burying his face in her shoulder. "Talk about what?" came the muffled reply.

"Whatever's bothering you," she answered, one hand moving with soothing strokes over the tense muscles in his back.

"You're killing me."

"What do you mean?" she asked, wide-eyed with worry.

Rafe reached up and cupped her face in his hands. "You make me see possibilities I thought were beyond me, make me see things as they are and not how I fooled myself into believing they were."

"But that's a good thing, isn't it?" Lindy asked with rising hope.

"It could be, but it hurts, Lindy. It hurts to admit certain things to myself."

"Like what?"

"Like the fact that, for a while, I hated my mother. I hated her for leaving me alone with this...this gift."

Lindy noted his use of the word gift instead of curse and her heart soared. "Rafe, you were a child, you were hurt and alone, it's perfectly understandable."

"I know, but I still feel guilty about it. I know she wouldn't have left me if she'd been given the choice." His voice shook.

Lindy could see the emotion roiling in his eyes as well as a sheen of unshed tears that gathered there. She wrapped her arms around him and pulled him close. "It's all right, it's all right, baby. Just remember how much she loves you and how much you love her. Nothing can change that, and all the bad things can just fade away. Just let it go, Rafe. Let it go."

For a moment he stiffened in her arms, then sagged against her as though a huge burden had been released. His long, muscular arms wrapped around her and he silently rocked, their bodies moving with a slow rhythm that soothed and calmed. Rafe eventually stopped the easy movement and pulled back to meet her loving gaze. His lashes were wet, and Lindy reached up to brush away the single tear that graced his cheek.

She gave him a tremulous smile. "Better?"

Rafe nodded. "You were right."

"About what?"

"I'm not an animal, I'm just a man with flaws and fears, and I've been given a very special gift."

"Oh Rafe, I'm so glad you can accept your mother's legacy now."

"That's not the gift I'm talking about."

"Then what?" she asked, puzzled.

"You."

"Me?" she asked as tears flooded her eyes. "I'm not a gift, I'm just...just me."

"You certainly are," he answered.

Rafe stood and guided her back to his tent, urging her inside. Without a word, he slowly undressed her while his hands and lips touched, caressed, and aroused. Deeply moved by the tremulously vulnerable look in her eyes, he whispered soft words of encouragement and praise, firing her blood and heating her body until he lay her down and slid between her thighs.

Lindy groaned, an orgasmic shudder shaking her as Rafe slowly eased his swollen cock inside, its girth spreading muscle and caressing the warm, wet length of her sheath until he was fully seated.

Rafe caressed her cheek and feathered a soft kiss over her lips. "This is my gift to you, a part of me no one's ever seen. Will you take it, Lindy, take this part of me?"

She reciprocated his move and lovingly caressed his face. "With pleasure."

Rafe smiled. "Always pleasure, sweetheart, always pleasure, I promise."

He began to slowly move, his hips undulating, his cock gently pushing and pulling inside, stirring the flames, building tension as he lost himself in the growing ecstasy in her eyes. On and on he moved, endlessly, the same slow, steady pace, refusing to be moved by Lindy's pleas until his own patience ended and a wild flurry of frantic strokes brought them both to a wrenching climax.

Outside the tent, Lindy's wails of pleasure echoed into the night, underscored by Rafe's muted, guttural roar.

# Chapter Six

## ℬ

Sometime in the early morning hours before the sun began to lighten the sky, they were awakened by a chorus of howls. Rafe was immediately alert and began gathering his clothes.

"What is it?" Lindy asked, confused and sleepy.

"Trouble. That's Cade's pack, they've spotted a potential poacher."

Waking up fast, Lindy stood and began throwing on her own clothes.

"Where do you think you're going?" Rafe growled.

"With you."

"No, you're not."

"Yes I am."

"No, you're not, Lindy. I—"

He was interrupted by the sound of a rifle shot.

"Fuck! I don't have time to argue with you. You stay behind me and do exactly as I say or when we get back I swear I'll blister that luscious backside of yours. Understood?"

"Understood," she agreed, grateful for his cooperation, no matter how grudging. It saved her from having to sneak out and try following him again.

They rushed from the tent and as soon as the terrain leveled out, Rafe began a fast and silent lope across the grassy meadowland. Light from the waning moon and stars was beginning to be replaced by light from the sun, which had yet to make an actual appearance on the horizon. Lindy uttered a silent thank you to the powers that be, glad for what illumination there was.

Rafe was pulling ahead of her and she was becoming afraid she'd lose him, when he began to slow. In the not-too-far distance she could see trees. They were closing in on a forested area. Panting and trying to silently suck in much-needed oxygen without drawing attention to herself, she caught up just as he disappeared into the trees.

Frowning, she mouthed a silent curse, she *was* going to lose him! Deciding the best course was just to go straight in, Lindy found herself on a lightly worn game trail and slowly picked her way through the underbrush, trying to be quiet while scanning the area for signs of Rafe or anyone else.

Just when she'd reached the conclusion that she was hopelessly lost, a shadowy figure loomed up at her from the side of the path. Her startled gasp was muffled by a large hand as she was pulled up tight against a warm, familiar body.

"Quiet," Rafe breathed in her ear.

Lindy nodded and he pulled his hand away and signaled for her to follow him.

Trying to calm her pounding heart, Lindy followed, staying so close she was nearly treading on his heels. She wasn't taking the chance of losing him again, especially if he was going to sneak up on her and inadvertently induce a heart attack. It wasn't long before she could hear some kind of movement up ahead. A light breeze blew over them and Rafe froze.

She watched him for a moment from behind. His body had gone absolutely still and rigid. Worried, she eased around him until she could see his face. His eyes were closed, a look of anguish on his face as he took deep, silent breaths. Lindy reached out and touched his arm. Rafe opened his eyes and swung his gaze to her. She swallowed a gasp of surprise. His eyes were a glowing, rich amber-yellow that blazed with tinges of red.

She watched in awed fascination as Rafe's hands came up, his fingernails lengthening before her eyes as he began unbuttoning his shirt. "It's him," he growled, his voice husky, rough and guttural. "The man who killed my mother." The last was barely recognizable.

"Are you sure?"

Unable to speak, he nodded and Lindy held back another gasp as his shirt came off. Rafe's body had begun to shift. Thick, dark hair had begun to run over his skin like water and he hunched over as his body changed. Claws tore at his jeans, shredding them, and there was a sudden blurring of the very air around him that—when it cleared—revealed a full-grown male grizzly at the very pinnacle of his power and grace.

Breathing hard, Lindy could only watch as the bear gave her one backward glance before rushing away. A shred of blue jean fabric stuck to one paw and she was reminded of someone leaving a bathroom with toilet paper stuck to their foot. The thought would have been funny, but it suddenly struck her that her lover, in the form of a thousand-pound, enraged grizzly bear, was going to confront, and probably kill, the man who'd killed his mother.

"Rafe, no!" She felt her heart stop at the sound of a rifle shot. "Oh God, no! No, please no." She uttered the prayer as she sprinted through the brush, unmindful and uncaring of the branches and brambles that slapped and tore at her.

She arrived at a scene of blood and chaos. Closest to her in the small clearing, a bull elk lay on the ground, blood seeping from the entry and exit wound that took its life. Across the clearing, a wounded and maddened grizzly bear stood over the terrified form of a hunter who saw his own death looking him right in the eye.

"Stop him."

Lindy jumped and turned to find the man Rafe had called Cade standing next to her.

"Stop him. You're his mate, you can stop him."

Scared to death, knowing she was going to put herself between Rafe and his vengeance, but also knowing what it would do to him if he killed this man, she walked across the clearing calling his name.

"Rafe, don't do this. Come back to me, baby. I'm scared, I need you."

The enraged bear turned his gaze to her, roared and made a mock charge at her. Lindy flinched but kept coming. "Rafe, please, you know who I am. Listen to me, don't do this." Tears flooded her eyes and streaked down her cheeks. "If you kill this man you'll regret it for the rest of your life. Please, we just found each other, don't let this come between us." The bear turned back to its prey and raised a huge paw, claws extended, ready to strike.

"I love you!" she screamed, and halted, sliding to her knees in the grass, her hands coming up to cover her face. Shuddering sobs tore at her throat. She'd never felt so lost and powerless in her life, until a pair of strong arms encircled her and pulled her tightly into the warmth of a familiar and oh-so beloved body.

"It's okay, baby, I've got you."

"Rafe," she breathed, and wrapped her arms around his body, squeezing him tight and drawing a gasping grunt from him. She drew back as a warm wetness soaked into her shirt and she looked down, finding blood. She quickly examined him. A shallow three-inch groove was carved across his ribs. "Oh my God, he shot you!" She searched for Cade and found him and a couple of his men standing over the hunter. "Call 911, get an ambulance, he's been shot!"

Cade ambled over, an impudent grin on his face. "Is she always so excitable?"

"No, she's usually quite sensible. I think she's a little shaken up."

"Shaken up? Shaken up! You're damn right, I'm shaken up!" Lindy yelled, wiping the tears from her cheeks while pulling a corner of her shirt up to press over Rafe's wound. "You went all furry on me and rushed off like a freight train on crack, and the next thing I know, I get elected to calm you down. Do you know what it's like to confront a thousand-pound grizzly bear?"

Rafe nodded in the affirmative. "As a matter of fact, I do. Remember, just the other day?"

Lindy frowned. "Oh yeah. But you have that Shoshone mumbo jumbo working for you, and your bear wasn't pissed off."

"Mumbo jumbo?" Cade repeated with a raised eyebrow.

"He spoke to the bear and it went away," Lindy explained. "I want you to teach me that in case I ever need it again," she ordered Rafe.

"I don't think you'll need it," Cade said with a smile. "What you said seemed pretty effective to me."

Lindy blushed. "Yeah, well, it probably wouldn't work with any other bear."

Rafe pushed her hand away and pulled her close. "It better not," he whispered, then he turned his attention to Cade. "What do we do about him?" he asked, indicating the hunter. "He saw me change."

"No, he didn't," Cade laughed. "He fainted."

Lindy and Rafe both looked around toward the man who still lay unconscious on the ground. "That's the man who killed my mother, I recognized his scent."

Cade nodded, all joking aside. "There'll be ballistics tests on his rifle to link him to killing the elk, hopefully that's the same rifle he used that night." Seeing the storm gather in Rafe's eyes, Cade forestalled any protest. "If it's not, considering the charges that are going to be brought against him, I don't think it will be too hard to get a warrant to examine any other firearms he might own."

Satisfied, Rafe stood and pulled Lindy up with him. "Then I'll leave you to it. I wouldn't trust myself around the bastard when he wakes up. This is too personal for me to be involved."

Cade clapped a hand on Rafe's shoulder. "Go on. I'll contact you if you're needed to testify."

Lindy put her hand out to Cade. "Thank you," she told him sincerely.

"No problem."

Rafe took Lindy's hand from Cade with a grumble that brought a smile to Cade's face. He watched them walk away, then called out to Rafe. "Hey buddy, that's a hell of a bruise you've got on your ass."

Rafe reached up, gave him the finger and kept on walking.

Cade grinned when he heard Lindy's voice.

"What bruise? What's he talking about? Are you hurt somewhere else I should know about?"

"Let it go, babe," came the disgruntled reply.

"No, I'm *not* going to let it go, let me see your ass."

Laughing out loud, Cade rejoined his men.

\* \* \* \* \*

Lindy and Rafe returned to their camp and after he allowed her to patch him up, they collapsed onto his sleeping bag and attempted to recover some lost sleep. Rafe's rest was disturbed by nightmares, as evidenced by his restless tossing. He woke once yelling her name, after which Lindy spent some moments soothing and assuring him that she was all right. Curling his body around hers and wrapping her securely in his arms, he was finally able to drift off, while Lindy lay awake for a while longer worrying. Rafe's subconscious was trying to deal with the recent trauma and was obviously having trouble doing so.

Awakening at midday, they enjoyed a leisurely meal and a final soak in the hot springs, then packed up their gear and headed back to base camp. Both of them were rather subdued, each for different reasons. Lindy was saddened by the fact that her time was up and that she would have to return home, especially in the light of her uncertainty as to Rafe's true feelings for her. It disturbed her that, despite the fact they'd slept so closely together, he'd bestowed only a brief kiss upon waking. He never mentioned the declaration of love she'd made, much less returned it.

Not wanting to press the issue, she kept silent and made no repeat of the words that had brought Rafe out of his rage and back into her arms. Despite the fact that his previous lovemaking had been both passionate and tender, and although she was sure she'd heard something in his voice that indicated he was more than just physically involved, how could she really know unless he told her?

With each mile that passed, Rafe's silence caused the knot in her stomach to grow until she felt sick, but she was determined that if anything was to happen between them, it was his turn to make a move. She felt she'd done her part, and any other action she could take was fraught with the possibility of humiliation and rejection. It was a chance she just couldn't take.

They walked on until Rafe called a halt for a quick meal. There was no stream here, so they made do with water from their canteens. Rafe actually made an effort to break the silence by pointing out a few things of interest like the varying plants that grew in the area and the different species of birds that occupied the tree branches above them.

Lindy responded with false interest, hoping that he wouldn't detect her rising tension, but it wasn't long before he fell silent and got them on their feet and moving again. By the time they reached base camp, she was exhausted and totally miserable.

They went straight to the Lodge and were greeted by David and Nancy, who'd received the news of the captured poacher from one of Cade's men. They dropped off the tents and other equipment in the storage room while relating the incident, neither one mentioning Lindy's declaration.

"I've got stew on the stove and biscuits in the oven. Come and rest and eat something," Nancy told the two of them and urged them in to the dining room.

While they ate, they talked about the trip and the bears and everything except the personal things that had happened between them. Lindy picked at her food, unable to force much past the lump in her throat, and finally gave up and took her plate to the kitchen counter, dumping the contents into the scrap bucket.

"Are you all right?"

Nancy had followed her and stood at her elbow with a concerned expression on her face.

"I'm just really tired, we had some short nights and a lot of interrupted sleep."

"Oh?"

Lindy smiled wanly at her inquiring tone but declined to elaborate. "I'm going to my cabin for a hot shower and then I just want to sleep."

She turned back to the table in time to hear David telling Rafe that Cade wanted to see him the next day. Rafe nodded his head in agreement, his gaze going to Lindy for a moment, his eyes shadowed and giving nothing away.

Lindy issued a soft and general goodnight to the company and walked out of the Lodge. At the door of her cabin she was hailed by Rafe.

"Are you all right?" he asked.

Lindy bit her lip, determined not to cry. "I'm fine, just tired. I've got to get some rest. My plane leaves tomorrow afternoon."

"I know."

"Will I…will I see you before I go?"

"I have to see Cade tomorrow morning, but I should be back before you go."

She nodded. "Rafe, did I…?"

"Did you what?"

She shook her head. "Nothing. Goodnight," she murmured huskily past the tears that clogged her throat. She turned and went quickly into her cabin before she lost control, never seeing the hand that reached out to her.

* * * * *

For his part, Rafe had lowered himself into a hell of his own making and was struggling to find a way out. The knowledge that Lindy loved him was so exquisitely wonderful that it made his heart ache — while it also terrified him down to his socks. He went to his cabin and dropped onto the bed, questions circling endlessly in his mind.

What had happened to all his vows of celibacy and his determination never to see his curse passed on to another generation? He knew the answer to that Lindy had happened. Not only had he not remained celibate, she might even at this moment be carrying his child. His mind boggled at the prospect. How could he have done that? Granted, she'd made him see that his ability wasn't the curse he'd always believed it was, but still, did he have the right to force it on another human being, his own child?

And what if something should happen to him? What if he couldn't be there for his child the way his mother had been unable to be there for him? The thought was an exercise in pure torment. Would Lindy be able to handle guiding their son or daughter into the gift, or would she withdraw from their lives the way his father had withdrawn from his? Was it even fair to expect her to handle such a thing?

There were so many questions to be considered that on their return trip he had distanced himself from Lindy in an effort to think clearly. Just being near her had a way of clouding his mind and made it impossible to think about anything but holding her and touching her, feeling the warmth of her in his arms and reveling in the unparalleled joy she brought him. While this was a very pleasant and desirable occupation, with all the serious issues he had to consider, he knew it wasn't fair to indulge his physical desires until things were settled between them.

Which brought him to another problem—Lindy herself. Although she had declared her love for him, he'd seen the fear in her eyes when he'd been lost in the red haze of rage that had filled him upon finding his mother's killer. What if he hadn't heard her pleas? What if he'd injured her? Was she really as accepting of his animal side as she seemed to be, or was she just fooling herself for the sake of new love?

Worst of all, he knew that his withdrawal was hurting her. But what could he do? Frustration and anger mixed with hope and desire and his own love for her until he felt he was going mad with it.

Unable to stay still a moment longer, he left his cabin and walked back to the Lodge. He went to the equipment room and retrieved the tent and other supplies they'd dropped off on their return, then went to the kitchen and pulled his sketchbook out of his pack.

He opened the page in the book that bore Lindy's image and hesitated, thinking he might leave it for her, but then a more urgent idea took root. He pulled his mother's necklace from under his shirt and over his head. His fingers traced the familiar contours of the beads and especially the carved bear that was the heart of it. Ripping a piece of paper from his sketch book, he wrote *For Lindy* in his bold script, and, leaving the note with the necklace draped over it on the table, picked up his pack and walked out into the night.

* * * * *

After half an hour spent sitting on the shower floor crying while the water cascaded over her, Lindy finally dragged herself out, dried off and threw herself naked into bed while pulling the covers over herself and Humphrey. Never had she felt so grateful for her bear's familiar comfort than at that moment.

Exhausted, she lay unblinking in the dark while disjointed thoughts swam through her head. Nothing made sense, only the deep and painful feeling of loss that left her feeling hollow inside. Her last thought, as she drifted to sleep, was that she'd never risk her heart again.

Eleven hours later she woke with a headache, swollen eyelids and eyes that stung with every bleary blink. She stumbled into the bathroom and into the shower, turning the water on as hot as she could stand. Afterward, feeling halfway human again, she dressed, packed her things and left them and Humphrey sitting on her bed while she walked to the Lodge.

She found Nancy and David sitting at the table and she took a cup out of the cupboard, poured herself some coffee and joined them. After an exchange of good mornings, she asked casually, "Where is everyone?"

"Sandy and Paul are still out in the field, they're not scheduled to be back for a couple of days now," David told her. "They asked me to tell you how much they enjoyed meeting you and that you had their votes to come back anytime you liked."

Lindy smiled. "That's nice of them, please be sure to thank them for me." She waited on tenterhooks for news of the one person she really wanted to hear about.

"Rafe's not here either, he left last night or early this morning. I know he had to see Cade, but he took his pack and a tent. I don't look to see him for a few days," David said in a gently apologetic voice.

"He left this for you," Nancy said quietly, and presented Lindy with his note and the necklace.

Lindy nodded, feeling frozen inside. It was over. After yesterday she should have given up, but hope had a way of keeping you hanging on until there was just nothing left. And now she knew.

She took a deep breath and put the necklace on, folding the note and tucking it inside her pocket. "Please be sure to thank him, too. He was a very good guide." She looked at her watch. "Well, I'm all packed, I guess we should be going if I'm going to make my flight."

David agreed and went out to bring the truck around, leaving Lindy and Nancy to say their goodbyes.

"What happened out there, Lindy?" Nancy asked, concern written on her face.

Lindy smiled sadly. "You were right, he *is* worth the work, but I guess he doesn't think *I* am."

"Oh honey, don't say that," Nancy admonished, giving her a hug. "I saw the way he looked at you, there's something there, don't give up."

"There's nothing to give up, Nancy, he's made that perfectly clear." David came in to tell her the truck was ready, and Lindy gave Nancy another hug. "Thank you for everything, most of it was pretty good," she teased half-heartedly.

David followed her to her cabin and carried her luggage back to the truck. Watching him while holding Humphrey in her arms, Lindy came to a quick decision and made a little side trip before joining him at the truck. She hopped inside, waved goodbye to Nancy and settled back, closing her eyes, determined to put this experience behind her. With that in mind, as she idly chatted with David, she set her thoughts on her company and the work she'd have waiting for her when she returned.

\* \* \* \* \*

It was mostly dark, with soft light just beginning to make its appearance on the horizon, but Rafe could see perfectly well. He stared out over the meadow, his thoughts at rest, not because he'd solved anything, but from sheer exhausted confusion. For the past few days he'd had little rest and no peace at all. Missing Lindy made it impossible for him to eat or sleep with any kind of enthusiasm. Staring sightlessly into space seemed to have become his favorite occupation and it was how Cade found him.

"She's gone," he said, sitting down on the log next to Rafe. It wasn't a question.

"What makes you say that?"

"You're here alone, mooning over her."

"I'm not *mooning* over her."

"A courageous man never runs from the truth. I know you're no coward."

Rafe sighed. "All right, I'm mooning over her, but it's the right thing to do."

"It's the right thing to make yourself, and the other half of your soul, miserable? I'm glad I'm not a bear," Cade said with conviction.

"Oh?"

"A wolf would never be so foolish."

"It's not foolish, I'm protecting her."

"To deny your life is foolish, no matter how much you talk yourself into believing that you're doing what's best for someone else."

"You don't understand," Rafe retorted angrily.

"I think I do. No one can predict the future, Rafe, but to run from life is wrong. You may save yourself some hurt, but all you'll end up with is regret. I prefer to chance the hurt, the rewards can be beyond your wildest dreams."

Rafe was silent for a time then admitted grudgingly, "You're pretty damn smart…for a wolf."

Cade threw back his head and laughed. "Go get your mate, cub. I expect to see you back here with her very soon."

The sun chose that moment to peek above the horizon, highlighting the sky with a palette of color. "It's going to be a beautiful day," Rafe murmured, before he stood, stretched and strode into his campsite, quickly and efficiently packing his gear. By the time he'd finished, Cade was gone. Rafe grinned and laughed like a man newly released from prison. He set off at a swift pace, a new confidence to his step.

* * * * *

The intercom buzzed.

"What is it, Cin?" Lindy sat in her office chair, staring out the window.

"There's someone here to see you."

"Tell whoever it is that I'm busy. I don't want to be disturbed."

"Not even by me?"

She gasped and swung around, her entire being electrified by that familiar voice. She was surprised to see only Humphrey sitting in the partially open doorway. Rising from her chair, Lindy walked toward the door, watching as it began to slowly swing open.

Rafe stood in the open doorway, a tentative smile on his face. Dressed in black jeans, a white shirt and a black leather jacket, he was more devastatingly handsome than ever. Lindy felt her heart racing as it tried to make a run for her throat.

He reached down, picked up Humphrey, stepped in and closed the door behind him. "He missed you. All he could talk about day and night was Lindy this and Lindy that. The poor guy couldn't eat or sleep. I thought maybe it would be for the best if I brought him back to you, but...you see, I've discovered I can't live without him. Do you think maybe we could share?"

Eyes filling with tears, she furiously blinked them back, her lips curving in a beatific smile. "I think that could be arranged."

Setting Humphrey down on a nearby chair, Rafe walked slowly across the room "Of course that would mean that we'd have to be close, very *very* close."

Lindy nodded with mock seriousness. "If you think that's for the best."

He stopped in front of her. "That would be the very best." He opened his arms and she flew into them, nearly taking them both off their feet.

Rafe staggered then laughed joyfully, swinging her around before kissing her passionately. He finally let her up for air and put his forehead against hers. "I love you, Lindy. Marry me. Have babies with me."

"Little bear cubs?"

"We only go cubby at puberty, remember?"

"Oh yeah. Still, I'm glad you want to have babies."

Rafe stilled and picked her up setting her down on the edge of her desk. He wedged himself between her thighs. "Are you pregnant, sweetheart?"

Lindy shook her head. "No. But if you go lock my door, maybe we could fix that." She waggled her eyebrows at him.

"Now there's the bold and brazen woman I remember." Rafe crossed the room with long strides, locked the door and started back, but paused where Humphrey was seated and turned him so that he was facing away from the desk. "Take a nap, Humphrey, we'll take you out for ice cream later."

As he returned to her, Lindy gave him a narrow-eyed look. "Did you have to do that? I can't do it now, not with Humphrey in the room."

Rafe moved between her thighs and firmly grasped her hips, holding her as he nudged his rising erection against her. His mouth moved to her ear and he whispered, "Are you sure?" before sliding his tongue in to do a sensuous tango.

Moaning at the shivers that slid up her spine, she squirmed against him and gave in "Okay, okay, I guess I can grin and..."

"Don't even think about finishing that thought."

"No? I really can't *bear* to leave a sentence unfinished."

"I'm warning you."

"Just *bear* with me."

"*Lindy...*"

"I'm just *baring* my thoughts to you."

"I swear, Lindy, just one more..."

"Okay, okay. Rafe? If we take our clothes off, we'll both be *bare*."

There was a short pause, then a huskily growled, "Now that one I can live with."

## *About the Author*

ഇ

Having been an avid reader of romance for years, and being possessed of an overactive imagination, Kate decided only recently to try her hand at writing. She discovered that, like reading, writing romance has become addictive. Whether writing about werewolves and otherworldly creatures or contemporary gay/erotic romance, she has found the perfect outlet and is thrilled to be part of the Ellora's Cave family.

Kate lives in a turn-of-the-century house located on three acres in the midst of Indiana farm country. Keeping her company is her family, dogs, and other assorted pets.

Kate welcomes mail from readers. You can write to her c/o Ellora's Cave Publishing at 1056 Home Avenue Akron, OH 44310-3502.

## *Also by Kate Steele*

ഇ

Chosen of the Orb

To Trust a Wolf

# Why an electronic book?

We live in the Information Age—an exciting time in the history of human civilization in which technology rules supreme and continues to progress in leaps and bounds every minute of every hour of every day. For a multitude of reasons, more and more avid literary fans are opting to purchase e-books instead of paperbacks. The question to those not yet initiated to the world of electronic reading is simply: *why?*

1. *Price.* An electronic title at Ellora's Cave Publishing and Cerridwen Press runs anywhere from 40-75% less than the cover price of the <u>exact same title</u> in paperback format. Why? Cold mathematics. It is less expensive to publish an e-book than it is to publish a paperback, so the savings are passed along to the consumer.

2. *Space.* Running out of room to house your paperback books? That is one worry you will never have with electronic novels. For a low one-time cost, you can purchase a handheld computer designed specifically for e-reading purposes. Many e-readers are larger than the average handheld, giving you plenty of screen room. Better yet, hundreds of titles can be stored within your new library—a single microchip. (Please note that Ellora's Cave and Cerridwen Press does not endorse any specific brands. You can check our website at www.ellorascave.com or

www.cerridwenpress.com for customer recommendations we make available to new consumers.)

3. *Mobility*. Because your new library now consists of only a microchip, your entire cache of books can be taken with you wherever you go.

4. *Personal preferences are accounted for*. Are the words you are currently reading too small? Too large? Too...**ANNOYING**? Paperback books cannot be modified according to personal preferences, but e-books can.

5. *Instant gratification*. Is it the middle of the night and all the bookstores are closed? Are you tired of waiting days—sometimes weeks—for online and offline bookstores to ship the novels you bought? Ellora's Cave Publishing sells instantaneous downloads 24 hours a day, 7 days a week, 365 days a year. Our e-book delivery system is 100% automated, meaning your order is filled as soon as you pay for it.

Those are a few of the top reasons why electronic novels are displacing paperbacks for many an avid reader. As always, Ellora's Cave and Cerridwen Press welcomes your questions and comments. We invite you to email us at service@ellorascave.com, service@cerridwenpress.com or write to us directly at: 1056 Home Ave. Akron OH 44310-3502.

# THE
# ☥ ELLORA'S CAVE ☥
## LIBRARY

Stay up to date with Ellora's Cave Titles in
Print with our Quarterly Catalog.

To recieve a catalog,
send an email with your name
and mailing address to:

## CATALOG@ELLORASCAVE.COM

or send a letter or postcard
with your mailing address to:

## Catalog Request
## c/o Ellora's Cave Publishing, Inc.
## 1056 Home Avenue
## Akron, Ohio 44310-3502

# COMING TO A BOOKSTORE NEAR YOU!

# ELLORA'S CAVE

*Bestselling Authors Tour*

# ELLORA'S CAVEMEN
## LEGENDARY TAILS

Try an e-book for your immediate
reading pleasure or order these titles in print from

## www.EllorasCave.com

## ELLORA'S CAVE
### The Best in Today's Romantica™

Make each day more *EXCITING* With our

# Ellora's Cavemen

## Calendar

www.EllorasCave.com

erridwen, the Celtic Goddess of wisdom, was the muse who brought inspiration to story-tellers and those in the creative arts. Cerridwen Press encompasses the best and most innovative stories in all genres of today's fiction. Visit our site and discover the newest titles by talented authors who still get inspired - much like the ancient storytellers did, once upon a time.

Discover for yourself why readers can't get enough of
the multiple award-winning publisher
Ellora's Cave.
Whether you prefer e-books or paperbacks,
be sure to visit EC on the web at
www.ellorascave.com
for an erotic reading experience that will leave you
breathless.